TAINTED LOVE

Stewart Home

First published in Great Britain in 2005 by
Virgin Books Ltd
Thames Wharf Studios
Rainville Road
London
W6 9HA

A catalogue record for this book is available from the British
Library.

ISBN 0 7535 1088 X

The paper used in this book is a natural, recyclable product
made from wood grown in sustainable forests. The
manufacturing process conforms to the regulations of the
country of origin.

Typeset by TW Typesetting, Plymouth, Devon

Printed and bound in Great Britain by Mackays PLC

CONTENTS

INTRODUCTION: BODIES OF EVIDENCE

When I was 40 I decided I wanted to meet my (m)other. Perhaps I should rephrase that because my words might be misunderstood by certain readers: when I was in my late thirties I decided to meet my (m)other on my fortieth birthday. My means of achieving this was quite simple. I would go to Finches on Portobello Road for a Sunday lunch-time drink, and my (m)other would be there to celebrate this event with me and a handful of close friends. It all seemed so simple and since I'd decided that my (m)other could time travel to hook up with me, it didn't really matter whether or not she turned up on the date I'd set. Even if I didn't meet her on my fortieth birthday, I would certainly have an almost tangible sense of my (m)other having been with me after the event. As an experienced time traveller, my mum could turn any day she wanted into 24 March, so there was no need for disappointment if it at first appeared she hadn't shown. At the time I made these fortieth birthday arrangements, I was under the almost mistaken impression that my (m)other had committed suicide in the 70s so I knew that she would have to travel through time or journey across the astral plane to meet me. It wasn't until the day after I'd arranged to meet my (m)other, that is to say 25 March 2002, that I discovered the exact date of her death to be 2 December 1979. The more I was able to look into the matter of my (m)other's demise, the deeper the mystery surrounding it became. However, once I got my hands on my mum's papers many of the matters that perplexed me were almost instantly resolved.

My (m)other had lived a few minutes' walk away from Finches during the early and mid-60s. To be more precise she'd rented a two-room conversion on the top floor of 24 Bassett Road. Finches had long been a bohemian watering-hole and my mum had been a beatnik, so if one was to make an educated guess about where my (m)other drank during the 60s, then Finches was as good a choice as anywhere. I now know with certainty that my mum drank at Finches, although she was equally fond of Henekey's and the Kensington Park Hotel. To inform my (m)other of my plan to meet her, I'd sent email messages to assorted friends. I'd figured that if my (m)other could time travel and traverse the astral plane, then she'd have no trouble reading emails I'd sent to various individuals I was in direct contact with but which were intended just as much for her.

On the appointed day I sat at one of the two outside tables on Elgin Crescent, since Finches is on the corner of this street and Portobello Road. Several weeks later I discovered that, after moving out of Bassett Road, my mum had lived for a time at 55 Elgin Crescent. However, on my fortieth birthday as I sat with a pint of Guinness in front of me and my back turned on Portobello Road, I didn't know I was gazing down the street towards a front door from which my (m)other might have emerged had I been able to travel back in time.

My reasons for believing my (m)other committed suicide were utterly straightforward: I'd been looking for her since 1985 and after sixteen years' failure, I decided the best place to continue searching was in the realm of mythology. So having opened a phone book not quite at random, I found someone with what had once been my mum's name living in Camelot Place. Actually this individual didn't quite share my (m)other's name, but the listing was as J O'Sullivan and my mum was Jilly O'Sullivan in most of the records I had seen at that time. This J O'Sullivan turned out to be called Justine rather than Jilly, but I didn't know this when I wrote saying I was a television researcher investigating links between Notting Hill's beatnik and hippie scenes who was looking for Jilly O'Sullivan. Justine wrote back to say she was not Jilly, but Jillian was a distant relative who as far as she knew had lived in London during the 60s and had killed herself at some point in the following decade.

Justine eventually put me in touch with one of my aunts and it was this older sister who gave me my (m)other's papers. My aunt had kept these effects, fully intending to read them one day, but having been very close to my mum and greatly saddened by her loss, she'd never felt able to tackle this task. My (m)other's papers were in considerable disarray but nevertheless proved to be of great interest since her life illustrates very well the cultural shifts of the 60s and 70s. My (m)other's biography and those of many women like her would not normally be accessible to the professional historian and this is a great pity, since access to the material in question completely transformed my understanding of both swinging London and much of what followed on from it.

The papers of my (m)other's that my aunt had preserved included journals, letters and a sketchy autobiography. I've assembled my (m)other's memoirs between these covers and as far as is possible I have tried to place them so that she is describing the events of her life in chronological order. However, the opening section is only the most obvious exception to this rule since while the incidents recounted in what I've placed first occurred some years after my (m)other initially arrived in London, it introduces the casual reader to the world she knew. This section of the book also appears to be the first thing my (m)other wrote when setting down this account of her life. Indeed, given everything my (m)other wrote about her life between the ages of sixteen and thirty-five was composed from the perspective of having reached her mid-thirties, as well as the way she switches between epochs with speed, it would have been impossible to organise her writing in perfect chronological order without destroying the coherence of what she recorded. I would also stress that it is extremely unlikely that the way I've ordered this material follows the exact sequence in which it was written, and that the loose sheets on which my (m)other scrawled her autobiography were badly jumbled when they came into my hands. The papers were housed in a large brown envelope addressed to my aunt in my (m)other's hand and postmarked LONDON W10, 1 DEC 79. The editing I have performed on these pages is light but some deletions proved necessary in order to reduce the number of repetitions. Rather more unfortunately it is not possible to include here all the material my (m)other wrote concerning her involvement in drug dealing and prostitution, since a number of the famous men she mentions are still living and might well object to the public circulation of material of this type. In the near future I hope it will be possible to provide a fuller picture of the demi-monde in which my (m)other moved, and the many ways in which it overlapped with the worlds of mainstream politics and entertainment. I have cut into the writings that it is possible to publish at this juncture two transcripts from the numerous reel-to-reel tapes that my (m)other made and which were left with my aunt for safe-keeping immediately before my mum travelled to the USA to undergo cancer treatment at the Mayo Clinic in the summer of 1976. Again, the fact that some of the notable personages whose voices appear on these tapes are still living means that it is not yet possible to issue the most interesting material contained within them.

I have taken the liberty of adding to the material assembled from my (m)other's effects testimony about her taken from some of her friends. I have edited this additional information together in the form of a film script. I may at some point make a short film based on this blueprint since it would provide an additional means of drawing attention to the shocking failures of the English coronary system. Finally, I must add that while I am extremely sympathetic towards the overwhelming majority of the opinions my (m)other expresses, what she has to say does not always dovetail with my own views. In relation to this I should point out that I have added chapter titles to my (m)other's unfinished writings and in places I have used these to signal how my own perspectives differ from my mum's. Since several of these chapter headings are taken from the names of songs of which I'm fond, they also hint at my love of soul music. Like all of us my (m)other was a product of the times through which she lived, and the world we inhabit today has in many ways changed beyond recognition from the one she knew not so long ago. I am, of course, extremely proud of my (m)other and find myself deeply distressed by the treatment she received at the hands of various authorities.

Lloyd O'Sullivan, London 24 March 2005

1. BETTER LIVING THRU CHEMISTRY

George was an American. He told me he was studying at Oxford. He said his family name was Wilde; I'm not sure that I believed him. I met George at General Gordon's Club, an establishment that back then was located on Brewer Street in the West End of London. When I was part of the hostess scene in the 60s it was rare to find anyone using their real name. On the sole occasion Bertie Grayson, who ran Gordon's, was foolish enough to leave me unsupervised in his office, a hurried search of a desk drawer revealed a passport in the name of Rudolph Stammler but bearing Grayson's photograph. Bertie's girls came and went, and those who'd gone and then returned inevitably reappeared with a new moniker, usually acquired from a marriage the length of which would be measured in terms of days rather than months.

Men did not go to Gordon's for the food, which was indifferent and overpriced. It is unlikely many went for the floor show, although that was rather grand. What attracted punters to Gordon's was the chance to sit with a hostess and buy her champagne. I was obviously made for this type of work since it provided me with the opportunity to get sozzled night after night, and the drunker I became the more I earned. I received a commission for every drink the men I sat with ordered. I would collect the specially designed cocktail sticks that were placed inside each glass and the pay I received varied according to the number I handed in at the end of the night. Most of the customers I entertained were middle-aged businessmen from the English provinces. They'd hector me about share prices and the absurd amounts of tax they'd been stung for. I'd pretend to be impressed since it was my job to be accommodating. Naturally, I preferred the younger guys from wealthy families who sometimes came to Gordon's, especially the group of Sufi boys whose fathers were oil sheikhs. George looked younger than any man I'd ever seen in the club, and like all Americans on a first visit, he was flabbergasted that this sort of establishment was able to flourish in London.

'Back home,' George told me in his southern drawl, 'this place wouldn't last five minutes. It would be closed down in a flash.'

'This isn't Little Rock, the Klan can't run us out of town.' I shouldn't have said it but I'd heard his line one too many times.

'I'm not from the south, I'm from the Big Apple. I grew up in Manhattan,' George lied.

'It's OK,' I said touching his hand.

'Don't treat me like a baby!' And as the words welled up from inside him I knew George was one of those guys who got an erection whenever he was angry with a woman.

'Look,' I said, 'Gordon's closes in an hour. If you want, when I've finished here I can show you the real hip scene.'

'Where's that?' George asked.

'The Cousins. Bert Jansch is on.'

'Where?'

'Lez Cuzzins.' I pronounced the name with the English intonation used by all Les Cousins regulars. That said, the Les prefix was universally dropped when the appellation was spoken.

7

'Now I understand, Lay Coo-zan,' Wilde echoed in correct French, instantly betraying the fact that he'd only read about the scene we had going and wasn't directly connected to it. 'That's a beatnik club. I've been told half the audience have John Steinbeck novels hanging out of their pockets.'

'It's cool,' I rejoined. 'It's named after a Claude Chabrol film.'

'Will we get to smoke reefer?' George asked hopefully.

'If you want we could get something stronger than that. Order me another bottle of bubbly and when we've polished it off we can hit the Cousins.'

At three in the morning we strolled across Soho. It only took a few minutes to get from Brewer to Greek Street. The Cousins was in the basement at number 49. Immediately above it there was a restaurant and on the upper floor an illegal gambling club. As we were about to descend into the folk cellar, I was accosted by my cousin Ziggy 'the Panther' Williams, who came racing out of the spieler located at the top of the building.

'Ah, Jilly, just the person I was hoping to see.' Ziggy beamed. 'I've had some terrible luck upstairs, and unless you can advance me a spot of cash I'll have to do a little job before I'm allowed to sit back down at the table.'

'George,' I said, making the necessary introductions, 'this is my Uncle Ziggy. He's the guy who stole Sophia Loren's jewels when she was filming at Elstree a few years ago. He's the best thief in Britain and probably the worst gambler in the world. He's on the nip right now; he needs welly to get back into a game.'

'Pleased to meet you, sir!' George announced brightly as he held out a paw.

'You can call me Ziggy,' my affable cousin told the polite American. Then he turned to me and panted, 'Jilly, give me a pony and I'll see you right next week.'

'What do you think, George?' I was deliberately drawing my escort into my cousin's predicament. 'Please bear in mind I was named after my father's elder sister who was also Ziggy's mother and . . .'

'But,' George interjected, 'that would make you his cousin. You just told me he was your uncle.'

'He is my cousin but I call him my uncle because of our age difference. Ziggy was already a grown man when I was a baby. Uncle Ziggy is drunk and he needs money. If he doesn't get dosh from us he'll be clambering over roof-tops trying to steal something the governor of the spieler will accept as a substitute for cash. Given the state Ziggy's in there's a fair chance he'll fall off a building and be dreadfully injured. Most cat burglars retire before they reach his age. Have you got a pony?'

'A pony? Back home in the States I've got a thoroughbred horse.'

'Horse?' a sleazy character hissed as he sidled up to us. 'My friends, I have the best horse. I got lucky when a fellow sufferer turned me on to a sympathetic woman doctor, you've maybe heard of her, Lady Frankau. She gave me a big prescription and I've just come here directly from the all-night drug dispensary in Piccadilly. After using what I need, I'm happy to sell the rest on for a fair price. What I'm offering you is of such fine quality that even the British Prime Minister Harold Wilson approves of it.'

I quickly negotiated a dope deal on George's behalf then, after explaining that a pony was 25 pounds sterling, persuaded him to hand the readies over to my Uncle Ziggy.

'You don't know what this means to me, Jilly my lovely.' Ziggy was already climbing the stairs to the spieler as he said it. 'You know I'll see you right.'

I was a paid-up member of the Cousins, so I signed George in and he covered the admission charge. The place felt packed if there were a hundred people inside. It only took a few score more than that to reach capacity. Although my arrival with Wilde must have taken the Cousins beyond that, we were allowed in. I was already familiar with the fishing nets hanging from the ceiling and the massive wagon wheel decorating one of the walls, but I tried to imagine them afresh as if through George's eyes. The stage was tiny but more than adequate for Bert Jansch and his introverted blues-folk-guitar act. I found somewhere to sit and sent George off to buy tea and sandwiches from the back room. We needed refreshments because it was hot and muggy in the unlicensed club. Eventually George returned and I quickly ascertained he was more impressed by the ambience than the actual music. The entire audience was stoned. The pot smoke was so thick that it wasn't necessary to toke on a joint to get turned on. I rolled some of my own wacky baccy and gave George a poke when Jansch did 'Needle of Death', his song about heroin. George liked the overall vibe, but clearly didn't appreciate just how good Jansch was on the guitar. My companion stared at me slack-jawed when after passing him a fat joint I praised a particularly fine legato.

'Where do all these people come from?' George asked as he gesticulated at the throng of part-time beatniks.

'Mainly the provinces,' I told him. 'If they come here it makes for a cheap weekend in London; there's no need to pay for a hotel when they can stay up all night.'

'Is that why a lot of them aren't paying much attention to the music? Back in Arkansas the liberal crowd listen intently to old-school protest singers of the Woody Guthrie type.'

'Forget about Pete Seeger. In the new protest culture everyone does their own thing.'

'If people pay to see Bert Jansch but don't listen to him, who do they really admire?'

'Bob Dylan.' And as I spoke this almost sacred name a spontaneous internal poetic stream-of-consciousness enlightenment machine was unexpectedly activated in my brain. 'What Dylan has to say about the absurdity of existence is cryptic; you can spend hours figuring out his lyrics. That's got to be better than some one-dimensional message that even when I'm wasted I can comprehend in three seconds flat. After listening to 'Subterranean Homesick Blues' more than a hundred times I still can't work out exactly what Dylan intends to convey. I understand the overall mood but the specifics elude me. After drugs, Dylan's systematic derangement of the senses is one of the best weapons we've got in the fight against mindless conformity. Listening to Bob on fab gear is a psychic elevator to higher forms of consciousness. Inner experience is the front line for those organising a permanent protest against crass materialism.'

'This is crazy talk; back home people like Tim Leary push a similar line. Who are the big names attaching themselves to it here?'

'Scotch Alex. We could cab it over to his place now if you like. He'll give you the rap and he's got the spikes we need to shoot the skag you just scored.'

'Is this dude a pusher?'

'Scotch Alex is the man. He'll blow your mind and put it back together the way it always should have been.'

'He sounds like low life.'

'He's cultured. He's written novels. Have you read *Cain's Book*?'

'No. I take it you're talking about Alexander Trocchi. I've heard he's a dope fiend.'

'Alex is no fiend; you'll like him.'

'If I go and meet Trocchi, will you fuck me?'

'You won't want sex once you're high.'

'I can pay.'

'You paid in spades when you gave Uncle Ziggy the pony. Money isn't the issue, what this is about is the best way of getting turned on.'

'Are you telling me I won't want to rut once I'm chilling?'

'That's right.'

'You underestimate my sex drive.'

'Do I?'

'I'll prove it to you.'

When we got to Scotch Alex's place the door was open and inside he'd nodded out. While I located a hypodermic syringe, George amused himself by reading Trocchi's blueprints for cultural revolution. Moments after I found a spike, Glasgow stirred.

'Alex,' I fizzed, 'where can I find a spoon?'

'Those who measure their lives with teaspoons waste their time looking at cutlery. The spoons have yet to manifest themselves.'

'It's you who's wasted,' I reassured him.

'Have you seen Terry? I wanted to ask him about heteroclite . . .' Alex was on the nod again before he finished the sentence.

'Did you want a spoon?' George asked. 'There's one beneath the pile of papers I'm reading.'

After I'd cooked the junk and drawn it into the syringe, I got George to tie his arm up so that I could give him a shot. The needle slipped in smoothly and he didn't feel a thing as the skag zapped him into oblivion. Now he finally understood what it was to be cool, really cool. Since I did odd bits of modelling, I wasn't about to put anything in my arm where the resultant scars might cramp my glam style. Sometimes I'd hit veins and sometimes I was skin popping. That night I slipped the spike between my toes and watched blood bloom in the dropper as I hit home. George and I lay back on our separate chairs, and for a long time afterwards neither of us spoke.

'You know,' Wilde said eventually, 'I feel so good that I'm gonna be totally frank with you. I'd planned to get my sexual kicks tonight by pretending to be JFK. Have you heard the inside dope about Kennedy being a full-on practical joker when he was a jock? Johnny built himself up as a real New York city slicker with this stuffy Californian co-ed, then after he had her creaming about how sophisticated he was and she'd allowed him to come in her mouth, he blubbed out that he didn't really grow up in Manhattan, but was from Jersey. The babe concerned felt so humiliated by this post-coital confession that she never spoke to him again. My initial intention tonight had been to re-enact this prank with you as my unwitting accomplice, but given how unnecessary I feel right now, I've decided to blow it off until I score with a chick who's certifiably uptight. That said, my libido is still every bit as potent as that of my role model. America needs leaders who understand that blow jobs are a matter of trust.'

For all I know, George may have talked on in this fashion for hours. We'd shot some good shit and I soon nodded out. When I awoke Wilde was gone. Scotch Alex was nowhere to be seen either, so I let myself out of the flat and walked back to my Ladbroke Grove pad. I straightened out with more puff and a coffee before crawling into bed. As I pulled the cool sheets over my head it struck me that I should have baited George into shagging me and then told him that I wasn't really a Londoner but came from Essex. Actually I grew up in Greenock in Scotland but after I'd moved to London, I'd become so assimilated to the local culture that most people mistook me for a native. In many ways Greenock was to Glasgow what Jersey was to Manhattan or Essex to London, although few of those I met in the Smoke had any idea of how my home-town was perceived back in Scotland. Exhausted, I slept longer than I'd planned and missed an anti-bomb demonstration I'd promised to attend. I'd metaphorically burned my duffel coat. The Campaign for Nuclear Disarmament had served its purpose. London was swinging and what us hipsters really wanted was better living thru chemistry.

2. THE VAGARIES OF NARCISSISM

One of the attractions of working at General Gordon's was the sheer range of people one met. Aside from businessmen I also got to meet politicians, aristocrats, entertainers and gangsters. The better class of criminal tended to avoid publicity and those who are best remembered now had little going for them. The most exemplary case of famous underworld two-time losers is that of Ronnie and Reggie Kray. On the surface the Krays appeared impressive but underneath they were complete phonies; their image had no more substance than the Hollywood gangster movies on which they modelled themselves. The Krays have been described as thieves' ponces but simply calling them pimps would be more accurate. Although they had the odd nickel-and-dime extortion racket going in the East End, up west, where the real money was to be made, they concentrated on introducing wealthy gentlemen to rough trade. However, for the Krays the real fun and profit came not from the poncing but the blackmail that inevitably followed it. That said, the Kray twins were every bit as keen on rent boys as their customers. Ronald was open about his sexuality whereas Reggie was a closet queen. In the early

60s homophobia was still legally sanctioned and backed up with prison sentences, which gave the Krays an edge when it came to their extortion rackets, but this situation simultaneously reinforced Reggie's sense of insecurity about himself. Reggie would pay girls from Gordon's to go up to a hotel room with him but once there he'd just drink. He thought being seen with a string of hostesses would give his hollow heterosexual image a boost. I'd been paid to sit with the brothers on a number of occasions, and it was only when I discovered I was pregnant that Reggie found a use for me that went beyond mere decoration.

I was seventeen years old in the summer of 1961 and I'd been living in London on my own for nearly a year. Since my line of work led me to sleep with many different men, I couldn't be certain whose baby I was carrying, although female intuition did provide me with a prime suspect who shall remain all but anonymous. Since Ronnie and Reggie knew what I did for a living, they understood that almost any man might be my child's father. That didn't matter to the Krays, who provided me with some money so that I might lose a paternity case against Reggie. Several women were paid in this way to lose legal actions against the ostensibly straighter of the twins, since even when a case was lost most people assumed there was no smoke without fire. By such means Reggie's fraudulent heterosexual standing received a bolster. To ensure that absolutely nothing went wrong, the Krays also set me up with a putative father who I first met some months after I actually became pregnant. Around this time Reggie was in and out of jail on a charge relating to an extortion attempt on Swiss Travel Goods in Finchley Road. I was living just up from Chapel Market in Islington, and this was considered uncomfortably close to Kray family territory in Hoxton and Bethnal Green, particularly since a local girl of my age called Frances Shea had been lined up as Reggie's trophy wife, and while I was pregnant she'd rejected his first proposal of marriage on the grounds of her youth. Shea did marry her beau a few years later but their unconsummated marriage was a sham and led directly to her suicide at the age of 23 in 1967.

A lot of rubbish has been written about the slumlord Peter Rachman, and although he tried to avoid the Krays, they forced themselves upon him and demanded certain favours. Since the twins wanted a flat for me in west London, Rachman put them on to Robert Jacobs, who'd taken over many of his properties after he sold up as far as slumlordism went. Jacobs in turn enlisted his lieutenant Michael de Freitas to find me and the putative father of my unborn child a pad in Notting Hill. De Freitas would later achieve both fame and notoriety as a black power leader known as Michael X. I first met the putative father of my child, Matt Bradley, after moving into the apartment. At that time Bradley was a nineteen-year-old student at St Martin's College of Art. Despite or perhaps because of his public-school background, Matt was also part of Ronnie Kray's retinue of boys. Michael de Freitas took me to the top-floor flat in Bassett Road, which would serve as my nominal home for the next five years. The flat had been tastefully equipped for me despite the fact it was being let as unfurnished. Who ultimately owned it I have no idea, but de Freitas was collecting the rent. Bradley arrived shortly after de Freitas ushered me into the pad. He was accompanied by Ronnie Kray and Lord Boothby.

'You make tea, girl, these men need refreshments,' de Freitas told me.

The kitchenette was attached to the main room so I could see most of what was going on while attending to my allotted task. De Freitas sprawled in an easy chair and rolled a joint. The three new arrivals stripped off. I quickly learned why the flat had been furnished for me. Lord Boothby lay under my glass coffee-table while Bradley, who I presume had taken laxatives, squatted on top of it. Ronnie Kray stood next to the table and, having dropped his pants and trousers, stuffed his erect manhood into Bradley's mouth.

'I like what you're doing,' Ronnie announced after Matt had been chewing on his plonker for a couple of minutes, 'and when I come you'll find the force of my ejaculation so great that I will oblige you to cack yourself.'

'You'd better prove him right, Bradley,' de Freitas put in before lighting the joint he'd just rolled, 'or else Ron and me will beat the shit out of you.'

It wasn't long before Kray was screaming incomprehensible obscenities and shortly afterwards a small turd plopped from Bradley's arse. Ron had come and his poshest rent boy had proved once again that he was able to shit on demand. As Lord Boothby crawled out from under the glass table, he was fondling an enormous erection. After pulling up his trousers Ronnie Kray stepped back from Bradley and proceeded to fasten his loose clothing. Matt hopped from the table to the floor and knelt in front of Boothby who he proceeded to suck off. As he was serviced, the Tory politician gazed intently at the turd that now decorated the table. I handed Ron a cup of tea and while I was doing so Lord Boothby groaned violently. Had I not known he was having an orgasm I would have been concerned that he was suffering a heart attack.

'You clean up the mess in this room, girl,' de Freitas snapped at me. 'You don't want your home looking and smelling like a slum.'

By the time I'd finished clearing up, my visitors had consumed their tea.

'You,' Kray was bawling out Bradley, 'keep your clothes off. We got some other geezers coming around, they want a gang bang.'

'Reggie's coming with them,' Michael added, before turning to me to say, 'You got nice silk underwear, girl? Reggie likes to wear lacy panties and a bra when he's having sex with a man.'

I went to get clean things from my case, but when I tried to give these to de Freitas he told me to change them for the stuff I was wearing. I went through to the bedroom to make the switch. This was perfectly acceptable to all those present since they weren't really interested in me. By the time I came back Reggie Kray and four other men who were never introduced to me had arrived at the flat. I handed Reg my dirty knickers and he complained he preferred clean undies. Ronnie and Michael laughed heartily, evidently enjoying his sense of dismay. Virtually everyone trooped through to the bedroom, leaving me alone with de Freitas.

'Listen, girl, I'll explain to you the way everything works,' Michael told me. 'You won't be working at General Gordon's again until you've had the baby. While you're up the duff there aren't so many men who'll want you. Ronnie has turned this loathsome public school brat Bradley into a rent boy by addicting him to amphetamines. The whole thing with a male hustler is that both he and his clients want to pretend that he's straight although it's obvious that he isn't. You're here to make Bradley's johns feel good. All you gotta do is take as big a slice of his money as you're able to grab. After Christmas I'll send you to a social worker. They can sort out an adoption for you. However, despite the fact we're gonna dump the baby you're to take Reggie to court over the paternity. You'll lose the case because the day on which you'll claim you had sex with Reggie will be one on which he was in jail.'

'What's the point of me taking a paternity suit out against Reggie and deliberately losing? Not that I'd be able to win, everyone knows he's into men.'

'Reggie has paid plenty of women good money to lose paternity cases against him. It's good for his image, it makes him appear as if he's straight. After all, whoever heard of a queer being sued for paternity?'

'That's crazy.'

'The twins are the craziest pair of ponces I ever met.'

'What about you?'

'I like money and women, in that order.'

'You make yourself sound like Mister Average.'

'Mister Average pays, I collect.'

'What are they doing in the other room?'

'Having sex. Don't think about it, just accept it. When those men came through the door I didn't see people; I saw pound notes. You take money from johns too, so what's the difference?'

'Are you going to give me a toke on that joint?'

'Girl, I like you, so I'll let you smoke. Have you tried charge before?'

'Sure, Christine introduced me to it at the club.'

'Peter's friend Christine?'

'Yeah, Peter's friend, Mandy's friend. As you know she's a showgirl like me.'

'You mean an expensive girl, one who won't walk the streets.'

'I mean a girl with class.'

'You're working class. These rich guys don't know how to place anyone from the middle classes on down, but I was born poor and I know you were too. When I was a boy I had to steal food to keep myself alive.'

'I shared a bed with my two sisters and one of my younger brothers until I was fourteen but I always had enough to eat.'

'Girl, you're lucky to come from the mother country because here they stopped starving the poor before you were born. I come from Trinidad, but although you ate better than me as you grew up, I still know you come from poverty.'

'You're right. On winter days I used to stand with my back to the oven wall of the bakery near my home to get warm. We only ate well when I was a child because my dad worked as a docker. Stealing goods from the ships that were being unloaded was one of the perks of the job.'

I could tell that on some level de Freitas liked me, and this feeling emerged partly from his idea that we were alike. As the years passed I got to know de Freitas well. I used to see him right up to the day he fled from England to avoid criminal proceedings, and after that I was mostly in touch with his wife Desiree. That first day I was sorry when Michael left with the Krays and their friends since I found myself alone with Matt Bradley in a flat I was condemned to share with him. This art student-cum-hustler was a pathetic human specimen. I made more tea and as we sat drinking it on the couch he went through the motions of attempting to seduce me.

'You know,' Bradley observed, 'I've just had seven different men spend their load in my bottom and my mouth. That's one for every day of the week.'

'If it's Ronnie it must be Monday!' I replied.

'Seven men just had their way with me and I haven't had an orgasm for weeks.'

'You've got two hands, a left and a right, so you've only yourself to blame.'

'I'm the putative father of your child, you could show a bit more concern.'

'It's not me who's been playing around with you. Didn't one of those seven men at least offer to jerk you off?'

'I'm not sexually attracted to men, I only do it with them for money.'

'What about women, then?'

'Well, I'd like to go with a woman.'

'What, you've never slept with a woman?'

'Would you show me what to do?'

'I can tell you, I won't show you. Go down to the Bayswater Road with some of that lucre you've just earned and ask one of the women standing on the pavement how much she charges.'

'But I'm almost the father of your child. In a few months, when you attempt to sue Reggie, the courts are going to hold me accountable for putting you in the family way, and from tonight we're sharing the same bed.'

'No we're not. You're sleeping on the couch.'

'Won't you get lonely in that double bed?'

'No.'

'I'll tell Ronnie you're mistreating me.'

'Your ponce won't be interested.'

'But I love you.'

'Give me a break, we've only just met.'

'I've seen you before, at General Gordon's when I've been in with Ronnie.'

'Well, I certainly don't love you.'

'You'd get to like me if only you tried.'

'I don't think anybody could like you.'

'What about my mother?'

'If she'd loved you then you wouldn't be so insecure. She must have rejected you. Did she prefer your siblings?'

'Do you think I'm insecure?'

'Yes.'

'I do too, which means we agree about something.'

'If we can agree about that then making suitable sleeping arrangements shouldn't be a problem either. I'll have the bed and you can take the couch.'

This pointless conversation continued in much the same manner until the small hours of the morning. When I did eventually retire to bed, Bradley waited until he thought I was asleep and then crawled in beside me. I had to punch him in the face before he accepted that his rightful place was in the other room. It was a war of nerves that went on for five years. Ronnie Kray and his associates made it clear that they expected me to stay with Bradley in Bassett Road. The Krays were frightening and you did what they said. In a fair fight, and I didn't always fight fairly, I could get the better of Bradley, but I didn't stand a chance against Ronnie Kray. I wasn't surprised when at the end of the 60s the Krays were banged up for murder. Their names were linked to some pretty gruesome crimes, and to throw people off the scent the cops put it about that their friend Freddie Mills was responsible for the murder of six west London prostitutes in the mid-60s. I'll write more about the nude murders and the uncaught Jack the Stripper later.

Despite spending several months a year away in Europe, it wasn't until 1966 that I was able to get a place of my own away from Matt Bradley. Even so, this was only around the corner in Elgin Crescent. Ronnie Kray never entirely lost interest in Bradley and I was instructed to keep the creep who spent five years posing as my common-law husband sweet. Once they got into you the Krays wouldn't let go. I couldn't win the paternity suit against Reggie but after the twins decided my son Lloyd was to be adopted they forced me to go through with it. I disappeared to Spain when the final papers were supposed to be signed, but when I returned to London months later, fully intending to be reunited with Lloyd, the Krays and their henchmen caught up with me and took me up to the adoption agency in Knightsbridge where I was forced to sign the final papers. The three busybodies who were present ignored my tears and the fact that I was flanked by two heavies who kept threatening to slash my face unless I signed on the dotted line. It was November and everyone present clearly considered me a nuisance for preventing the whole deal from being tied up back in the summer when what they all referred to as my 'business transaction' was supposed to have been completed.

'Adoption is the best thing for Lloyd, dear,' a middle-aged social worker told me. 'You can't offer him any sort of future. You're not married, and the stigma would ruin his life and yours too.'

I haven't got much time for the social workers or the Krays, but more than anyone else I blame Bradley for the fact that I lost Lloyd. Bradley liked showing me off to his johns but he didn't want a baby in our Bassett Road flat. Ronnie had the hots for him and that was why he was able to pressure the Krays into forcing me to give Lloyd away. In more normal circumstances it would have been a matter of indifference to the twins what happened to my baby. It was after I'd finally managed to leave 24 Bassett Road that Ron introduced Bradley to a man called Alan Bruce Cooper, who some years later they both discovered to their cost was an agent of the American Bureau of Narcotics and Dangerous Drugs. Cooper had offered to set the Krays up in a drug-smuggling scam where Pakistani officials would use their diplomatic immunity to import large quantities of hash into Europe. Ron was interested but Reg refused to get involved. In the end the project was passed over via Bradley to Tommy Graham. The resultant smuggling operation ran smoothly for a few years, then in 1970 Bradley and Graham were busted driving a substantial quantity of dope across the Swiss border into Germany. Bradley pretty much lost his nerve for drug trafficking after serving time in a German jail, but Graham is still working the scam with able assistance from men like Dennis Howard Marks.

3. EROTIC BOREDOM

When you've worked for much of your life as a hostess you have one circle of friends who understand what such employment entails and another circle who don't. The overwhelming majority of women who worked with me at clubs such as Gordon's or Kennedy's would be outraged if they were called prostitutes, since for most people the term conjures up images of destitute girls dressed in cheap clothes hawking their bodies on a public highway. That simply isn't how things were done at Gordon's, and it probably accounts for why those publicly connected to the political scandal that made the club infamous deny there was any impropriety involved when they received money from the various men they'd slept with. A hostess doesn't have sex with just anybody; interested men must first court her with champagne meals and flowers. At Gordon's I drank an awful lot of bubbly because I received a £5 commission for every cup consumed at my table. £5 was a lot of money in London in 1960. Likewise, when physical intimacy occurred with men I'd met in my capacity as a hostess, it tended to take the form of an ongoing relationship and the money that changed hands wasn't always directly linked to sexual acts.

A good-time girl knows the men she sleeps with by name, and even in the early 60s accepted cheques as well as cash. I began working as a hostess when I was sixteen and nearly twenty years later I'm still seeing a man I met during my first week at Gordon's in 1960. Albert Redwood is married and he has children. He's a businessman who's been sexually obsessed by me for years. He says he can't leave his family despite the fact that apart from his wife they've already left him. His youngest son is away at university, and his other children have families of their own. Bert's told me that if I refused to see him he'd track me down and kill me. I don't like it when he says things like this but I need his money. His mental balance is slightly askew but he's been a steady client and I almost like him.

Most of the men who develop a relationship with a hostess have some sort of emotional problem. They all like the status of being seen with a pretty girl, especially those who are self-made and didn't acquire the accoutrements of wealth until they reached middle age. There is one really well-known figure who can be invoked as absolutely typical of the clientele at Kennedy's or Gordon's, although to the best of my knowledge he never went to either club, and that's Peter Rachman. He wasn't the evil figure the press made him out to be after his death, although he made a more than healthy profit from the slum properties he rented out, and he was engaged in all the dubious practices beloved of the successful businessman. That said, Rachman was less exploitative than those who bought up the west London slums he owned a year or two before his death as he sought to consolidate his holdings by moving out of the rented sector. Rachman was fat, bald and spoke in a high-pitched voice, but he was also a kind man who took an interest in those around him. He was generous to a fault. The first time I met him, he gave me a 22-carat gold watch he'd bought from the jeweller Kutchinsky. As was my habit then as now, I sold it on and I got a good price for it. Rachman had a hygiene fetish and didn't like to eat or drink in any establishment where he couldn't inspect the kitchens, which was why he wasn't to be seen at Gordon's. The Nazis had placed Rachman on a chain gang building an autobahn after they invaded his native Poland. Having escaped from the clutches of Hitler's henchmen, Rachman was caught by the Russians who placed him in a Siberian labour camp. Rachman starved and to survive he told me he had to eat human excrement. He'd seen his parents dragged off to a concentration camp by the Nazis, and despite endless enquiries he was never to learn their fate. Rachman had led a rough life by the time he died from a heart attack in 1962 at the age of 42. Despite his middle-class background he was reduced to working as a factory labourer when he first arrived in London.

It was Michael de Freitas who put me on to Rachman, and for this service I slipped him a fiver from the sale of the gold watch I was given by his former landlord. Michael couldn't set me up directly with Rachman since there were unresolved differences between them. Instead he told me to go to the coffee shop in Queensway where Peter took his lunch and to sit around looking pretty. Michael had been forceful when he insisted it was more than worthwhile to enter Rachman's orbit and he assured me I wouldn't have to make the first move. Michael was, as I quickly discovered, unnervingly accurate about where and how easily money might be copped. I was pregnant, and although a judicious choice of clothes enabled me to disguise my condition, for the time being working at Gordon's was out of the question. Michael told me not to worry: I could still work – it was just a matter of taking the right approach. I was blooming and Albert Redwood wasn't the only regular from Gordon's who still wanted to sleep with me. Nevertheless, despite being bunged a few drinks by the Krays, now that I wasn't at the club every night my income had dipped. Michael warned me not to mention the Krays to Peter; he told me Rachman was petrified of them. He'd also said not to mention my condition unless Rachman noticed it. Michael told me he knew a few guys who'd pay extra to make it with a pregnant woman, especially if she was heavily pregnant, but that Peter wasn't one of them. I was nursing a coffee when Rachman entered the café in which Michael had told me he took his lunch. Having donned my war paint and false eyelashes, I was by far and away the prettiest girl in the coffee shop and Peter's eyes soon alighted on me.

'Look over there at that beauty.' I overheard Rachman saying to his companions. 'Do you think I could have her?'

'She's classy, Peter, and young too, but you might as well give it a try. The worst she can do is tell you to get lost.'

'Excuse me, dear,' Rachman said as he made his way across to me, 'but do you know the time? My watch has stopped.'

'I don't wear a watch,' I told him.

'But my dear, to make a success of oneself in the 1960s one absolutely must wear a watch. I want you to take mine.' As he said this Rachman pulled a 22-carat gold watch from his pocket.

'I don't know if I can take it,' I lied.

'Don't worry, dear, I have another. At the very least you must try it on.'

Peter helped me put the watch around my wrist.

'Is it gold?' I asked, hoping the question sounded naïve.

'Yes, my dear, solid gold. It looks so pretty on your wrist. You absolutely must keep it, I insist.'

'I couldn't.'

'It is rude to refuse a present. I'm a very wealthy man and this is a trinket. You must keep it, and to repay me come over and keep me company while I have my lunch. Would you like something to eat?'

'I'm not hungry.'

'Well, then, you must have another coffee.'

'Yes, I'd like another drink. Thank you very much.'

And with that we walked across to Rachman's companions, who had evidently seen him make pick-ups of this type dozens of times. That said, they remained impressed by his front.

'What's your name?' Peter asked.

'Jeanette,' I replied, since this was what I was calling myself professionally at that time.

'I'm Peter, and this is Gerry and my other friend is Serge.'

'Hello,' I said.

'Hello,' Serge and Gerry echoed.

'Given that you weren't wearing a watch I presume you're not on a lunch break and have plenty of time.'

'I'm free all day. I work in the evening.'

'What do you do?'

'I'm a showgirl at General Gordon's Club, or rather I was. I'm taking a break from it right now.'

'Ah, very good, very good. Look, here's another coffee. How many cups did you drink before I arrived?'

'Two.'

'You get £5 commission on each cup at the club, don't you.' It wasn't a question, it was a statement, despite Peter's singsong voice. He proceeded to pull a huge wad of notes from a pocket and counted out £15.

'That's the commission I get for each champagne cup I drink at the club. It's a ridiculous amount to give me for drinking coffee in here.'

'They don't serve champagne at this establishment, so I'll pay you the same for drinking coffee at lunch-time as you get for downing bubbly at the club.'

'That's very sweet of you.'

I picked up the notes that had been placed on the table in front of me and flashed Rachman a smile as I folded them. I noticed Peter was drinking cola although his associates were imbibing coffee.

'Do you live nearby?' Rachman asked.

'Bassett Road.'

'Too far to walk. May I drive you there? My car is just outside.' Peter jerked his thumb and indicated a Rolls Royce.

'Yes, that would be lovely.'

'I'll see you guys later.' Peter's friends obviously knew what was in his diary since they didn't ask where to find him.

We got into the Roller and before I knew it we were home, or at least I was home. I invited Peter up to the flat. He said nothing about it although it wasn't any better than the slums he used to rent out. At least the place was clean. Michael had told me to make sure it was spotless in case Rachman wanted me to take him back there.

'I want to lie down on the bed,' Peter told me. 'You will sit on top of me with your back to my face. I don't want you to turn around and look at me.'

I was happy to do whatever Rachman wanted. He wasn't exactly good-looking, so being told not to ogle him during sex was no loss to me. I wriggled above Peter and once he'd come he wanted to get up and leave. He dressed and then pulled out his wad of notes and peeled off £20. It had been a profitable encounter for me.

'I find lunch-time sex clears my head and makes me a better businessman in the afternoon. Now I must go because I have many things to attend to. However I like you. May I see you again?'

'Certainly,' I said.

'Here's my number,' Peter said as he handed me a card. 'Call me at the office next week. We'll meet for lunch and I'll find somewhere we can retire to afterwards. Your flat is lovely but I find that changing the surroundings keeps sex interesting.'

'OK,' I said.

'I'll see myself out.'

I lay down on the bed wondering whether or not Rachman had realised I was pregnant. If he had, then he'd decided to say nothing about it and he'd arranged to see me again regardless. His own belly was larger than mine, the result of suffering from starvation during the war years and then bingeing when he finally got the chance to eat as much as he wanted. Michael had warned me Rachman was sensitive about his size and to say nothing that might indicate I considered him to be fat. When I saw Peter the following week he noticed my belly as I got up from the hotel bed. He'd apparently been oblivious to it while we had sex. He gave me extra money for the baby and told me to contact him again after the child was born. Rachman liked his girls young and at that time I was still seventeen. When we rekindled our relationship late in the spring of 1962 he only had seven months to live and I was away in Spain for nearly half of that time.

After Lloyd was born I was able to resume my work as a showgirl at General Gordon's, so I had less need of Peter's money and he was both ill and busy. In total I had sex with Rachman no more than half a dozen times. He didn't demand much and he was generous with his roll. When he elected to spend time with me he proved to be good company and this more than made up for his lack of looks. Of course Rachman had a wife and a regular mistress. I've no idea how many other girls like me he enjoyed on the side but I certainly wasn't the only one. When Rachman died he was an obscure London businessman, but within a year he became notorious as the most evil landlord of all time. Peter was an ideal target for politicians like Ben Parkin who wanted to stir up a debate on housing issues. The dead are unable to defend their posthumous reputations. Likewise, the newspapers could write what they liked about Rachman without fear of libel writs. His business practices, usually only just this side of legal, were no different to those of any other tycoon. If one wished to condemn Rachman then it was hypocritical to do so without simultaneously indicting all those capitalists who made money from property deals. He was, if anything, slightly better than the majority of them.

Sex with Rachman, as with all the businessmen I met at Gordon's, was essentially meaningless. I found it funny that rich men would pay me to go to bed with them. The best thing about Peter was that he treated our lunch-time sessions with a casualness that matched my indifference about his lack of skill as a lover. Sex to Rachman was akin to taking a bath, something which for whatever reasons he felt obliged to attend to at least twice a day. That was what made Peter such a good client. He liked my body but we both knew he didn't love me. He wasn't like Bert, who claims that if only he wasn't trapped in a sexless marriage there is nothing he would rather do than live with me full-time. That, I'm afraid, is a drag, and I'm very glad Redwood is encumbered with a wife since I don't want to set up home with him. A man twice my age has never been my idea of an ideal husband. I don't mind men who are a little bit older than me but twenty to thirty years is way too much of a difference when it comes to a serious relationship. Giordano, my soul mate from the mid-60s onwards, was five years older than me and we lived together off and on from 1966 until 1976. Now I'm living with Garrett, and although he tries to keep his age a secret, I know he was born nearly a decade before I made my first appearance in this world. I never expected to fall for Garrett the way I have, but dealing with the ten-year age gap between us isn't a problem now I've reached my mid-thirties.

4. MOTHER OF SHAME

I'm enjoying writing about my life because setting it down helps me place it in perspective. That said, there are incidents that I find difficult to address, and chief among them is the way in which I lost my son Lloyd. One of the things that I'm amazed by is how much European society changed between the early 60s, when Lloyd was born, and the swinging London era that took off just a few years later. In 1962 abortion and homosexuality were still illegal in the UK, whereas by the end of the decade both social attitudes and the law were less rigid. Indeed, by the 70s the pill and women's liberation had become an integral part of everyday life in London. If Lloyd had been born in the mid-60s things would have turned out very differently for both me and him, since by then there was a psychedelic community around who'd have given us support. In 1962 it really wasn't acceptable for a girl to keep a baby born out of wedlock. Even in the beatnik circles I moved in it wasn't easy to bring up a child outside of marriage. I knew other prostitutes who lost children they'd given birth to at eighteen. It was only working girls who'd reached their twenties who'd stick to their guns and raise children as single parents. Of course, I knew where to get an abortion but that was the last thing I wanted. Few of the club girls I knew who fell pregnant had terminations. The culture in our circles was very much to have the baby even if we didn't intend keeping it.

It was Michael de Freitas who told me to go to St Stephen's Church in Shepherds Bush to ask for help in getting my unborn baby adopted. St Stephen's was where the West Indian girls in the neighbourhood went when they found themselves in the family way. Since it was High Church with an ethnically mixed congregation, Michael figured that a girl like me with a Catholic family background would fit in reasonably well. I'd heard horror stories about nuns and priests mistreating illegitimate Catholic children who were placed in their care, and so I didn't want to risk my baby ending up in a religious institution. Likewise, since the man I believe is Lloyd's father was Catholic like me and had many enemies, I concluded that those with evil on their minds who might seek out my child were less likely to be successful in their mission if I placed him with a Protestant family. It was at the time extremely unusual for a Catholic baby to be adopted outside the Roman faith.

Michael said all I needed to make a paternity suit against Reggie Kray was my baby's birth certificate, so he figured the best thing to do was sort out an adoption before the child was born. On 17 January 1962 I took a tube from Ladbroke Grove to Shepherds Bush in an attempt to resolve my situation. I'd turned eighteen ten days earlier and, being seven months pregnant, my condition showed. I found a priest and he immediately sent me around to the church hall where I met Sister Wesson, a moral welfare worker. I had to provide various details including my name, date of birth and address. I gave a false date of birth, something my father always did when dealing with the authorities since it made you harder to trace. I claimed to be a year older than I actually was. I felt this might be to my advantage since I was determined that my family should never know about

Lloyd and it seemed my wishes were more likely to be respected if I appeared to be older than I really was. As far as employment went I claimed I'd been working as a nanny for a private family, since I thought it unlikely the Church of England would help a showgirl and hostess who'd fallen pregnant. Besides, if I said I was a hostess then the moral welfare workers were bound to conclude I was a prostitute.

'Well, dearie, anyone can see what your problem is. Why didn't you come earlier?'

'I was intending to marry the father but that's not going to happen now.'

I didn't want to admit that I hadn't tried to sort out an adoption when I was still seventeen in case the authorities informed my parents of my condition. My mother was desperate to get me home and she'd even sent a couple of my brothers down to London with instructions to go to the police about me. After seeing the rozzers my brothers had come to visit me. The Met had told them that since I was seventeen and had a roof over my head no one could force me to return home. My brothers told me this and then said I should go back to Scotland with them anyway since ma was worrying herself sick about me. I told them that London was my home. Living in Greenock really didn't suit me. The moral welfare worker's voice woke me from my reverie.

'Will it be possible for me to interview the father?' Sister Wesson enquired.

'Yes.'

'What is he called and where does he live?'

'His name is Matthew Bradley and he lives with me.'

'What! You want my help and yet you're living in sin! Didn't your parents teach you right from wrong?'

'We were going to get married but my fiancé's parents wouldn't allow it.' I'd already agreed this story with Matt Bradley.

'Do you want to keep the child?'

'I'd like to keep the baby but Matt wants him adopted.'

'Well, for the baby's sake you can't keep the child unless you're married and I can't help you with an adoption unless you leave the father.'

'But you're asking me to leave my home! It's just a small upstairs flat, but I love it.'

'Will the father leave this accommodation?'

'There's no chance of that.'

'Then you'll have to go.'

'But I don't want to move and I don't have anywhere to go.'

'Can't you go home to your parents?'

'I couldn't possibly do that. They're getting on and it would be a terrible shock for them to learn about my condition.'

'Are they very religious?'

'They're Roman Catholic.'

'Never mind, dearie, your family are Christians and you can at least be thankful you're not Irish!'

'I was born in Greenock but all four of my grandparents were Irish.'

'We all have our crosses to bear.'

'I'm not a practising Catholic.'

'Do you go to church?'

'I'd like to but I'm unsure if I'd be allowed to go to the Anglican Church seeing as I'm Catholic.'

'The Lord welcomes all his children to the flock, dearie. When did you last go to mass?'

'More than two years ago.'

'That's absolutely shocking!'

'Well, I didn't know that I was allowed to go to your church and the family priest attempted to molest me every time I went into the confession box back in Greenock.'

'Did you tell your father?'

'Of course not, it would have upset him.'

'Will you go to an Anglican church this Sunday now I've told you that you can?'

'Yes. I will, I'd very much like to do that.'

'That's what I like to hear! Now, if your baby was to be adopted, what religious denomination would you like the child's new family to be?'

'Anglican,' I shot back, figuring this was what Sister Wesson was hoping I'd say and that by providing her with the right answer I might induce her to help me.

'A wise choice, a very wise choice indeed,' Sister Wesson told me. 'I can see you're a sensible girl. Now, if you're prepared to leave the father of this child, I'll certainly arrange for you to go into a mother and baby home.'

'But couldn't you help me with an adoption and let me stay with the father?'

'That isn't possible, my dear, no one will help you while you're living in sin. By doing this you're not simply ruining your own life, you're tainting your unborn child. I have a background in the Church Army, you know, which is why I have the title Sister Wesson, and I came to Shepherds Bush directly after working for many years as a missionary in India. Let me tell you something in confidentiality: when I came back to England in 1953 I was shocked to find how far our country had drifted away from being a properly Christian nation. Young people have become so used to doing whatever they want that when they are faced with a real temptation they don't know how to say no. I can see this is precisely what has happened to you, although I have to admit you were disadvantaged to begin with, coming as you do from an Irish Catholic family. But I can see you're an intelligent girl, and let me tell you this. England is going to the dogs, and I blame both the Labour Party with its secular values and a sorry Tory leadership who lack the gumption to fight against the trades unions and abolish the welfare state. The Bible teaches the value of charity because it is something that can be used to lead sinners back on to the path of righteousness. When government assistance becomes a universal right then the poor are robbed of their role as the moral backbone of our national community. Instead of the deserving poor receiving help from those of us kind-hearted enough to provide it and undeserving scoundrels either mending their ways or going to the wall, all the incentives for the working class to walk the straight road God has laid down for them are removed. It is morally wrong to allow the working man jam every day; this is a privilege that in a sane world would be reserved for the better classes!'

Since I'd already told Sister Wesson my father was a docker, she was less than keen to hear my opinions on this matter but I let rip anyway. Initially I was rather heartened by how my outburst led her to conclude the interview. As I left Sister Wesson told me not to return unless I was ready to move into accommodation that was suitable for an unmarried woman. I caught the tube back to Ladbroke Grove and told Matt Bradley what had happened. He in his turn informed Ronnie Kray and not long afterwards this heavy made it plain that unless I found someone else who'd help me arrange an adoption for my baby, then I would have to take Sister Wesson up on her offer of a place in a mother and baby home. Ronnie quietly explained that if I failed to sort something out by the middle of March, then he personally would punch me in the stomach until my unborn child lay dead in my womb. Kray also made it plain that if I attempted to run away from him so that I could keep the baby, he would track me down and when he found me he'd kill my child and cripple me. As a direct consequence of these threats I went to see a number of social workers and all of them refused to help me while I was unmarried and living with a man. In the end I went back to Sister Wesson and since I was willing to do her bidding she arranged for me to move into the Haygarth Witts Memorial Home in Wimbledon. When I asked if it would be possible to find somewhere nearer to my friends, Sister Wesson informed me that all the mother and baby homes in west London were full. However I suspected I was being shuffled off to the southern fringes of the city precisely to remove me from what this moral welfare worker perceived to be bad influences.

Sister Wesson handed me a letter to take with me to the Haygarth Witts Home. I was instructed to return to Ladbroke Grove and to stay in my flat no longer than it took me to pack a suitcase. I would be expected in Wimbledon that very night. I attempted to con Sister Wesson out of a few quid with the excuse that I'd fallen behind with the rent but she was having none of that. Since the man she believed was responsible for getting me into trouble was staying in the flat she said it was down to him to sort out any difficulties with the landlord. Sister Wesson had interviewed Matt Bradley once I'd accepted the strings which came attached to her offer of help, and she did not like him one bit because he'd refused the offer she'd made him of help from the Church.

'I am pleasantly surprised to hear that you're intending to return to live with your parents in Greenock,' Sister Wesson informed me after she'd swallowed a whopping helping of bullshit I'd fed her on this score. 'The fact that you are going to have a baby and you'll have to part with the child has made you think! To be fair to you society is very much to blame for the situation you find yourself in. It has provided you with too many carrots and not enough sticks. I want you to remember that God is a jealous master, and the only way to deal with that is to throw yourself down before Him and beg Him for forgiveness and mercy. Admit that you are a miserable sinner and you can enjoy eternal life, but if you should fail to abase yourself before the Lord then you'll fry forever in hell.'

It didn't take me long to pack. What I'd told Sister Wesson about returning to Greenock once the baby was born was an outright lie. I intended to stay in Bassett Road, so I left most of my possessions there. Sister Wesson had given me the train fare to travel across the city, and so with a suitcase in my hand, I took the tube. There were an incredible variety of girls in the Haygarth Witts Memorial Home: some were still at school and a few had just recently left. All of the really young girls were in local-authority care and would be returned to orphanages once they'd given birth and had their babies taken from them. That said, the majority of girls resident in the mother and baby home were in their late teens, while the oldest woman amongst us was 36. Hannah Smith had been deserted by her husband and wasn't able to cope on her own. She was due to give birth on the same day as Mary Cressingdon, who at 23 was the second eldest inmate when I arrived at the home. Most of the residents in the home were English although Susan Sheba, who I liked best, had come over from Trinidad to train as a nurse in London. The only other girl from Scotland was fourteen, and since Marion MacBeath came from the east coast and had suffered a hardcore Presbyterian upbringing, we didn't have much in common.

There weren't any girls over from Ireland in the Haygarth Witts Memorial Home and I knew this was because when they were sent to London to have their babies they were placed in Catholic institutions. We were organised into what were called dormitories, although to me they seemed more like wards. While resident in Wimbledon I was forever aware of the fact that I was living in an institution with sounds and smells very similar to those you'd find in a hospital. I arrived on 14 March 1962 and the ten days I endured there before I went into labour seemed to constitute an eternity. I was assigned a number of chores, but given my condition these were not onerous. I read and made baby clothes to help pass the time. I would chat with the other girls and there were endless interviews with busybodies during which I had to pretend I thought that everything being done for me was truly wonderful. The chaplain was by far and away the most tedious of the numerous nitwits I was forced to deal with. He took a special interest in me because I came from a Catholic family background, and he saw this as an opportunity for making a successful conversion. This windbag was deliriously happy when on an application form I filled out for the adoption agency, I gave my religion as Church of England. Through ruses of this type I managed to avoid the confirmation classes the chaplain wanted me to attend. I've always been deeply spiritual and as a result everything about the Church of England rang false to me. At base this institution amounts to no more than a scam set up to glorify her royal lowness the Queen of England.

If the Mother and Baby Home located in London SW19 seemed bleak, then Nelson Hospital, with its considerably less prestigious London SW20 postcode, can only be described as more so. Wimbledon was seen as posh, while neighbouring Merton, in which the hospital was situated, simply didn't carry the same cachet. However, these social niceties were the last thing on my mind when on 24 March I gave birth to Lloyd. My labour was short at just three hours, and when Lloyd popped into the world at five minutes before midnight, he weighed a healthy seven pounds and ten ounces. He had fair hair and blazing blue eyes. Lloyd was bonny and since his appearance was similar to mine it gave mercifully few clues about the identity of his father. Holding my newborn baby boy in my arms made me deliriously happy and I didn't give a damn about the surroundings. I was on the most amazing high, a state which I was never able to replicate no matter what chemicals I experimented with in later life. But my happiness was tainted by the knowledge that the time I had with Lloyd was limited. All I wanted to do was cradle my beautiful baby son in my arms and gaze at him. Being with Lloyd was like walking on air and I hardly noticed when I was moved out of the hospital and back to the Haygarth Witts Home. In retrospect I wish I'd been able to breast-feed Lloyd but since he was being put up for adoption I was told he should go straight on to a bottle. While he was with me, Lloyd was on a strict regime of four-hour feeds and I loved watching him guzzle his milk. The six weeks we spent together sped by. I took Lloyd out for walks because I knew the spring air did him good. Towards the end of April the two of us paid a visit to Russell's Photographic Studio in Wimbledon. I went back a few days later and picked up a number of snapshot-sized portraits. There were several of Lloyd on his own and in others I was holding him. Across these black and white photographs, rubber-stamped in blue ink, were the words: PROOF. A. RUSSELL AND SONS, WORPLE ROAD. I didn't have the money to pay for the full-sized portraits, and so the pictures of Lloyd I've carried with me for the past seventeen years are marked in this fashion. As the only memento I have of my time with Lloyd, these have been the greatest treasure of my adult life. I've learnt to live with the stamps, and since none of them touch Lloyd's face, they've never bothered me when I look at the pictures.

Since I'd insisted I didn't want my parents to know about Lloyd, we were allowed to live together at the Haygarth Witts Memorial Home for six weeks after his birth. Then on 3 May 1962 a social worker called Mrs Lichenstein came and tore us apart. She took us to Wimbledon station and Lloyd cried all the way. Although it was a warm day I'd dressed Lloyd up in several sets of clothes so that he'd have plenty to wear when he left me. He was hot and unhappy and I felt wretched too. Mrs Lichenstein accompanied us on to the tube train. I'd have preferred to enjoy the final hour I shared with my baby free from the distraction of a do-gooder's idle and meaningless chatter. We changed trains at South Kensington and Mrs Lichenstein chaperoned me all the way into the offices of the London Children's Adoption Agency in Knightsbridge, that dreadful building in which I last saw my son. After I'd handed Lloyd over to a ghastly woman who didn't know how to cope with either his or my tears, I was ushered out on to the street. In my pocket I had a one-way train ticket to Greenock via Glasgow which Sister Wesson had purchased for me. As I walked across Hyde Park to Notting Hill there were tears streaming down my face. I couldn't face catching a bus since I didn't want the sympathy strangers might tender if they saw the state I was in. I still had a key for 24 Bassett Road, so I was able to let myself into what should have been

Lloyd's home. It was my bad luck that Matt Bradley was around. He made me some tea but offered no soothing words about what I was going through. I was pleased about that because sympathy was the last thing I wanted from him. After I'd had a brew, Bradley handed me various papers I had to sign in order to set the ludicrous paternity suit against Reggie Kray in motion.

5. FOUND NAKED AND DEAD

Pursuing the life of a working girl I've met more than my fair share of weirdoes, and among this lumpen refuse from all classes there have always been a disproportionate number employed as Old Bill. While the Jack the Stripper slayings remain officially unsolved, it is widely known that the man responsible for the murder of six west London prostitutes in the mid-60s was a cop. Having met the nude murderer I find myself in the unenviable position of being able to finger him. John du Rose, who oversaw the investigations into these grisly crimes, claims that although the killer is dead he should remain anonymous because the feelings of his relatives count. This is simply a case of a cop protecting his own and pronouncements of this type are rather rich coming from someone who has publicly ventilated his highly ambivalent attitudes about prostitutes by claiming that not even they deserve to die. Clearly, John du Rose was not a man who should have been entrusted with protecting working girls. Likewise, since Jack the Stripper never married, there are no close relatives and as far as I'm concerned the six women he slaughtered count for far more than the posthumous reputation of a perverted sex-fiend.

Elizabeth Figg and Gwynneth Rees were not nude murder victims. That said they've sometimes been linked to the Jack the Stripper serial killings and while I have no idea how they came to breathe their last breath, I know it was not at the hands of the man I'm going to identify. Figg died in 1959 and Rees in 1963; it is merely the fact that they were both known prostitutes which led to speculation that they might have been the earliest nude murder victims.

Jack the Stripper's first victim, Hannah Tailford, was an acquaintance of mine. She was a decade older than me and had come to London from Northumbria. I got to know her at a late-night beatnik café in the West End called Coco's, where we scored pills. Both Hannah and I popped reds, whites, blues, downers, sleepers, Nembutal, Seconal, Tuinal, Amytal, Luminal, call them what you will. Likewise each of us smoked what was in the street jargon of the time called 'charge'. Hannah enjoyed recounting curious tales of her life in the sex trade, and after the Profumo scandal broke she became particularly fond of reciting how in 1960 she'd been picked up by the osteopath Stephen Ward, who had in the intervening period become an object of media fascination. It was Ward who introduced Christine Keeler to both the Tory war minister John Profumo and the Russian naval attaché Eugene Ivanov. As everyone still recalls, Harold Wilson and the Labour Party opposition hammered away at the security implications of a leading government minister having an affair with a girl who'd simultaneously taken a Soviet spy as a lover. Although Profumo was forced to resign from his Parliamentary position, as far as most people from my more immediate circles were concerned the entire affair was designed to divert attention from saucier goings-on in the White House.

Returning to Tailford and her story, she told me that after she accepted £25 from Ward, he drove her in his car to an orgy being held by Prince Philip's cousin, the Marquess of Milford Haven. The service Hannah provided was to make love to a man in a gorilla suit while a group of his cronies looked on. As well as straightforward flat-backing, Tailford used to pose for dirty pictures and she was sometimes employed as a dominatrix. Hannah had done plenty of kinky stuff in her time but she insisted that the group of perverts centred on Ward and the Marquess of Milford Haven were the sickest johns she'd encountered during the course of a long and extremely chequered sex industry career. Given her well-paid work with high-society rakes, I never understood why Tailford often resorted to street-walking, nor why she took photographs of tricks to earn extra money by blackmailing wealthy clients. I was shocked but not that surprised when Hannah was found dead on the Thames embankment near Hammersmith Bridge on 3 February 1964. She had been stripped naked, although her stockings were still around her ankles and her panties had been stuffed in her mouth.

Irene Lockwood was the second nude murder victim. She lived not too far from me in Denbigh Road. Irene was found naked and dead on 9 April 1964, three hundred yards from where Hannah Tailford's body had been discovered two months earlier. It was after the death of the pregnant Irene that the media hullabaloo about the nude murders began, and for almost a year there was saturation coverage. I used to see Irene in the pubs around Portobello Road and would sometimes chat with her. Irene was not simply a pavement pounder who provided straight sex; she also did perversions and posed for photographs. Like Tailford, when the opportunity arose she'd blackmail the better-off among her clientele. In terms of brazen scams Irene went even further than Hannah, since she took men to rooms for sex where she'd steal their wallets and then run off without even providing the service she'd promised. I've always considered it safer to rely on a smaller number of rich clients who are either met in clubs or through the doormen who work them, so I never pull tricks like that even when I'm desperate for money. I always wondered why Irene continued with these activities, especially after our friend Vicki Pender was murdered at her flat in Finsbury Park in March 1963. Like Irene I'd last seen Vicki Pender alive in the Nucleus Club on Monmouth Street not long before she died.

Whenever I wanted to lift a wallet I'd use my skills as a pickpocket on strangers, not people who knew me by name, even if that was as Jeanette Geoffries rather than Jilly O'Sullivan. To me prostitution was always a good source of income and I didn't want to damage my ongoing relationships with rich clients. Tailford and Lockwood lacked my longer-term views on these matters; revelling instead in the idea of criminal activity and projecting to the world at large a self-image of belonging to the demi-monde, they simultaneously placed themselves in jeopardy and scared away the least troublesome johns.

The third nude murder victim, Helene Catherine Barthelemy, left her Talbot Road flat for an evening in the Westbourne Park Road Jazz Club before she was murdered. She was found on 24 April 1964 in Brentford, less than a mile from where the previous bodies were dumped. The fourth victim, Mary Fleming, lived on Lancaster Road in Notting Hill and her body was found on 14 July 1964 in Chiswick. According to the papers, like many other west London prostitutes, Fleming was a heavy smoker, drinker and consumer of pep pills. I didn't know Barthelemy or Fleming, but both of them were friends of the penultimate nude murder victim, Margaret McGowan. I saw McGowan in the Warwick Castle on Portobello Road just before she died: she was making bets with her streetwalker friends as to who the next Jack the Stripper victim would be. I exchanged a few words with McGowan but since I was not a pavement pounder and I wasn't familiar with all the names that were being bandied about I didn't get involved with the gambling. McGowan's body was found on 25 November 1964 on waste ground in Kensington, with a dustbin lid placed over her face. The final victim, Bridget Esther O'Hara, was found on 16 February 1965. She'd been murdered more than a month before, and after being kept in storage under a nearby electrical transformer, her body was dumped on a west London industrial estate. I didn't know O'Hara but she knew at least one other nude murder fatality.

There was plenty of talk back in the mid-60s about the Jack the Stripper slayings being a continuation of the cover up that began with the Profumo affair, and this is correct as far as it goes. I put the story of what really happened together from many sources and over a number of years. The bare bones of how I did this will become apparent from what I'm about to relate. The fifth victim of the anonymous serial killer was Margaret McGowan, who had testified at the trial of Stephen Ward, using the pseudonym Frances Brown, when he became the fall guy for an establishment being rocked by a scandal that was of considerably less consequence than some of the stories it functioned to divert attention away from.

A procurer of young girls for his high-society friends, Doctor Ward was found guilty of living off the immoral earnings of Christine Keeler and Mandy Rice Davis. By committing suicide Ward escaped a spell in jail. As more and more people are beginning to realise, the Profumo affair was orchestrated by various western security agencies as a cover-up to prevent the exposure of a prostitution scandal involving the US president John F. Kennedy. The fact that Kennedy was a philanderer is now public knowledge, but a decade and more ago the intimate details of his peccadilloes were merely gossip and rumour within tightly restricted political circles and my own demi-monde. Mariella Novotny isn't the only prostitute I know who was paid by the dead president to perform sexual acts with him.

Kennedy was assassinated in November 1963 by his own security men because they knew that his sexual escapades were a political liability, and that it was impossible to keep the lid on them while he remained alive. After JFK had been iced, those members of the US establishment who'd orchestrated the murder were free to nurture the myth that the era he'd presided over had been a golden age for free-market democracy. By this means the cynical Kennedy was post-humously dressed in the garb of a slain hero and elected to the status of a capitalist saint whose fable became one of the capstones of American cold war propaganda.

As I've said, I got to know all this by putting together information from a wide variety of sources, but I was canny enough not to admit to it when I had my collar felt by a couple of uniformed cops as I left General Gordon's late one night. I found myself whisked off to see Detective Chief Superintendent Tommy Butler of Scotland Yard's Flying Squad. Butler was a bald and wiry middle-aged man who still lived with his mother. He was a career cop who lived for his work and who reached the top because he was considered a good detective by his colleagues. That said, even within the Metropolitan Police he was considered unsociable, obsessive and eccentric. Butler's extended working hours were a matter of legend among his colleagues, and he had a reputation for securing enough material to convict a suspect before having them hauled up before him. Therefore I was terrified to find myself being interrogated by this weirdo with only a large and extremely battered wooden desk separating us.

'I want you to get this straight from the beginning,' Butler informed me. 'I'm down on whores.'

'Prostitution isn't a criminal offence in England and I would never take to the streets to solicit.'

'Don't try to get clever with me!' Butler snapped. Then, pointing at his crotch, he added, 'My pecker kills lewd bitches.'

'Is that how Hannah Tailford and Margaret McGowan copped it?'

'I choked all six of the sluts with Henry and you'll get it next if you don't play ball with me. Do you understand that I'm in deadly earnest when I say this to you?'

'Yes.'

'Do you know what all the stuff with Keeler and Stephen Ward was about?'

'No.'

'It was a warning to harlots not to reiterate anything they know about JFK. Gossip about the president plays into the hands of Ruskie propaganda.'

'I don't know anything about JFK. Why use Profumo to fire a warning shot over the bows of club hostesses?'

'Profumo had become a liability, and worse yet, he was repeating gossip he picked up from the strumpets he socialised with.'

'Right.'

'Dead right. Now, as you may perhaps recall, John Kennedy visited London in June 1961.'

'He was also here in June 1963.'

'That's correct, but don't think you can get clever with me. If you were really smart you'd have never left Greenock, you'd have never come to London and you'd have never set up shop as a tart. Do you regret the life you've been leading?'

'Yes,' I lied, since this was clearly how I was expected to reply.

'That's better. Now I want you to cast your mind back to June 1961. I want you to tell me whether or not you conceived a child at that time.'

'My son Lloyd was born several weeks overdue in March 1962, so he'd have been conceived in June 1961.'

'And pray tell me, girlie, where is Lloyd now?'

'I don't know.'

'Well I do.'

'Where is he?'

'I'm not telling you. I just want you to know that if I gave the order he could be brought here in less than an hour. Do you care about what might happen to your son? Do you want him to live long enough to become a man?'

'Yes.'

'In that case you'd better think carefully about the questions I'm about to ask you and provide suitable answers. The whores who died were all gossiping about you and Kennedy; they believed you'd been to see him when he was over here in June 1961.'

'I saw him but only from a distance, and it was nothing professional. I took part in a Campaign for Nuclear Disarmament protest against his cold war policies.'

'So you're telling me that there is no truth to the rumour that you were paid to have sex with John F. Kennedy.'

'Yes.'

'And that your son Lloyd O'Sullivan is not the illegitimate offspring of this murdered US president.'

'Yes.'

'In that case, who is the father?'

'Officially Matt Bradley, unofficially I don't know.'

'So you gave birth to a bastard?'

'Yes.'

'And you're absolutely certain this bastard is not the illegitimate offspring of the late president of the United States.'

'Yes.'

'Very good, trollop, I like your answers. In fact I like them so much that I'm going to let you and your bastard son live, for the time being at any rate. However, I want you to remember something: I'm a top copper and that makes me untouchable. I'm not some expendable squirt like Challenor. I've killed six whores and I got away with it. I could off another six and I'd still get away with it. I'm down on whores but I'm also a disciplined man: I only liquidate vermin when I've been ordered to do it.'

'Who's behind all this?'

'Who do you think?'

'Does Harold Wilson know about it?'

'No.'

'Are you working with the Americans?'

'No.'

'Who, then?'

'God, that's who. God told me to do it. You look shocked, but you've a bigger shock to come yet. When you die you will have to answer to your maker for your degeneracy. God will judge and God will find you guilty! My sole purpose is to ensure that what God wants to pass in this life is realised here and now on His earth.'

'You're going to let God judge me when the time comes?'

'That's right. God will judge you, and having done so He will cast you into the black pits of hell, you filthy, disgusting, disease-ridden, pox-spreading, degenerate whore. My God is a jealous God and you've let him down.'

'I'm sorry.'

'Is that all you can say? Sorry isn't enough – you must repent before your Saviour or else you're going to burn for eternity, tortured by the Devil himself. You are going to suffer forever, and all for a few paltry pleasures in this vale of tears. I want you to take your clothes off.'

'What?'

'I want you to take your clothes off and come and kneel before me. Then I want you to take my member in your mouth.'

'I don't think that's a good idea.'

'Why not?'

'You might not be able to restrain yourself.'

'Restrain myself from what?'

'Killing me, and if I died you'd have to get my body out of the building without your colleagues seeing you doing it.'

'God would help me.'

'Not if He hadn't intended that you should kill me.'

'God would forgive me.'

'Not if He is a jealous God.'

'God would save me.'

'Not unless you repent.'

'Sergeant!' Butler screamed. 'Get this whore out of here, throw her on to the street, I don't want to see her again.'

Immediately after this interview I wasn't too worried by what I'd been told since as everyone knows coppers are the world's biggest bullshitters. They're used to running around in a uniform and ordering people about, so the idea that someone might question the veracity of anything they've said generally doesn't occur to them. Certainly I was horrified to find myself hauled up before Tommy Butler, but once I was out on the street again my confidence quickly returned. I'd realised from the very beginning of my interrogation that Tommy-Boy was acting out a psychodrama and its purpose was to frighten me. The moment Butler came out with the phrase about being down on whores, which was straight out of the original nineteenth-century Jack the Ripper casebook, I immediately understood that what I was being put through was an exercise in intimidation. Tommy-Boy wanted the rumours going around that my son Lloyd was the illegitimate child of JFK scuppered, and obviously offing me wasn't going to help to achieve that. At the time I figured Butler's blarney about God and Jack the Stripper was a theatrical put-on which he hoped would divert my attention away from the fact that he'd been instructed by his political masters to do the Americans a favour. However, after people like the London gangster Jimmy Evans fingered Tommy-Boy as the nude murderer I started to get apprehensive, and once I'd checked out the evidence I was petrified. That was a couple of years down the line from the events I've just described, and it was one of the factors that led to my leaving London for eighteen months in the late 60s. India beckoned at that time, but discovering the truth about Butler gave me the push I needed to make my own personal journey to the East.

TAPE TRANSCRIPTION: SESSION 69 WITH R.D. LAING

R.D. Laing: This is Ronnie Laing having a talk with Jilly O'Sullivan on the 10th of January 1976, and I'm paying Jilly to help me work through some of my sexual-cum-psychoanalytic fantasies. My current thing is Patty Hearst, which Jilly handles very well despite the radical ways in which the role-playing during our sex sessions has changed over the years. Patty, in session 68 you said that you felt flat and that your feeling flat is connected to you wanting to be honest in your autobiography, but finding that this isn't possible given your current situation.

Jilly O'Sullivan: Knowing that I'm not able to be honest, or at least not while I'm dependent on my family. The one time when I'm OK is when I'm writing. I got hold of a typewriter to do all the notes and the agent really liked them, but I still need to flesh them out and put more detail into them. The agent wants two chapters to show publishers, and when I'm typing the notes I'm really happy. I just sit down at the typewriter and the hours flash past, two or three hours can pass without me realising it. It takes me quite a while to come back down to earth again. My family have been looking at the notes, and they're not happy with everything I'm doing, and they want me to revise my story. However, this week I lied to my family and took unrevised notes to my agent instead of the version they'd approved. The agent said this was the best material she'd seen from me. I find it very easy to work on the first draft, but doing the revisions my family want proves almost impossible. I've finished the unrevised notes and today I want to work on the two chapters my agent wants, an account of my first night locked in the broom cupboard after the kidnap and an erotic episode, an account of the first time I had sex with our family gardener when I was fifteen.

R.D. Laing: Tell me about your relationship with your agent.

Jilly O'Sullivan: I went to see Jordan this morning and we had a very good meeting, we discussed the business side of things. I told her the minimum amount of money I'd need to live on if I broke with my family and they were no longer supporting me. She said I'd get a lot more than I need as an advance against royalties. She wasn't going to give an exact figure, but she said what she was going to do was auction my story, she'd targeted six different publishers and she was going to sell my story to the highest bidder as long as I liked the editor I'd have at that publisher. She needs the notes and the two chapters to take to these six publishers. After that she'll set up a series of meetings with the editors who'd deal with me, and she needs to do this before August because nobody does any business then. Her colleague who does the film rights at their firm is also very excited about my notes, but both Jordan and I agreed we'd get the book done before we started thinking about anything like that.

R.D. Laing: So how do you feel about your family?

Jilly O'Sullivan: I'm finding my family absolutely excruciating, especially as they are always talking about future plans and about restructuring their business concerns. Something in me keeps wanting to scream in their faces 'I'm not going to be here, I'm going to run out on you and tell the whole world what really happened and what I really think of you.' But until Jordan has actually sold my book to the publishers . . .

R.D. Laing: You can't afford to.

Jilly O'Sullivan: I can't afford to. I feel very uncomfortable with my family. I'm not interested in them . . .

R.D. Laing: You have no interest in your family?

Jilly O'Sullivan: I just want to be on my own, so that I can write about being locked in that broom cupboard with the radio on day and night, examining the way my relationship developed with those government men.

R.D. Laing: Government men?

Jilly O'Sullivan: Government men, revolutionary men, CIA, SLA, whatever.

R.D. Laing: But why have you lost interest in your family when you used to have so much conviction about their importance to you?

Jilly O'Sullivan: I feel like I've reached the end of the line with them; they won't admit that everything has changed and that while I was away I found a new family. They're trying to pretend that everything is still the same. My heart's not with my family any more, my birth family, I'm not committed to them. I just find myself sitting with them and finding them unbelievably boring. I'm sick of them. I feel so flat. I'm missing Cinque, he did what he had to do but I can't reconcile myself to the fact that he's dead. I keep having these thoughts that at least he isn't making love to somebody else. I know the SLA planned to abduct Jane Fonda, and the idea that he might have made love to some big Hollywood film star makes me very jealous. I know this is stupid . . .

R.D. Laing: No, it's not stupid, just look at Charles Manson and Sharon Tate. What we need to talk about is to what extent does jealousy bother you?

Jilly O'Sullivan: It bothers me a lot; it's not a revolutionary emotion. After I'd been locked in the broom cupboard

I didn't want to feel jealous again. I went through all that with Steven Weed. I always felt insecure and I convinced myself that he'd leave me for someone else, someone with a more normal family background. I am a media heiress and there is a big downside to that. It isn't just a matter of someone marrying money, there are a lot of responsibilities and expectations that go with it. At least with Cinque and the other revolutionaries, I knew they were into me, into my body. If they took money from my family it would be with menaces, so everything I did with Cinque was for real. I have a terrible insecurity with regard to men, there are always traumas over infidelity. My mother believed my father was repeatedly unfaithful to her, so I grew up hearing her bitterness over that. When my mother took a lover, she used to go on and on at her lover about how he was or wanted to be unfaithful. The lover would be faithful to her but in the end her insecurity always broke up what could have been a happy relationship, and she stayed with my father. I really thought that each of my mother's lovers would be my escape from the family, that they'd bring me up. So when I was in the broom cupboard, Cinque became my surrogate stepfather. I've found that through all the relationships I've had with men, the basic problem is that I'm never able to trust them.

R.D. Laing: What do you think goes on inside the mind of the man? Firstly, when you see the man you want and he's not having a relationship with you but he has one with someone else, and you decide to start an affair with him. Secondly, I want to know what you think the man feels when you start cutting the other woman out.

Jilly O'Sullivan: With Cinque I hardly felt jealous at all. I don't really feel any jealousy now, it's just the odd thought. My opinion of men is that they are able to have emotionless sex very easily.

R.D. Laing: I think that there is some truth in that.

Jilly O'Sullivan: And I realise that if Cinque had been sleeping with somebody else, like some big Hollywood actress, it would have been a case of emotionless sex.

R.D. Laing: It would make you less jealous if it was emotionless?

Jilly O'Sullivan: Yes, I enjoy masturbating and I know that's emotionless. I just think of faceless naked bodies when I masturbate, and I could compare it to that.

R.D. Laing: You've just said men can have emotionless sex, and the implication of this is that women can't.

Jilly O'Sullivan: I'm generalising, since I know women can have emotionless sex too; that's what most professional women do to stay sane.

R.D. Laing: Can you have emotionless sex, and what are your attitudes about it?

Jilly O'Sullivan: It's been a long time since I've had emotionless sex. It's never really been completely emotionless. When it's been with someone I've just met there's always been a little bit of me that's wondered if there's the possibility of a relationship. I had a boyfriend I never lived with, and over the years our relationship mellowed into friendship. I liked him a lot as a person, he was totally honest about being unfaithful, so it was very on and off, because I'd get jealous. Eventually I broke it off, and he said he'd change for me, but then I realised I wasn't in love with him, but we continued to be friends. Then years later we ended up sleeping together and it was good fun, and since then we've made love whenever we've seen each other, every six months or so, and there is no expectation of a relationship. We always land up making love when we meet, but we're just good friends.

R.D. Laing: Are you jealous of the fact that he makes love to other women?

Jilly O'Sullivan: Not at all, we can talk quite openly and easily about other people in our lives.

R.D. Laing: And yet you still want to make love to him?

Jilly O'Sullivan: Yes.

R.D. Laing: So what's the difference between that and what a man does when he has emotionless sex?

Jilly O'Sullivan: One of the things this former boyfriend said to me the last time we had sex was that he was not a monogamous man. It was just something that he said, but the conviction behind the words was not really there.

R.D. Laing: I'd like to ask you to what extent are you sensitive to men who are attracted to you?

Jilly O'Sullivan: (*pause*). When I'm in love with someone, I'm not sensitive to other men. I don't pick up on flirting or sexual vibes. If I'm not in love, I'm very sensitive to sexual innuendo. When I get these nasty visions of Cinque, it's always this thing of him making love to famous women. These are women who have achieved something by themselves, they aren't famous because of their family or because they've been kidnapped. That's what bothers me about the idea of Cinque making love to them: these are women who've achieved a lot more than me, they haven't just been handed everything on a platter. Women like Christine Keeler or Mandy Rice Davies come from very ordinary families.

R.D. Laing: Is this tied to your feelings about your family and the autobiography you're working on? Do you want to demonstrate that you can achieve something on your own?

Jilly O'Sullivan: Yes, I want to stand on my own two feet. My first autobiography was ghost written, I want to prove that I can write a book myself.

R.D. Laing: The important question here is whether the thought of Cinque making love to a Hollywood sex bomb triggers a feeling of inferiority in you?

Jilly O'Sullivan: Yes it does, and that's irrational because he's dead.

R.D. Laing: If there had been no feeling of inferiority would you still be jealous?

Jilly O'Sullivan: I don't know. What I do to get rid of these visions is tell myself that I'm special, that I can really achieve something with my book, that Cinque did love me quite apart from who I was, and that I should stop having these stupid feelings of insecurity. Besides, I know that when I've seen these Hollywood actresses after they've had a night on the tiles they don't look as good as they do on celluloid.

A lot of them are rather bland-looking in real life; their beauty is an illusion created by lighting, camera angles, make-up artists, hairdressers and wardrobe people.

R.D. Laing: Do tell me this, when Cinque masturbated did you mind?

Jilly O'Sullivan: Not at all. He really enjoyed jerking off. I used to get him to do it right in front of me, and he'd come in my face.

R.D. Laing: What about if he was thinking of another woman as he masturbated?

Jilly O'Sullivan: (*pause*) It wouldn't bother me because I don't think of him when I masturbate.

R.D. Laing: What do you think about when you masturbate?

Jilly O'Sullivan: It's very visual, a kind of porn film made with the budget of a Hollywood blockbuster. I never think about making love to other men, not even film stars. I think of watching other people make love but I never see their faces, just two bodies. Sometimes I'll look at a film or a picture as I do it. If I watch a blue movie, it has to be well lit with good camerawork and attractive-looking people who are obviously enjoying what they're doing.

R.D. Laing: You could think of images that would make you lose interest in masturbating, and there could be other images that would heighten your interest in masturbation.

Jilly O'Sullivan: (*pause*). What heightens my interest is other people engaged in the act of intercourse. Most of the time it's a man and a woman, sometimes it's a man and a man, and sometimes it's a woman and a woman. I liked the idea of the Douglas Fairbanks Junior home movies, but the bad lighting and camera work turned me off.

R.D. Laing: As you talk about this do you feel some tinge of embarrassment?

Jilly O'Sullivan: Yes I do, because to me masturbating has always been a very private thing. I like watching other people masturbate, but I've never masturbated in front of someone else.

R.D. Laing: You find it is something you can't share?

Jilly O'Sullivan: I can talk about it. I've got a couple of girlfriends who often talk with me about masturbation. I could talk to Cinque about it, but I would never masturbate in front of him. It's something I do on my own, not something I do with anybody else. I feel embarrassed right now because I'm afraid I might shock you, which is really silly.

R.D. Laing: It doesn't shock me. What makes this subject important?

Jilly O'Sullivan: (*long pause*). I don't quite understand. What is the importance of masturbating? To me masturbation is to have an orgasm, it's a way of relieving tension. I never have such intense orgasms when I make love to a man. My orgasms are much better when I masturbate.

R.D. Laing: How do the orgasms differ when you masturbate and when you make love?

Jilly O'Sullivan: They're completely different sensations. When I masturbate I only stimulate my clitoris, I don't use vibrators or anything like that. It's very quick and very easy. It's a very intense physical feeling. Whereas when I'm with a man I don't get the same physical sensation. There's a difference between a clitoral and a vaginal orgasm. When I'm with a man there's a feeling of love. I get more satisfaction from his orgasm than mine.

R.D. Laing: There is in all nature an utterly fundamental mechanism which is the pleasure-pain principle. The function of all pain is to act as a warning against that which can become damaging to the whole of your life if it gets intensified. That's what makes you draw your hand away if you put it into a flame. It makes you recoil. Now pleasure is the opposite of this. Pleasure is the in-built mechanism which tells us which directions are right for us. It's true that one can fool pleasure mechanisms artificially. You can give drugs that fool you into thinking they're pleasurable when they're harmful, therefore you can get people addicted to pleasures that are totally artificial and wrong. But if you don't vitiate the pleasure principle, then the pleasure mechanism is a reliable indication of the direction in which you need to go to grow and develop. Do you understand?

Jilly O'Sullivan: Yes, I do understand.

R.D. Laing: Now in both emotional and sexual relations intense pleasure is possible as you know, and what has happened to us from an evolutionary point of view is our sense of pleasure in relation to anything sexual has been severely interfered with by civilisation, so that we have developed what Wilhelm Reich calls character armour. This needs to be reversed, and the revolutionary movement with which you have come into contact is an attempt to correct this, although it is often a one-sided attempt. The sexual dishonesty that's been developed in modern society consists firstly in forbidding pleasure or at least attempting to forbid it, although that is less common these days. What is *important* is to break down our character armour and let everything hang out sexually.

Jilly O'Sullivan: Cinque used to ask me if I would masturbate with him, and he tried to stimulate me, but I couldn't stand it.

R.D. Laing: When you say you couldn't stand it, what do you mean?

Jilly O'Sullivan: Masturbation has always been something I've done on my own. It's something which I do very quickly and very easily.

R.D. Laing: But also very well. When you masturbate, the characteristic of the masturbating situation is that you perform the action, and you also experience the sensation that results from your action. Now when someone else masturbates you, the difference is that he performs an action without actually knowing the sensation he is creating in you. Therefore unless he is very sensitive, you're going to experience him as clumsy and as not really satisfying. But let's imagine a man who can give you even better orgasms through the act of masturbation than you get when you jerk off yourself.

Jilly O'Sullivan: Wonderful.

R.D. Laing: Not only would it be wonderful, but it would also create a terrific emotional bond if he actually knew what the experiences he gave you were like, and meant you to have them.

Jilly O'Sullivan: Yes, Cinque said men like that are called pimps. He also said pimps must cultivate indifference, that any man who cannot show coolness towards a woman will end up under her thumb. Cinque also talked about what he called the overlay, and he said that more than anything else this was something a pimp had to watch out for in his women. According to Cinque, when a woman puts another woman down what she's really doing is giving her own game away. Therefore when a hooker tells her pimp she doesn't like another whore because that doxy doesn't hand over her entire take to her man, the pimp better watch out because it's what his dell is doing to him.

R.D. Laing: The whole situation of sexual pleasure-giving is one that can be magnified in a love sense far beyond anything Cinque ever imagined if he associated it with pimping.

Jilly O'Sullivan: Yes, but maybe I don't feel I can show that one bit of me that is private, which is me.

R.D. Laing: You said that you can't show the bit that is you, the innermost you, to somebody who doesn't show enough commitment to you. That's right. To me that means that the bit that I'd like to have seen revealed in the relationship you had with Cinque wasn't explored sufficiently. Your lack of self-confidence results in a lack of affirmativeness towards pleasures such as masturbation.

Jilly O'Sullivan: Yes. Definitely. (*long pause*). I knew how to give Cinque pleasure; it gave me intense pleasure to give him pleasure by caressing him. I knew what gave him pleasure, and it gave me pleasure giving him pleasure.

R.D. Laing: But you didn't turn that situation around!

Jilly O'Sullivan: Yes I did, I felt intense pleasure giving him pleasure.

R.D. Laing: I meant the intense pleasure it would have given him to give you intense pleasure.

Jilly O'Sullivan: OK. (*pause*) Why?

R. D. Laing: This didn't happen for two reasons. Firstly, it would appear from your account that he didn't have any great desire to give you great pleasure, and secondly he didn't have the ability to give you great pleasure.

Jilly O'Sullivan: He wanted to make me come. He was always demanding that I tell him what to do to make me come. That was the stumbling block. It would have made him joyous knowing he was giving me great pleasure. But I couldn't tell him how to do it.

R.D. Laing: You couldn't because you get embarrassed.

Jilly O'Sullivan: Yes, I get embarrassed. I feel ashamed.

R.D. Laing: The heightening of your pleasure is not something to be embarrassed about since it is connected to your own growth as a human being. The more intense the pleasure you experience, the more powerfully this will protect you from any repercussions in terms of guilt.

Jilly O'Sullivan: I've had nothing but hurt and disappointment from both Cinque and men in general. I mistrust men. When I've had pleasure from men it has always been connected in some form or fashion with sex and me feeling let down. Usually they're also having sex with one of my girlfriends, and the emotions that accompany such betrayal are unbearable. I feel insecure and inferior. I like women a lot, but I can't trust them around my man. My girlfriends have let me down too many times in the past. It isn't just my girlfriends, it takes the man to betray me too. The first sexual experience I had was with a gardener employed by my father, and he was simultaneously fucking most of my friends, my girlfriends. At the age of fifteen I had no idea how to assert myself in a relationship. I told this gardener not to make love to my friends because it really hurt me, but he ignored my pleading. I couldn't understand why he was doing it. I don't understand why every man I have ever loved has done this.

R.D. Laing: (*long pause*) Why would a man leave you for another woman if he liked you better?

Jilly O'Sullivan: Because there's something wrong with me, because I'm not as attractive as a professional model or a Hollywood movie star.

R.D. Laing: If you knew a man was tremendously attracted to you sexually, and he wanted to find out whether he could be equally attracted to a Hollywood screen queen, and did make love to her, but found the experience unsatisfying, what would you feel?

Jilly O'Sullivan: I'd take it as a compliment.

R.D. Laing: Your insecurity would dissolve because you'd have the evidence that in real life the movie star couldn't compete with you.

Jilly O'Sullivan: Yes. That's fine, but there's only been one or two occasions when I've had the type of orgasm I get when masturbating in an actual love-making situation. Once was in the broom cupboard with Cinque, but it only happened once. Another time was with the gardener. But I have orgasm difficulties, let's talk about that!

R.D. Laing: If pleasure is sufficiently intense you don't forget it any more than you forget extreme pain. If someone chopped your hand off you wouldn't forget it.

Jilly O'Sullivan: So why do women who've experienced the pain of childbirth allow a pregnancy to run to term more than once?

R.D. Laing: Masochism.

Jilly O'Sullivan: OK. So supposing I said it was the setting and the circumstances of the broom cupboard that made my relationship with Cinque so intense. Once I came out of the broom cupboard it just didn't work.

R.D. Laing: The man who has no sensitivity to the needs of his woman becomes sexually unattractive. Bonding is incredibly important.

Jilly O'Sullivan: Bondage is important?

R.D. Laing: Bonding. Let me ask you another question, have you ever had an abortion?

Jilly O'Sullivan: Yes.

R.D. Laing: How did it make you feel?

Jilly O'Sullivan: It made me feel hideous, it interfered with my hormones and gave me mood swings.

R.D. Laing: For how long?

Jilly O'Sullivan: About a week.

R.D. Laing: Why?

Jilly O'Sullivan: The very thought of anyone having an abortion upsets me.

R.D. Laing: No matter how early it is done? In the first two weeks you can use suction, it is painless.

Jilly O'Sullivan: It's still an emotive subject. If I'd had Cinque's baby, then there'd be a part of him still with me.

R.D. Laing: Let's forget about Cinque for a moment. My feeling is that the pleasure you can get from making love to a man is very much greater than anything you've experienced yet. It goes far beyond the difference you describe between your clitoral and vaginal orgasms. My feeling is that you're vaginally desensitised.

Jilly O'Sullivan: Oh yes, I'm aware of this and physically it doesn't make much difference to me whether or not a man wears a Durex. But I am afraid of getting pregnant, so psychologically whether or not a man wears a Durex makes a difference.

R.D. Laing: If you develop your ability to experience pleasure, intense pleasure, on a much deeper level, you're going to find that your insecurities will melt away.

Jilly O'Sullivan: That would be nice. (*pause*). Understatement.

R.D. Laing: Am I right in thinking you're a little more relaxed about this subject now we've talked it through?

Jilly O'Sullivan: Yes, yes. I told you about going to see that analyst who wouldn't say anything, and I was just supposed to talk. I hated it.

R.D. Laing: You must have loathed it. I was trained for six years in Freudian analysis, but through many long years of practice I've rebelled against it.

Jilly O'Sullivan: I am aware of times when I have more heightened pleasure and other times when I do not feel very much at all.

R.D. Laing: This is very significant. Do you know why you sometimes feel more pleasure than at other times?

Jilly O'Sullivan: No.

R.D. Laing: We can look at this empirically. Just because you don't know what really turns you on doesn't mean that somebody else can't find out. Give me enough time and I'll discover what you really like. I can improve your orgasms.

Jilly O'Sullivan: The texture of loving with Cinque was fine.

R.D. Laing: So you were having good orgasms.

Jilly O'Sullivan: Yes, I had one really great orgasm in the broom cupboard. If I really had to analyse it I suppose I did a bit more than Cinque did. (*pause*) He used to get wound up because after I came out of the broom cupboard, most of the time when we fucked, I didn't come. But on the whole our love-making was very good. However, I did notice it always seemed to be me who initiated it.

R.D. Laing: I'm really not bothered about that.

Jilly O'Sullivan: When I showed I wanted to make love, Cinque responded immediately. The urge to have sex was never an issue.

R.D. Laing: You do make it sound all right for as long as you were in the broom cupboard, although I haven't heard you say it was absolutely wonderful. You've said it was very good.

Jilly O'Sullivan: I suppose I should have said it was wonderful. I've never had such good orgasms at any other time in my life, even if the best ones were when I was alone listening to the radio and jerking myself off. I'd imagine Cinque coming back into the cupboard and catching me masturbating. After the tension of the kidnap, when we finally made love in the broom cupboard, all the bad vibes melted away and there was a real bond between us.

R.D. Laing: You told me your love-making with the family gardener was extraordinarily good in its time, so how would you rank the two in order of greatness? How does Cinque compare with the gardener?

Jilly O'Sullivan: (*long pause*) Very similar actually. Joint first, I guess.

R.D. Laing: That indicates a past experience that was a peak experience was repeated with Cinque.

Jilly O'Sullivan: When I think about it, the only time I can compare making love to Cinque to making love to the gardener is when it was very good between us. When I was with the gardener I used to fantasise I was Lady Chatterley, but when I was with Cinque in the broom cupboard he seemed to be the real thing, the leader of a revolutionary organisation, so I didn't have to fantasise. Then one night I heard Cinque talking in his sleep about his controller, and when he woke up I asked him if he'd been turned into a CIA patsy while he was in jail. I don't think Cinque ever trusted me after that, and our love-making was never as good.

R.D. Laing: The things we are talking about are very important, and if it helps your family and the government understand what went on then that is fantastic.

Jilly O'Sullivan: I'm sorry? Helps who?

R.D. Laing: If it helps you break with your family and understand how evil our government is, then talking about these things is very important. Did you by any chance discuss the Frank Sinatra film *The Manchurian Candidate* with Cinque?

Jilly O'Sullivan: No, we didn't. Wasn't Janet Leigh Sinatra's co-star in that movie?

R.D. Laing: Yes she was. Now did you ever discuss Project Artichoke or MK Ultra with Cinque?

Jilly O'Sullivan: No.

R.D. Laing: We are all of us a living raw material as well as what we've made of this raw material. To date I've not made any attempt to look at the reality which lies beneath your own self-image, the real you that on a conscious level you're completely unaware of. You may ask me, how do I know who the real me is?

Jilly O'Sullivan: How do I know who the real me is?

R.D. Laing: You don't, not consciously, but I will remake and remould you, so that you can be yourself.

6. MR SELF-LOVE AND DRUNKENNESS

Of all the crazy freaks Michael de Freitas knew, perhaps the very straightest on the outside and the most mixed-up underneath was Colin MacInnes. Colin authored a trilogy of novels, of which the best known is *Absolute Beginners*, that rather too self-consciously set out to mythologise both youth and the Notting Hill area. Given that MacInnes loved rough trade, he was also Michael's perfect mark. Colin provided Michael with access to the oxygen of publicity, while what he got in return was not simply the opportunity to cruise teenage arse but just as importantly almost unlimited access to innocent young minds. Colin and Michael needed and exploited each other in the way only two such world-class egomaniacs could do. Together they set up Defence, not simply to organise resistance to ongoing police racism but also to serve other less noble ends. Colin was mad for life, mad for black rough trade, mad to break with the grey values of the adult world which he had never properly joined, but above all he was mad to meet characters that might bring his rather contrived novels to life. Michael de Freitas deposited MacInnes in my Bassett Road flat one Saturday afternoon and this new visitor made return visits on his own for many months after that. MacInnnes like to hear himself speak and I'd listen to virtually the same diatribe every week.

'Ah yes,' Colin mused between slugs taken straight from his bottle of Bell's whisky, 'this world is monochrome no longer because now the teenager has shekels in his pocket: life has become a series of garish Technicolor explosions. Those first grey post-war years were the grimmest in living memory, and it was only during the thirteen long years of Tory misrule that the young found their feet. We've never had it so good, and with the brutal enthusiasm of teenage bank-holiday brawlers we're going to stick it to those oldies who've tried to dupe us with slogans about the white heat of technology. Loot, kiddies, loot, that's what really matters. A booming economy provides the fuel for youthful rebellion. If I could have my time again then I'd be born yesterday, so that I might enjoy the coming aeon in which the oldies will no longer count for anything and the young will strut about in peacock fashions rather than mimic dull parents who adhere to dreary suburban values. Now that Harold has taken the pipe between his teeth, sucklings, things can only get better for the youth.'

'Ring-a-ding,' Matt Bradley put in. 'Vote Labour and make the world a better place in which to wig out, daddio!'

'It's not voting Labour that makes the difference,' MacInnes insisted. 'It's the way we walk and talk, the clothes we wear and our desire to achieve everything and nothing in the here and now. It's having a ball in the present and allowing the future to take care of itself.'

'To build a world in which love is not compromised,' Bradley suggested.

'What would you know about uncompromised love?' MacInnes snarled. 'You're fake rough trade for those whose noses would shrivel if they encountered the real thing. You're a brown stain on our day-glo age. The way you're dressed anybody would think you were heading out for a barn dance somewhere in the sticks rather than getting ready to spend Saturday night in Soho! It's 1965, and today's hep cats know they need to look sharp in Italian suits if they want to embody style while getting their kicks.'

'How could I improve the way I look?'

'You need to drink more and think less, that's the surest route to leaping up the evolutionary scales of sartorial elegance!'

MacInnes would carry on in this way for hours, blissfully unaware that he came across as a refugee from the 50s who was utterly clueless about the new hippie fashions that were emerging from the womb of swinging London. Thus although I was initially thrilled to have the bestselling author of *Absolute Beginners* and *City Of Spades* grauching out in my pad, I quickly realised he was a leech who hoped to bleed me dry solely to the end of adding a touch of authenticity to whatever fictional abomination he was in the throes of concocting. MacInnes continued to churn out pot-boilers long after his brief and undeserved moment in the limelight had passed. In sharp contrast my genuinely gifted friend Alex Trocchi ceased publishing fiction when he had nothing left to say.

Unfortunately Bradley didn't have it in him to turn MacInnes away whenever he arrived on our doorstep. I guess I was lucky in that, by the time I met MacInnes, this ersatz teenager was well past his prime as a chronicler of all things youthful, and while he clearly viewed me as prime material for a novel, unlike some of our mutual friends I was never identifiably served up in a shoddy slice of his would-be contemporary fiction.

The one good thing MacInnes had done for me was to provide an introduction to Bobby Naylor, who lived close by in Ladbroke Grove. Naylor had been a teenage hustler with a job in a Soho amusement arcade when he'd first met MacInnes at the tail end of the 50s. Colin used Bobby as a model for the title character in one of his books and simultaneously encouraged him to write, since he fancied grooming a protégé to carry his banner once he'd snuffed it.

Naylor, like me, was more interested in producing poetry than fiction. Bobby's motivations to write were anything but commercial. Naylor made plenty of dough selling charge and leapers, as pot and speed were known back then, and the verse he knocked out was heavily influenced by the endless joints he consumed. Bobby also had a weakness for the company of prostitutes, so we were a pair of chancers tailor-made for friendship. Naylor was amused by the way MacInnes had exaggerated the prowess of his fictional double as a pimp, he might have been offended by the book he'd inspired if its author had shown any signs of understanding the realities of his life.

'Jilly,' Naylor said to me one day, 'did you know that my girl Hetty has a regular trick who is a chemist and he knows how to manufacture LSD?'

'The heaven and hell drug?'

'Yup, the very same.'

'Have you been dropping it?'

'Yeah, it's great, like smoking thousands of reefers in a single puff.'

'I've been tripping out too. Hetty keeps me supplied with acid and I often take it before I service my johns.'

'Do they notice when you're out of your skull?'

'No, but I can see right through them.'

'To the other side of the room?'

'Sometimes, but more usually it's just the skin that kind of melts into rainbow colours and I find myself making love to a skeleton. It's great, you get the ultimate orgasm when sex and death become the same thing.'

'Would you make love to me when you're on acid?'

'Would you pay me to do it?'

'No, we're friends and I never pay for sex. So would we become a beast with two backs if we got high together?'

'It would depend on whether I felt like having it off with you when I was tripping. I went down on a girl during one LSD session and that was a good laugh. I enjoy ingesting acid when I'm on dates with johns, it's a real scream pretending to be straight when I'm so gone I could hold a conversation with a week old cadaver. I'm up for pretty much anything when I'm that out of my tree.'

'Three in a bed sounds nice.'

'In your dreams.'

'Perchance to dream, and there you were just a few minutes ago claiming you liked nothing better than erasing the dividing line between sex and death.'

'Sex is death, that's why the French call an orgasm a *petit mort*. However, I only die so that I can be born again. I know I'm not ready to exit the circle of rebirth.'

'I was John Dee's scryer Edward Kelly in a previous incarnation.'

'I'd like to be able to tell you I was once the Queen of Sheba, but I've never been anybody important in this life or any previous one.'

'Better luck next time!'

Bobby and I had our own very private and secret Notting Hill drugs and magic group. The other key players were Hetty and Norma Cowsil. Norma was another high class prostitute with literary aspirations and a taste for drugs. Like Hetty she was ten years older than me and had grown up in the north of England. Bobby, who grew up in London, had spent time in Tangier hanging out with local mystics including Hamid the Handsome and Walid the Mute. In a room hung with Berber rugs, Naylor, these locals and some carefully selected Americans would get stoned and then proceed to project their thoughts on to the tapestry. This was a very traditional form of magic, an attempt to materialise the immaterial. The scene in the room became whatever the person with the strongest thought form was projecting. Bobby initiated me into practices of this type when he formed a new magic group after his return to London in the spring of 1964. When the group started we used grass and it was pretty crazy, but things got even wilder once we moved on to dropping LSD, and the conversation I've just recorded was Naylor's prelude to this.

Bobby wanted to turn on the whole of London, and while he wasn't solely responsible for the massive increase in the use of psychedelics, he played a major but largely un-recorded role in the phenomenon. Before long I was also selling this instant means of pursuing the systematic derang-ement of the senses, as advocated by Rimbaud and other poets of the French school, to anybody interested in exploring inner space. LSD was still legal in 1965, so while we were discreet the dealing wasn't always as clandestine as some of our other activities. Likewise, it was only when Colin MacInnes decided he wanted to participate in our psychedelic experiments that my quest for the absolute was transformed into a season in hell. I was against admitting MacInnes to our charmed circle but Bobby and Norma thought it would be a laugh. I loaned Colin various works by Henri Michaux to prepare him for the session but he didn't bother to read or return them. We met at Hetty's because during term-time, when her daughter was away at boarding-school, she was the one amongst us whose two room apartment provided the most space. We all popped LSD-laced sugar cubes into our mouths and once these had dissolved inevitably it was MacInnes who spoke first.

'I don't feel anything. Are you sure this drug is any good?'

'Patience,' Naylor announced. 'It takes time to have any effect.'

'Patience!' MacInnes spat. 'Patience! Don't berate me with the values of the adult world. I'm not some ageing stockbroker and I don't like being told to wait for my kicks. Deferred gratification is the credo of the suburban middle classes, not of the juvenile delinquent seeking thrills. Age is as much about attitude as it is about years passed. The teenager is impatient because impetuosity is the metier of youth. I want to remain forever young and that means wanting everything and wanting it now. I don't have time to wait. I'm not going to repeat myself. Repetition is the vice of those who've resigned themselves to waiting for life instead of grabbing it by the throat. You don't wait to live, you only wait to die, and teenagers are immortals. Action is a necessity when it comes to this way of life, contemplation is death. I don't want a living death. I'm going to live fast and die in my prime. I'm going to drink myself to death. It is only because I have chosen life that I will be able to choose the moment of my death and thereby become immortal. To live is to live in the present. Death is not true, it can only occur in some non-existent future.'

'Right on!' Norma put in, and as she said it she raised her right fist in a salute.

'You see, Bobby, she agrees with me!'

'She's being ironic.'

'Irony is craven, it is a mode of deniable disclosure, the last and most desperate resort of those benighted with a slave mentality. Irony is a refuge for white would-be hipsters and other bounders and scoundrels. Contrast that to cool, which is a way of leading by example. Because I am cool my acts and attitudes do not require any form of justification or explanation. I purely and simply embody rebellion against authority without the necessity of recourse to verbal articulations. Cool is an imperceptible gesture, the cut of my clothes. The irony of squares is reduced to dust and rust when it's exposed to the straight-from-the-fridge chill of my new and cool world.'

'I guess that is one of the things *City Of Spades* was about,' Naylor suggested.

'Your barely ironic attempts to trick me into repeating myself will get you nowhere. I'm too glacial for that, too cool. I embody hipness, I am my own authority, I transvalue all values and this makes me the Jesus of cool. I don't need to impose myself on my peers through recourse to verbal tricks. I merely shift my weight in a chair or move a bottle of Bell's towards my mouth and conversations shift in accordance with my whims. When I speak I always use words with great economy and the same is true of my body language. I have very little need of speech which is why the words I do utter have such a devastating effect. Everything

I do say is uttered without recourse to repetition or emphasis or even very much thought. In this and much else I embody ease. For me actions speak louder than words and that ultimately is the great value of the teenage world that has overtaken the grey values of parents and priests and police officers. I never work myself into a tizzy because ranting and raving are the province of the fascist demagogue. I leave that to the likes of Oswald Mosley, as anyone who has read and understood my books well knows. The devastating effect of my speech is my ability to get directly to the point without repeating myself and that is a rare feat indeed. I may drink heavily but my utterances remain even more economic than those of a trappist monk who has taken a vow of silence. I am everything that those would-be hipsters who accept even a single value adhered to by the oldies can only talk about becoming.'

'Yeah, we can dig that.' Norma whispered. 'Colin is a synonym for cool.'

'To be cool is to be a bird's nest of drunkenness,' MacInnes continued as the acid began to hit. 'Cool is wearing a battered old coat and simultaneously becoming the height of sartorial elegance. Cool is knowing that anyone who attempts to merge their art and their life understands nothing of art or of life. I am my art, I embody it and the novels I write are but a vehicle through which I can recreate myself and act upon the theatre of the world. Cool is never having to repeat yourself, it is a never-ending act of personal creation and recreation. Cool is to embark on the ultimate reality trip, it is a way of channelling anger until one is angry no more. Cool sees through the world and in doing so acts upon it. Cool is when good becomes bad and bad becomes good. It is a teenage knee-trembler in a dark alley on Saturday night. Cool is what I am, not merely what I hope to become. Cool is an obscure hobo who knows how to ride the omnibus of art. What is not cool is to be endlessly explaining oneself. It is not cool to be anything but economic in one's gesture and one's speech. It is not cool to go on and on and endlessly repeat oneself. The cool say more with a single gesture than the square can articulate with their millions of words of self-justification or their raised fists and massed tanks and artillery and armies and nuclear weapons. It is not cool to use speech as a defence mechanism. A cool cat does not need language because they embody truth. Those who are cool do not need to speak and whenever they find it convenient to utter the odd syllable they absolutely never, and here I must place great emphasis on the term never, repeat themselves. To be cool is to be silent, to know when not to speak. The cool never complain, they chill. Irony makes me puke. If you want to join the new world of teenage rebellion then you need to follow my example and like me learn to embody its truths.'

'You're not a teenager, you're a middle-aged drunk,' Norma observed.

'Drunk, yes!' MacInnes roared. 'I'm drunk on life, drunk on kicks, drunk on this new teenage world of action and ultra-violence. I'm drunk on cool. I'm like a victim at the stake signalling through the flames. I'm so cool I don't feel the heat. I'm the Jesus of cool. A man who absolutely refuses to repeat himself. When I raise an eyebrow this embodies greater truths than you could even imagine. I have no need to speak or to write, which is why I am able to do both to such devastating effect. I gave teenagers life and speech in my novels so that they could forever bask in the icy silence of cool. The books of a charlatan like Samuel Beckett are more talked about than read, whereas my novels are read and read again. I do it all for the kids. Nothing I have said requires explanation. My speech takes those who know how to listen beyond speech. I am the beginning and the end. The alpha and omega. The first and the last. That which follows and that which came first . . .'

MacInnes continued in this fashion throughout what quickly became a bum trip. After this session he showed no interest in taking acid again and if he had we would not have been prepared to trip with him. Colin was a bore and I was glad when he stopped coming around to Bassett Road. I saw very little of him after this acid session at Hetty's.

7. THE BLOOD BEAST

Matt Bradley held me back. Once the Krays had set us up together and forced me to stay with him, I lost the five years in which I had the best chance of making a good marriage. However it wasn't simply my age which was against me, it was the changing times in which I lived. When I'd arrived in London in 1960 traditional class boundaries were still very much observed, and if, as many of the hostesses of my acquaintance did, you slipped over them then this was done in a discreet fashion. Likewise, as the myth of swinging London was spread across the pages of the international media, the idea of social advancement lost its importance for me because class distinctions appeared to be a thing of the past. I'd always enjoyed living in two worlds, the world of wealth and the world of bohemia. The age of equality we appeared to be entering further tarnished the faded glamour of the aristocracy while adding to the lustre of being a drop-out. Most of the other girls at General Gordon's married into the aristocracy or at least into money, but I did neither. As the 60s progressed my teenage conviction that I should snare a wealthy husband became increasingly shaky. I valued freedom more than wealth and creativity above decorum. However, I remained a sucker for degenerate members of the upper classes and always placed far too much of my trust in them. Matt Bradley came from a comfortable nouveau riche background but he was hardly a catch, and not merely because he'd sunk into amphetamine addiction and was working as a rent boy. I had to sham along pretending Bradley was my husband under threat of violence from the Krays, and while this was going on I missed several very good opportunities to better myself, although whether I'd have seized them if I'd been absolutely free I have no idea.

In the mid-60s I made one last-ditch attempt to improve my circumstances. Although I enjoyed the beatnik scene and the drug experimentation that went with it, I didn't want to pass my entire life living in a Notting Hill slum. What I did was enrol for a Lucie Clayton charm course. I'd already mastered doing my own make-up and applying false eyelashes, but some of the girls I studied with still needed coaching in such mundane matters. However I did learn more about social protocol and I honed the skills I already had that enabled me to get on in polite society, although by the time I passed out from Clayton's I lacked any real desire to do so. I learnt poise from walking around with a book on my head. I also learnt the correct way for a lady to get in and out of a car. You must slide in gracefully and above all else never allow your bottom to stick out. The funny thing was that every time I saw the middle-aged woman who taught us how to do this emerging from or disappearing into a taxi cab, her arse would be protruding from the passenger door and I'd have to restrain myself from slapping it. I guess it was a matter of do as I say and not as I do. This particular piece of etiquette was no doubt redundant if you were old and ugly like my teacher. No one was likely to become over-excited at the sight of her bum.

I emerged from Clayton's with a modelling portfolio and the contacts that enabled me to secure the odd bit of professional work. In London my height went against me as far as fashion modelling was concerned: at five feet five I was considered too short. When I was in India in 1968 and 1969 I was better able to secure fashion modelling engagements, mainly for newspaper and magazine display ads. There were fewer Caucasian models competing for this work in Bombay and although I did well there my desire to pursue a career as a mannequin wasn't as strong as the urge to consume drugs. My use of opiates spiralled out of control and I'm amazed no one seemed to realise I was completely out of it during my modelling assignments. Eventually I figured that things must have chilled with various creeps including Tommy Butler and I returned to London. In London during the mid-60s I fared far better as a film extra than a model and secured work with many famous directors including Joseph Losey and Peter Glenville. That said, although this extra work was well paid it certainly wasn't glamorous, since to secure it I had to get up at the crack of dawn and I considered myself lucky if my face was visible on screen even fleetingly. I had plenty of contacts in the London movie world but they never really took me anywhere.

Inevitably it was younger filmmakers like Donald Cammell and Michael Reeves with whom I actually became close. Cammell always claimed he wanted to die young and in a manner of his own choosing, but as I write he remains a suicide in waiting. Michael Reeves, of course, overdosed in February 1969, immediately before I returned from India. I'm told the coroner concluded his death was an accident, but being familiar with one of the sources from which he secured finance for his films and Michael's inability to provide the returns the gangsters in question expected, my own suspicion is that he was murdered. Unfortunately I now find myself in the position of owing the very same family money, which is why I'm in hiding in this basement flat in Cambridge Gardens which my boyfriend rented using a pseudonym a couple of weeks ago. I stay in all day and amuse myself by writing out episodes from my life on these endless sheets of paper. If I go out it is only late at night to visit one of the men who've provided me with an income for many years, or on odd nights to socialise with Alex Trocchi. I earn a living and my current boyfriend Garrett supplies me with smack. If Michael had done what I'm doing and dropped out of sight for a while he might well still be alive. I guess I'm living out my own private version of *Performance* – but Michael actually made a couple of films that were better than that.

Returning for a moment to Donald Cammell, when I first met him he was working as a scriptwriter and he was extremely angry about what Hollywood had done with his output. I always thought of Cammell as a bit of a character because he used to go about claiming that the occultist Aleister Crowley was his godfather. Regardless of whether or not this is true, I know for a fact that Donald can't channel because back in the 60s he tried to contact the spirit world for me. The only time Cammell used my professional services was when he wanted me to make up a threesome to impress some film-industry colleague, and rather than giving me money he was supposed to repay me with psychic work. His attempts at channelling were embarrassing and he ended up slipping me mean greens to make up for it. I didn't ask for money, Cammell just didn't want me to mention his fakery to any mutual friends.

Donald shot most of his first film as a director while I was in India: the aforementioned Mick Jagger vehicle *Performance*, on which he collaborated with Nick Roeg. I'd have liked a bit part in *Performance*, but by the time the film was made I was already an embarrassment to Donald because I could see right through him. If I'd been around I'd have been lucky to get taken on board as an extra, let alone anything else. Cammell didn't have a lot of luck with his movie career and he didn't get to direct another feature until a couple of years ago, the 1977 sci-fi flick *Demon Seed*, which bizarrely features Julie Christie being raped by a fantastically intelligent computer and she then goes on to

THE BLOOD BEAST

have its child. I wanted to like *Demon Seed* but when I saw
it I was disappointed: it simply didn't live up to the promise
of *Performance*. Cammell's co-director Nick Roeg was the
one who went on to make great movies, but then he already
had a background as a cinematographer on films ranging
from Roger Corman's *The Masque Of the Red Death* to
Francois Truffaut's only English-language feature, *Fahren-
heit 451*, in which coincidentally Julie Christie also handled
one of the leading roles. I haven't seen Donald for a while:
he went off to Hollywood and married the daughter of one
of Marlon Brando's girlfriends. I guess that was what finally
enabled him to make a second film. As for Nick Roeg, he
quietly disappeared from my life too.

Cammell is a decade older than me and when I was
hanging out with him it always felt a little like being with
one of the more artistic clients from Gordon's or Kennedy's.
He was someone I felt I had to humour and perform for in
order to nurse his bruised ego and make him feel younger
than he really was. Michael Reeves was my age and most of
the time we got on like a house on fire. Of course we'd have
mammoth rows: that was inevitable given our personalities
and it was also a part of our being friends. We'd go to the
movies and discuss what we'd seen afterwards over drinks.
By this time I'd also run into the abstract painter Giordano
de Holstein in Spain and I was interested in him. We'd got
it together on the odd occasion but had yet to become a
regular item. I knew that horror actor Vincent Price had
been buying Giordano's paintings. In the early 60s Price
made an agreement with the American department store
Sears Roebuck to purchase original works of art for them;
a large quantity of high-quality but affordable paintings by
relatively unknown artists, which were sold as having been
personally selected by this cracked actor. Price actually
trained as an art historian before going into films, and his
private collection of paintings is quite legendary since it
includes original works by the likes of Jackson Pollock,
bought at a time when the prices charged for the canvases

of this abstract expressionist could still be met from the earnings of a B-movie star. In the early to mid-60s Price's working arrangements with Sears Roebuck resulted in him buying art from a great many painters, but the fact that he was Giordano's main patron made me interested in him, and I made a point of going to see all the films in which he appeared.

As a consequence, I dragged poor Michael Reeves along to see *Dr Goldfoot and the Bikini Machine* which is definitely one of Price's lesser movies. The film had a good theme song performed by the Supremes and, like many American International Pictures, a tasty animated title sequence, after which the movie goes seriously downhill. In the picture Vincent, costumed in gold lamé slippers, plays Dr Goldfoot, whose lifelike man-hungry nubile robots are sent off to seduce and marry the world's richest men, so that their creator might by stealthy means appropriate vast financial holdings. Craig Gamble, played by Frankie Avalon clad in a trench-coat rather than his more customary swimming trunks, is a spy who falls in love with the sexiest of the robots to emerge from Dr Goldfoot's Bikini Machine. The plot is clearly intended to be zany but this spoof spy thriller merely creaks along, and some of the cast members would have trouble injecting life into even the most brilliant of scripts. Forced by his contract to appear alongside the pop idol Avalon, who couldn't act to save his life, Price had no choice but to ham it up and make the best of a bad job. Indeed, given how wretched the film is I felt it was to Vincent's credit that he manages to be enjoyable to watch.

Needless to say, when we emerged from the cinema Michael was in an absolute rage about the piece of crapola we'd just seen. He was particularly irritated by Price's overacting and it didn't surprise me to learn that when this horror veteran was cast against Michael's wishes as the star of his third and final feature *Witchfinder General*, Vincent was continually being forced by my director friend to tone down his performance. Curiously Michael's second feature

The Sorcerers had starred another seasoned horror veteran, Boris Karloff, who by the time they worked together was reduced to making schlock like *Ghost in an Invisible Bikini*, which is every inch as bad as *Dr Goldfoot*. Before he made *The Sorcerers*, I overheard a conversation between Michael and Tom Baker about a script for a science-fiction musical which was supposed to be a vehicle for Cliff Richard's former backing band the Shadows. As a consequence I thought it might be helpful if I introduced Michael to Alex Trocchi, since I liked the notion of these two friends of mine working together. I dragged Alex along to Michael's Knightsbridge cottage in Yeoman's Row, and the meeting started off on the wrong foot since it quickly transpired that it wasn't Michael who was working on the Shadows' script but a couple of his friends.

'I'm glad to hear you're not involved in this ridiculous attempt to remake *Les Parapluies De Cherbourg* as a sci-fi vehicle for the Shadows,' Alex informed our host, 'and since you're clearly a sensible man, I'm led to wonder if you've ever considered making a movie about drug use?'

'I work in the horror genre, which at its best is a material manifestation of the collective unconscious. I think that relates very closely to the expanded horizons experienced by those of us who experiment with drugs.'

'So what exactly are you working on right now?'

'I'm finalising a deal for a psychedelic odyssey which will, if all goes according to plan, star Boris Karloff.'

'So in this psychedelic movie what drugs do the protagonists ingest?'

'They aren't seen consuming anything illicit, the drug connection is implied rather than explicit.'

'In that case, what drugs have you tried?'

'Pretty much everything, weed, speed, acid.'

'Have you ever taken smack?'

'No.'

'You don't know the first thing about drugs until you've tried heroin, it's better than sex.'

'That's all very well but is it better than a Don Siegel movie?'

'It will make you look at *Invasion of the Body Snatchers* in a cool and objective light.'

'My favourite Siegel movie is *The Killers*.'

'I don't like *Body Snatchers* either, it's paranoid right-wing crap.'

'Don't run Siegel down, he gave me my first break in the business. He put me to work shooting various film tests for the female supporting roles in the Elvis Presley vehicle *Flaming Star* when I was just sixteen.'

'The only Elvis celluloid that interests me is his home porn.'

'Have you seen any of it?'

'No.'

'Well, that's where I have an advantage over you. I've not only seen them, I have copies of several. Would you care for a screening?'

'Certainly, and if you'll do me that kindness then you must allow me to repay you by giving you a shot of smack.'

'OK, it's a deal.'

Michael liked nothing better than an opportunity to show off his pirated Elvis material. His house was sparsely furnished and a section of it functioned as a projection room. He owned projectors for various sizes of film. The Elvis material he had was spliced together onto a continuous reel but was obviously made up from shorter films since the girls kept changing. Most of the action took place in a bathroom. You couldn't actually see Elvis but the same thing kept occurring. A naked man who was unidentifiable since his head remained above the top of the frame would stand by a bath and piss over the face and hair of a naked girl sitting in bubbly water. After the male, who was allegedly Elvis, had urinated, he would be given a blow job by the girl he'd just humiliated. The girls were predominantly blonde and appeared to be in their late teens or early twenties.

'That could be anyone,' Trocchi complained. 'I can't see his face so I've no way of knowing whether it is or is not Elvis.'

'It's Elvis,' Michael assured him.

'How do you know?'

'Because I shot the footage for him.'

'In that case why didn't you include some head shots?'

'Elvis didn't want his face included in case these movies were ever pirated.'

'If he was worried about that why did he bother getting you to make them in the first place?'

'He enjoyed watching himself in action but he also wanted to avoid unseemly court cases. A fan admitted into the company of a big star like Elvis will consent to almost anything in the heat of the moment. Later on she might feel degraded and come to regret what she's done. She might even claim that she was raped or by some other means forced into performing sordid acts. Before any groupie is allowed to have sex with Elvis it is explained to her that this must be filmed so that if any disputes arise the footage can be produced in court to prove that what went on was consensual.'

'You're putting me on.'

'Straight up.'

'This shit is too much, let's get mellow while we watch it.'

'OK, I'll turn the projector off while we shoot up. I'm curious to see whether the footage can hold our attention while we're on heroin.'

So that's what we did. The smack didn't initially agree with Michael and it caused him to throw up. That happens often enough the first time someone gets a shot. I nodded out but to the best of my knowledge the porno footage held Alex's interest. Afterwards Trocchi questioned me closely about Michael. He clearly wanted to believe he'd been watching the King of Rock engaged in some seriously sick sexual perversions but he had yet to become fully convinced of this. I wasn't the person to persuade him that he could accept Michael's claims about this without reservation, since I had no idea whether or not the home movies were a genuine document of Elvis getting his jollies. Like any film director worth their salt, Michael enjoyed manipulating people's emotions. Alex's convictions tended to grow over time, and all that was really required for them to harden was for stories about this film screening to be incorporated into his repertoire of amusing anecdotes. Once Trocchi began telling other people he'd seen Elvis Presley's private sex films, he came to believe it himself.

Alex's capacity for self-delusion was quite extraordinary. When Trocchi first moved to London he claimed he was living in the premises where the wrestler Fred Rondel had pulled out the eye and bit off the ear of a pimp, and he continued making this claim even after he moved to Observatory Gardens. In the instance of Trocchi's initial residence such an assertion may have been true, but despite the fact that he appeared to believe it the story was blatantly false when carried over to Observatory Gardens. I don't think Alex ever knew Peter Rachman, who owned the house in which Rondel carried out his assault, and Rachman was considerably more horrified by it than the local cops, who had a whip-round for the aggressor. The fuzz in Notting Hill are notoriously racist and the victim of the attack was West Indian. I was introduced to Trocchi by Michael de Freitas, and at that time the latter was certainly in a position to house Alex in a property that had formerly been owned by Rachman. Michael's then employer Robert Jacobs had taken over a great deal of that much-maligned landlord's Notting Hill empire.

8. WHITE RABBIT

I'd seen John Lennon around. He was hard to avoid in London in the mid-60s but equally difficult to meet. The public image of Lennon's group the Beatles was that they were loveable moptops and he was clearly the least approachable member of the band. Lennon used to sit and sulk in a corner of the Ad Lib when that club was the place to go. Once the 60s really started to swing I'd clock him at the Speakeasy and the Scotch of St James. By this time there was always too much of a crowd around Lennon for someone like me to get close to him in anything other than a professional capacity. During the first flush of the psychedelic era he finally appeared friendly although the atmosphere of bonhomie he exuded was very obviously chemically induced.

A shrink of my acquaintance called Ronnie Laing used to tell some of his mentally disturbed patients to go round and see the most sociable Beatle, Paul McCartney, at his London home. I wasn't one of Ronnie's clients; indeed it was the good doctor who'd slip me a regular monkey for entertainments provided. Like a lot of men who pay for their jollies Ronnie was lonely and wanted to talk. Laing fancied a session of steamy chat predicated on the Beatles so he told me to get myself invited into Lennon's stockbroker belt mansion Kenwood. Obviously Laing considered this pop-music fantasy figure more interesting as a phenomenon than as a musician, and it was the mythic dimension of Lennon's life that most attracted him. Ronnie knew I'd rise to the occasion because I did not want to lose the 500 knicker he contributed towards my living expenses every other month. Talking my way into Lennon's home on the swanky St George's Hill housing estate in Weybridge was a difficult task. I figured I could do with a little help from my friends Alex Trocchi and Michael de Freitas, who already knew the great man.

Alex and Michael decided that I should drive the car down from the Grove. I'm not sure exactly where the Ford Zodiac came from; I have a feeling Michael commandeered it from a supporter. It was an uneventful trip; Alex nodded out on the back seat and Michael sat up beside me. By this time de Freitas was known the length and breadth of the British Isles as Michael X, since after becoming the first man to be jailed under newly introduced race relations legislation, he'd been built up by the media as Britain's primo black-power leader.

'You know, Jilly, I'm sure glad you and Alex is Celtic, because once this race war gets going we're all gonna be offing whitey.' Michael liked to practise his rhetoric on me. I'd hear him repeating things pretty much word for word with other people later. 'You know the Celts came from Persia and since the Celts are de facto African they have always been welcomed with open arms by black power organisations, starting way back when with the Moorish Science Temple and coming right on down to my own Racial Action Adjustment Society. So anyone whose family comes originally from Scotland, Ireland, Wales, Brittany, the Isle of Man or Cornwall, well, they are my brothers and sisters, and they must join my battle against the English honky. And we all know that the English honky has to answer for both slavery and falsely taking the credit for the scientific and cultural achievements of the brothers from Egypt, Ireland, Scotland, everywhere. You look at movies today and the big stars, the great actors, they're not honkies but men like Sean Connery from Scotland. Now you told me one time you met Connery in some club and I was wondering if you could go out and meet him again and get me an introduction. That cat is making serious money and once he understands he's an African he'll see it is in his own best interests to support the Racial Action Adjustment Society in its fight against whitey.'

Michael carried on in this vein for the entire journey, stressing among other things that John Lennon, who we were going to visit, could trace his family roots back to Ireland, like Paul McCartney and George Harrison. He needn't have worried about this. Everyone knew the Beatles were an easy touch, since to use a phrase that Michael was fond of applying to any potential sponsor, they had money falling out of their assholes. When we got to Kenwood I drove straight up to Lennon's front door. Alex and Michael already had an in with this Beatle, and they were determined to exploit it to hit him up for every penny they could get. However, driving right up to the door was clearly something of a mistake, since it didn't give Alex time to wake up properly. Michael and I bundled Trocchi out of the car but we'd missed the opportunity to walk him up and down to raise him from his drug-induced stupor. Moments after we rang the bell, the housekeeper opened the door and announced that John was waiting for us. The house had been very tastefully decorated and then wrecked. A year or two later I'd have run straight around to the outdoor swimming pool to check whether any expensive consumer goods or Rolls Royce cars had been dumped into it, but the rock demi-monde didn't really accelerate to these levels of decadence until we'd crossed over to the other side of the summer of love. After being ushered into Kenwood we found Lennon sitting bug-eyed in an easy chair with a huge grin on his face. A TV was on but the sound was drowned out by the Dylan platter blasting from a hi-fi.

'Curiouser and curiouser,' Lennon announced to no one in particular as he flicked a switch without getting up and the Dylan record stopped playing. 'Now I'm opening out like the largest telescope that ever was! Goodbye feet. Oh my poor little feet, I wonder who will put your shoes and stockings on for you now, dears? I'm sure I shan't be able! I shall be a great deal too far off to trouble myself about you: you must manage the best way you can; but I must be kind to them or perhaps they won't walk the way I want to go! Let me see: I'll give them a new pair of boots every Christmas.'

'Sit down, all of you, and listen to me!' I replied, having instantly picked up on where Lennon's acid-addled brain was at. 'I'll soon make you dry enough. This is the driest thing I know. William the Conqueror, whose cause was favoured by the pope, was soon submitted to by the English, who wanted leaders, and had been of late much accustomed to usurpation and conquest.'

'Mother!' Lennon cried in ecstasy. 'Mother, is that you? Don't come in, I'm sleeping.'

Quick as a shot de Freitas bustled me out of the room. 'You're doing well, girl, his mind is fried and he thinks you're his mother Julia. I'm going back in there, so when I call you I want you to come in and jerk him off.'

'What do you mean?'

'Give the man a fucking hand job, he's got a thing about his mother and you can help him with it.'

'Are you sure about this?'

'The gossip goes around, don't worry about it. When I call you in you'll see I'm right.'

So I stood by the door for a couple of minutes and when Michael called me Lennon had his pants around his ankles and was doing the five-knuckle shuffle. Alex was staring into space, oblivious to everything; Michael simply looked on impassively – he'd seen it all before.

'John!' I said as I walked across to the rock god. 'You've found something, beautiful John!'

'Mother!' Lennon panted. 'Julia! Julia!'

I stroked John's member, then took it firmly in my right hand and wanked him off. I used my left hand to tickle beneath his balls. I held Lennon's love muscle until it went limp, then dipped my fingers into the spunk that had splattered across his stomach before placing them in his mouth. Lennon licked my pinkies as if they were coated in the mother of all acid trips. Out of the corner of my eye I saw that Michael was giving Alex a speedball; he wanted to wake him up. Once the moptop had licked my digits clean, I allowed my hand to drop from his mouth. I sunk down beside him and drummed my fingers across his chest. There wasn't much I could do for the Beatle now beyond talking to him, and it was this as much as anything that the men I dealt with professionally wanted and most liked.

'Now,' Lennon frothed, 'take a good look at me! I'm one that was made a Member of the British Empire by the Queen, I am; mayhap you'll never see such another; and to show you I'm not proud, you may shake hands with me!'

Lennon doubled up in his chair as he leant forwards and offered me his hand. If he'd smiled much more the ends of his mouth would have met at the back of his head, leading me to wonder if this might have caused it to fall off.

'There are seven levels of consciousness,' the Beatle announced, 'and after the fifth you don't need sex. I'm stuck at the fifth despite using LSD as a psychic elevator because the switch on my brain-blood volume is jammed.'

'You don't stop having sex at levels six and seven,' I assured this special John. 'It's just that it stops being physical and becomes telepathic.'

'Are you my guru?'

'I can be if you want me to be.'

'Mother is my guide and mother is simultaneously my other.'

'Yeah, yeah, yeah.'

Lennon laughed hysterically until his attention was caught by a game of football being relayed on the TV. I walked across to a white leather sofa and lay down on it. I propped my face in my hand and joined John in his appreciation of the soccer. The Beatle was mumbling that England could never win against a team of spiders because with eight legs and no arms the opposition had 88 ball-kicking feet against our 22. As far as possible, I ignored the men kicking the ball around and focused my attention on the grass, which was beautiful. The speedball Michael had administered to Alex had kicked in and they were huddled in conversation. After a while they broke apart and Alex began preparing a shot of junk.

'Jilly, this man requires sedation; he is a well-known figure from the world of popular entertainment so I must insist that you slip the spike in somewhere the mark won't show,' Alex yelled as he handed me the needle and pointed at the Beatle. 'The last thing Mr Lennon needs is for there to be a public scandal about his perfectly reasonable use of heroin. That said, my patient is under an intolerable burden of stress, so this recourse to medication is perfectly legitimate.'

'You can find a vein just as well as I can,' I protested.

'You're his imaginary mother,' Alex scolded me. 'He gets off on you nursing him. Do what you're told, Jilly – or do I mean Julia?'

'OK,' I acquiesced, 'but cook me up something too.'

As Alex prepared my shot, I told Lennon to open his mouth and slipped the needle beneath his tongue, where any mark it left would pass unnoticed. When Alex handed me a second spike I gazed skywards but all I saw as I slipped the hypodermic into the underside of my eyeball was the ceiling. When I clicked back into focus on the room, it didn't surprise me that Michael was going through Lennon's possessions and slipping anything expensive and portable into his voluminous pockets. The Beatle was oblivious because he was being sucked in by the spiel Scotch Alex was running past him.

'Mr Beatle, the last thing you'd want is to be mistaken for a cockroach and yet you're heading down a slippery path thanks to your uncontrolled experimentation with psychedelic drugs. You're popping acid as if it was a sweetie, taking several doses a day, leaving yourself on a permanent high with no opportunity for your brain to recover. This is a head drug and while it will expand your consciousness, you simultaneously run the risk of frying your mind with it. I've come here to save you with a body drug. Used sensibly heroin won't harm you, it will help preserve your body and it certainly won't have any detrimental effects on your mind. You have an addictive personality and it is clear to me that the only way to pull you away from your overindulgence in LSD is to put you on to a stabiliser such as smack. Some of the greatest works of English literature were written on opiates. Indeed the best writing produced by the Romantics, including the cream of Coleridge and de Quincey, would not be with us today were it not for their enlightened use of self-administered drugs. My friend Bill Burroughs writes on smack, and my own masterpiece *Cain's Book* was composed under the influence of this marvellous mental stabiliser. Mr Beatle, I implore you, accept my heroin prescription because it is the only thing that will save your mind and thus ensure that posterity is able to enjoy the full panoply of your talents.'

Lennon was all blissed out. We spent the night at his place and when he was coming down the next day, Scotch Alex showed him how to mellow everything out by chasing the dragon. I'd done a great deal of opium smoking and I was beginning to find it an expensive and inefficient way of getting the drug into my body. That's why with increasing regularity I was shooting up. That said, I was still careful not to inject anywhere the tell-tale needle scars would be visible to a casual observer. Lennon didn't need to worry about the expense of inefficient drug delivery since he was loaded. I'm convinced the pep talk Alex gave the Beatle saved his mind from acid burn-out. I rather envied the nice little habit Lennon proceeded to cultivate. I went down to Weybridge maybe half a dozen times after that first night, both to play mother and deliver smack. John liked me to pretend I was Julia Lennon, and he'd get very steamed up whenever I found him jacking off, so it usually took only a few strokes from my hand before he'd come. This relationship didn't last long because my Beatle became increasingly involved with the Japanese conceptual artist Yoko Ono. I found myself blown out once a new heroin connection was forged. As a junkie I was highly amused when Lennon spent increasing amounts of time in bed supposedly as part of an anti-war campaign. To someone like me it was obvious that John was more interested in nodding out than promoting perpetual peace. Still, you have to hand it to him, he understood the basic principles of magick. Here he was besieged by the press when all he wanted was an endless slumber party. If Lennon had attempted to goof off in this way at home, the media might have rumbled that he was smacked up. Instead of attempting to cloak his habit with the mantle of privacy, John invited the world's press into various hotel rooms to watch him at it. By presenting such behaviour as a selfless political and artistic act, Lennon grabbed his time on the nod without a single journalist from the straight world raising a hue and cry about him being a drug addict. There is a lot to be said in favour of being rich and famous.

9. BLONDE ADONIS

When I got back from India in June 1969 London had changed and I'd changed too. Those of us who'd been a part of the nascent counterculture of the very early 60s were by this time suffering from post-hippie burn-out. I was twenty-five and the smack habit I'd acquired served as a badge of a ten-year immersion in the alternative society. I'd been using opiates for the better part of five years and I returned to London heavily addicted. I'd undergone my first attempt at a clean-up in Greece in the summer of '67, and as a consequence had discovered that getting off smack wasn't difficult but staying off presented a serious challenge. London wasn't swinging the way it had been when I'd left the capital – instead, by 1969, it was dying. From among my own circle the film director Michael Reeves was already dead by the time I returned, as well as a host of unknowns, and almost always as a consequence of a drug overdose. Beyond a re-acquaintance with my habit and some newspaper clippings of my work as a model I had little to show for the eighteen months I'd spent in Afghanistan, India and Nepal. I'd journeyed to the East with Giordano in an attempt to get my life together, but it fell apart once again before we even reached our initial destination. Our attempts at spiritual illumination had proved abortive. The various self-styled mystics we encountered were more interested in making money than direct connections to the Godhead.

After our car broke down during the outward journey to India, Giordano had abandoned me in Kabul. He had with him a large painting that had been commissioned by a gallery in Bombay and he needed someone to transport it there. The transport turned out to be Mary. She had a withered leg from childhood polio, a car and money. Mary's sparky character made her Giordano's type and they began an affair. Mary was an American drug dealer who'd come up to Kabul to purchase wholesale supplies of hash which she'd then retail at a considerable profit among the western drop-outs who'd overrun Goa. By the time Giordano left me in Kabul, I'd run through the money I'd saved for the trip. However, I knew how to find gainful employment and I was far from destitute. That said, even working as a topless go-go dancer on the fifth floor of the Spinza Hotel, which was extremely well paid work by local standards, I wasn't able to make enough money to cover the airfare to India. Things would have been better in the summer, when there were rich tourists about with money to burn. During the winter the only patrons of this western-style hotel were wealthy locals. These men were much better off than most of their fellow countrymen but they couldn't splurge dollars on me the way visiting American businessmen might. In the end the local representative of the Subud organisation gave me the money for a flight to India, alongside various items she wanted me to deliver to assorted mystics and which she felt unable to entrust to the post. Having dispensed with these duties I caught up with Giordano and enticed him away from Mary. This wasn't particularly difficult since she'd fulfilled his most immediate needs.

Having travelled the length and breadth of the Indian subcontinent, Giordano and I were living in Bassett Road – not in my old flat but at the end of the street furthest from

Ladbroke Grove. We were arguing constantly and furiously. Like me, Giordano was addicted to heroin but he also greatly enjoyed shooting speed. I'd mainline amphetamines but my drug of choice remained smack. We were also dropping a lot of acid. We had a brief stab at a rigorous regime of meditation but without much success since we both lacked self-discipline. We'd hoped to find spiritual enlightenment while we were away but every master we'd encountered in India was self-evidently a phoney. Subud was not fraudulent; I knew it provided a way of directly experiencing God but I couldn't convince Giordano of this. I'd been involved with Subud for as long as I'd been into smack, and although I knew drugs hindered my spiritual progress I was unable to give them up. If I'd been able to get further with devotional practice then I could have done without the drugs. Chemical stimulations held me back from becoming earthed and centred but at the same time they were the only thing that made my life bearable. At least Giordano and I ate healthily, mainly rice and vegetables with vitamin supplements. I knew speed wasn't good for our constitutions but keeping up an otherwise healthy lifestyle minimised the damage. My concern was very much with Giordano's health. Despite media hysteria about heroin, it is considerably less harmful than amphetamines or alcohol. Heroin retards your emotional and spiritual growth but if you've got a pure and regular supply and you look after yourself, it has little impact physically. My problem was a taste for speedballs, since without them I couldn't keep up with Giordano, who was totally and constantly wired.

So I was back in London and working as a club hostess. I was on the night shift at Kennedy's because I was too old for General Gordon's; Bertie Grayson, who still ran the latter club, was fixated on teenyboppers and his patrons expected really young girls. Kennedy's was a similar set-up to Gordon's, with a show and girls at the tables. At Gordon's I had worked as a showgirl but now I was merely a hostess. In India I'd used opiates as a way of enduring really long bus journeys; back in the Smoke I used them to help me through what I found to be tedious nights at Kennedy's. It gave me a kick being really fucked up on drugs as I entertained the rich businessmen who paid me so well for my services. The overwhelming majority of these johns would have been gutted if they'd known I was a junkie and was virtually sleeping through my encounters with them. I was being paid to bolster their egos, to foster the delusions they had about being studs. It felt good getting completely loaded, knowing that not one of the straights I half-interacted with would notice that my interest in what was going on around me was entirely feigned.

In the late-60s and early 70s Trocchi was coerced into carrying out street deals. It was some time before I learnt who was grabbing a big slice of his profits and if I'd known I'd have stayed well away from him. That said, it wasn't easy to stay away from the bastards running Alex if you were a junkie living near Ladbroke Grove. Making Trocchi do street deals was a way of humiliating him. The situation changed in the mid-70s, when the last wave of bent coppers to imagine themselves untouchable were removed from office and those who moved into the vacuum left in their wake went easier on people like Alex, although they continued their predecessors' hardcore and heavy exploitation of pretty girls like me.

Trocchi still had his rock-star clientele and he was working closely with Garrett, who before I'd split for India had stalked the Grove dressed in a purple cape. By the end of the 60s he favoured a more inconspicuous sartorial style. Garrett was running a few girls, and despite the fact that these were streetwalkers who were completely lacking in class, there was a mutual attraction between him and me. We were too fucked up to have much sex but the feeling was there, despite the fact that Garrett was living in Cambridge Gardens with a blonde junkie called Cat and Giordano was my common-law husband. I was doing some dealing for Trocchi and the best of this was when I was working with Garrett. As soon as I got back to town I'd gone around to Trocchi's to score, and since I lacked the readies to pay for the gear I found myself selling drugs for him once again.

'Do you like Winnie the Pooh?' Garrett asked about ten days after I'd arrived back in London.

'Sure, I remember the stories from when I was a kid, but these days I filter my understanding of Winnie's addiction to honey through the prism of smack. I don't go along with the idea that he's a bear of little brain; my view is that he's got a habit. The real problem is that straights don't understand junkie logic, they have no knowledge of what addiction will make you do.'

'So do you want to go down to Cotchford Farm in Sussex where A. A. Milne wrote and set the Winnie the Pooh stories?'

'OK.'

'Show some fucking enthusiasm.'

'Great! There are serious existential implications to Winnie the Pooh eating too much honey and becoming stuck in a hollow tree trunk. However, I don't think we're going down to Hundred Acre Wood to consider these philosophical conundrums in their original setting. Obviously something else is on the agenda.'

'We're going to see Sinatra.'

'Who's Sinatra?'

'He's a builder who's renovating Cotchford Farm for the new owner.'

'So why's he called Sinatra?'

'It's his name.'

'Come on, that can't be his real name, he's acquired the moniker and he'll have done so for a reason . . .'

'He sings like a canary the minute he's put under a bit of pressure.'

After further banter we got into Trocchi's Mini Cooper and headed south. Garrett was obviously peeved about something and I eventually figured out it was the fact that I hadn't exhibited any curiosity about the new owner of Crotchford Farm. Once I'd asked about this Garrett took great delight in telling me that Pooh Corner had recently been acquired by Brian Jones of the Rolling Stones. Actually the guitarist had just been sacked from the group he founded so if I'd wanted to be pedantic I could have picked Garrett up for failing to describe Jones as an ex-Rolling Stone. Although Garrett was going to see Sinatra, my job was to entertain Jones so that he could have a nice private chat with the builder. Back then I didn't know who Nobby was although he cropped up with alarming frequency in conversations between Garrett and Trocchi. Garrett was on his way to relay some messages from Nobby to Sinatra, and also to supply this contact with a special form of speed that had only recently been synthesised. I assumed some sort of drug deal was going down but clearly other business was involved too. I'd long ago learned not to poke my nose into illicit activities that had nothing to do with me. There are many things it is better not to know.

As I just said, while I'd been in India I'd got into the habit of taking opiates as a way of getting through long cross-country bus journeys. The Mini Cooper Garrett was driving was perfectly comfortable and our journey wasn't of any great duration, but nevertheless once we'd spent some time travelling through the wastelands of south London I took a shot of smack and nodded out. The heroin cured me of all curiosity about what Garrett was actually doing. At the end of the day it didn't matter. More importantly the heroin helped blot out the feelings of loss I felt whenever I journeyed through the southern extremities of London, since this was where I'd given birth to Lloyd. I don't know how long the journey took but after we'd arrived at Cotchford Farm, Garrett slapped me a couple of times and I woke up. Garrett complained that he'd wanted company on the boring drive and that although he knew I was a junkie he hadn't expected me to nod out. I promised to stay awake all the way back to London and that mollified him somewhat. Garrett knocked on the main door and it was answered by Brian Jones.

'This is Jilly. She's a peace offering from Nobby,' Garrett informed the musician. 'I'm here to see Sinatra?'

'Nobby's a bastard!'

'Just keep bunging him money and you'll be all right.'

'I haven't paid him for a while.'

'In that case Jilly can't be a present, she must be a reminder.'

'Does she know Nobby?'

'No, she's a pro, a hostess at Kennedy's. She worked at General Gordon's in the early to mid-60s when she was still teenage.'

'My girlfriend is asleep upstairs.'

'Well, if she's nodding out what's your problem? Too much speed, is that it? You can't get it up?'

'Are you telling me to take her through to the back of the house?'

'Yes. I want a private word with Sinatra. If you won't let Jilly entertain you then you'll have to entertain her; my business is with Sinatra.'

'Is Nobby angry with him too?'

'Curiosity will be the death of you.'

'Sinatra saw Nobby up in town yesterday; this is all very odd.'

'Just tell me where I can find him.'

'He's round the back, sunbathing by the pool.'

'Nice work if you can get it. I thought he was renovating the house.'

'He prefers goofing off, I pay him regardless.'

Jones led us through the house and showed Garrett out the back. I was taken into a darkened room set up with an eight-millimetre projector. There was a reel in the machine and Brian started it up before sitting beside me and putting his arm around my shoulder. The home movie showed Jones at a party with other members of the Rolling Stones.

He was sitting in a chair masturbating with several beautiful girls looking on adoringly. His smug smile gave away the fact that he was very pleased with himself. Jones might have had any one of the girls present but preferred to bring himself off. When the reel finished Brian rewound it and then put on a film which showed him having sex with two girls in a hotel room. At the start of the reel a blonde girl was beneath him and a brunette to their side. After about a minute the camera had been turned off to make a crude edit. Following the jump cut, Jones was shown bucking above the brunette with the blonde lying beside them. There was roughly 60 seconds of this and then a further jump cut. In the final section of the film Brian was lying on his back, his head turned to one side so that he could kiss the brunette while the now-kneeling blonde could be seen jerking the guitarist off with her right hand, while the middle finger of her left hand was worked in and out of his arse. This film, like the previous one, was silent, but from his muscle spasms Jones looked as if he was approaching orgasm. However the reel ended before Brian shot his wad.

'Do you like them?' Jones asked.

'Sure, they're beautiful. Who are the girls?'

'I don't know their names.'

'Who shot the film?'

'Have you ever balled a chick?' Jones parried my question with one of his own.

'Sure, but only to entertain guys; a lot of blokes like to watch two girls getting it on.'

'Would you ball my girlfriend?'

'Would she want to make it with me?'

'I'd have to ask her.'

'Do you want to do anything with me?'

'Garrett was right, I can't get it up. Too much speed.'

Jones stood up and dropped his trousers. His tool was flaccid. I reached out to touch it and as I did so it bounced upwards. Brian stepped towards me and I guided his cock into my mouth. Then he started to yank at my hair, so I grabbed his balls with both hands and pulled hard while simultaneously biting into his manhood. The guitarist yowled and as I let go he stepped back. I stood up and swung my fists into his face. He went down and I kicked him. It might have been the warmest July in years but I was still wearing the knee-high black leather boots I'd just bought for my hostess work at Kennedy's. I didn't have any other footwear, since by the time I reached London the shoes in which I'd returned from India were worn out.

'You fucking prick!' I spat at Jones. 'You used to be a hero of mine but you aren't any more. Just because I'm not charging you doesn't make it OK to push me around.'

The former Stone had curled up into a foetal ball so I just left him where he was lying with his pants around his ankles. I strode out to the swimming pool, but when I got there Garrett, who was deep in conversation with Sinatra, motioned me back into the house. I'd had enough so I made my way out of the front door and sat down in the driver's seat of the Mini. The keys were still in the ignition so I started up the car and revved the engine as loudly as I could. I revved furiously until Garrett emerged from the house and sat beside me.

'What the fuck's up with you?' he asked as he slammed the passenger door.

'That creep Jones thought he could get his kicks by knocking me around.'

'I thought I heard a scuffle when I was out by the pool.'

'So why didn't you do something? I thought you were a pimp who believed in looking after your girls.'

'Sure I look after my girls, but until you start handing me most of what you earn you can look after yourself.'

'I'm not earning anything here, I was doing you a favour handing it out for free. Are you going to fulfil your obligations by getting back in there and kicking seven shades of shit out of that scumsucker?'

'Forget it, just drive.'

'I'm not going to forget it.'

'OK, if I tell you what's gonna happen to Jones tonight do you think you could forget that?'

'I can forget anything I don't need to know.'

'Nobby's into drugs and protection. Jones hasn't kept his payments up. Sinatra has instructions to organise a little accident for our friend. Tomorrow he's gonna wake up in the Sussex County Hospital. He won't be making any music for a while because that hand he broke belting Anita Pallenberg is about to be refractured.'

'I thought he had a climbing accident.'

'That was just one of the many stories the public relations people invented to cover up the fact that Jones is in the habit of beating up his girlfriends. The guy's a creep, you know that now. It's why Pallenberg left him for Keith Richards.'

'Stop,' I interrupted as I slipped the car into gear. 'I've already got more than enough to forget. Let's just get out of here and home to the Grove before the ambulance chasers arrive looking for a scoop. If Sinatra is going to see that Jones gets what he deserves then there's no need for you to attend to it.'

As everyone now knows Jones didn't wake up in hospital. He didn't wake up at all on 3 July 1969 because he was dead. He'd drowned in his swimming pool, with Sinatra the last person to see him alive. Garrett said afterwards he'd had no idea Jones was going to cop it. He told me the same thing eighteen months later after the daughter of a prominent Tory was murdered. I chose to believe him then and I still do now. I don't have much choice in the matter.

10. A WOMAN IS A WOMAN

When I was small the highlight of my week was going to the Saturday-morning matinee at the pictures. Our local cinema had all the standard Universal and RKO serials ranging from *Flash Gordon* to *Commando Cody* but my all-time childhood favourite was an old twelve-episode series made the year I was born, called *Zorro's Black Whip*. It starred Linda Stirling, who played Barbara Meredith, the owner of an Idaho newspaper who would secretly don leathers and a mask to become a crime buster known as the Black Whip. Barbie was such a dab hand with a pistol and a bullwhip that the villains didn't realise she was a woman. Even at the age of eight I rather envied her curves and I couldn't understand why the men she fought never cottoned on to her gender when she had such a luscious figure. If the Black Whip was my first role model, ultimately it was French and Danish actresses such as Catherine Deneuve and Anna Karina who provided me with more enduring templates upon which to fashion myself. That said, as soon as I started to covet the life of Barbara Meredith I knew I wasn't going to stay in Greenock. The bright lights of bigger cities beckoned even when I was eight. Greenock was extremely grey, wet and cold in the 50s, or at least that's how I remember it.

I arrived in London at the age of sixteen in 1960 and immediately found myself mixing with those the *Melody Maker* had labelled modernists, in other words hipsters who gathered in clubs such as the Flamingo to listen to records by the likes of Sonny Rollins and Miles Davis. Dancing away those nights that were free from my hostessing work, I got to know various students from the Slade School of Art. The boys in question attended lectures on movies given by a professor called Thorell Dickenson, and they were also involved in the college film club. I'd go along whenever French flicks were being screened. It was at the Slade that I first saw many of Godard's movies, including *Une Femme Est Une Femme* and *Vivre Sa Vie*. I loved *A Bout De Souffle* but Godard's follow-up features starring his wife Anna Karina were of far more importance to me. In 1961's *Une Femme Est Une Femme*, Karina plays a stripper who desperately wants a baby. The plot is slight and it is Karina's charm that carries the film. At that time I was teaching myself French by watching undubbed movies and I greatly appreciated the fact that in this flick Karina's character Angela is scolded for her failure to fully master the language. In their 1962 feature *Vivre Sa Vie*, Godard and Karina moved even closer to my home territory. The movie is about a girl called Nana who dreams of making it as an actress but ends up working as a prostitute. It was almost my life story, and after first seeing *Une Femme Est Une Femme* I'd already dyed my blonde hair black because I thought Karina's dark locks looked so fantastic. *Vivre Sa Vie* has several incredible scenes, including one where we see documentary-style images of Nana as a working girl while on the soundtrack she and her pimp discuss the mechanics of the Parisian sex trade.

A couple of years after *Vivre Sa Vie* was released I caught Catherine Deneuve's first film, *Les Parapluies De Cherbourg*, a musical in which every line of dialogue is sung.

What plot there is in the movie has been strung around an unplanned pregnancy and the shattering of youthful dreams. I loved the day-glo colour and romance of *Les Parapluies De Cherbourg* but it was Deneuve's appearance in *Belle De Jour*, directed by the surrealist Luis Buñuel, that cut far closer to home. In this 1967 feature Deneuve plays an upper-class woman called Severine who indulges her penchant for sadomasochism by doing daytime stints in a high-class Parisian brothel. Severine's work as a prostitute apparently enables her to enjoy some sexual intimacy with her rich and strait-laced husband, who is an incredibly unsuitable match for her. This being a Buñuel film, you can never really tell what is fantasy and what is reality, so the issue of whether Severine really has an economically privileged home life while secretly working as a prostitute remains open to doubt. That said, what really appealed to me about Severine was her breeding and aristocratic manner, which enabled her to earn more money than the women she worked alongside. Severine has poise and good clothes and it is these surface appearances that constitute her enduring appeal to men. I know from my own experience that such things are of supreme importance to a working girl who covets a better class of client. Severine in *Belle De Jour* is blonde, and after seeing this movie I reverted to my natural hair colour and even enhanced it with some highlights.

What I liked about these films was not that they reflected my own experiences, but rather the ways in which they provided me with roles I could take on as a means of enhancing my life. I've always thought of myself as an actress rather than a prostitute, even if a hundred or so years ago these two terms were generally treated as synonyms. Obviously when I have sex with a john I am acting out a role for his benefit. I have to pretend to find every man I sleep with physically attractive and, height of absurdity, that I would be gagging to have sex with them all regardless of whether or not I was being paid to do so. In taking on

such allegorical roles I must necessarily become an arche-
type of what it is to be a woman and I am always very
conscious of the many ways in which what I do can be
traced back to the notion of 'everywoman' to be found in
medieval morality plays. I am enjoyed and discarded as a
whore because I play up to the stereotypes of being a 'tart
with a heart of gold' and 'an English rose'; I become a
stucco Madonna and by such means I remain both desirable
and in some queer fashion almost chaste in the eyes of my
johns. Sex is pure surface, it is nothing but role-playing, so
what you see is exactly what you get. Since my tricks know
nothing of my long hard struggle to erase my Scots
working-class background, to them I really am a middle-
class English girl. In their eyes I am able to simultaneously
realise and suppress the bourgeois bifurcations of the
Madonna/Whore syndrome.

When I came back from India with a monkey on my
back, I tried to get a job at the Playboy Club but I was
turned down. Victor Lownes was always extremely fussy
about which girls got to work in the clubs he managed and
he unfortunately knew far too much about me from various
third parties. Having connections in all the right places can
be detrimental when the keeping up of pseudo-respectable
appearances becomes a matter of supreme importance.
Officially Bunnies were not supposed to turn tricks with the
Playboy Club clientele, but there was nonetheless a big
demand for just this type of service. Doormen at this
establishment immediately seized the chance to grab a slice
of this action and I came to an arrangement with one of
them. For a percentage of my earnings, Derek the doorman
sent me off to plush hotels where I'd have sex with men who
were wealthy enough to pay for a session with a Bunny Girl.
Since the arrangements were made through a Playboy Club
employee and I had a Bunny uniform to wear on these
dates, everybody was happy. In the early 70s a lot of the
Bunny action I saw involved Arab men. Having been to the
Middle East, I know most Arabs are poor, but at that time

it was only those who'd managed to grab a hefty slice of their respective countries' oil money who were in any way visible in London. Usually these men avoided telling me their real names, and since most of them had enjoyed the dubious benefits of a western education, they often adopted an English alias. Peter was typical.

'Hi!' I said when we met at the bar of his hotel in Park Lane.

'Hi,' he echoed.

'Shall we have a drink here or would you like to go straight up to your room?'

'We'll have a drink here. What would you like?'

Peter, like many other men, was enamoured with the idea of being seen in public with a Bunny Girl. Like a sports car or a great big house in the country, I was a status symbol to be ostentatiously and very publicly displayed. I had vodka and orange, Peter drank whisky and coke. I enjoyed the charade of being a trophy; if only this poor mark had known the truth. We chatted about our respective schools. Peter had a plummy English accent and he told me he'd attended Rugby. My line was that I'd been educated at St Felix, an all-girl boarding school located on the outskirts of the Suffolk coastal town of Southwold. This sounded more impressive than admitting I'd attended a state school until I was sixteen and that I'd paid my own way through a brief albeit expensive charm course at Lucie Clayton's in 1966. After acquiring Dutch courage and having made sure he'd been spotted by several acquaintances with me on his arm, Peter was ready to go upstairs.

'Do you want me in my uniform?' I asked once we were in Peter's room.

'Yes.'

'Shall I change in front of you or would you rather I got Bunnied up in the bathroom and emerged miraculously transformed?'

'How long does it take?'

'A few minutes.'

'OK, change in the bathroom.'

I knew Peter would still be dressed when I appeared in my Bunny outfit. He wasn't the type to strip off and lie naked on the bed waiting for me, wearing nothing more than a smile. Peter offered me a second screwdriver from the mini-bar in his room and I accepted it. He sipped at another whisky and coke.

'I read a book by a prostitute called *Streetwalker*,' Peter informed me, 'and in it the girl said she hated going on hotel dates and much preferred taking men to a room she rented for professional purposes. In her autobiography this anonymous prostitute described being attacked on a hotel visit. Does it worry you to be meeting a strange man at the Hilton?'

'You're not strange,' I reassured him. 'You're very nice.'

'But you didn't know that before you met me.'

'No, but Derek fixed this up and if anything happened to me he'd come around here with some of his boys.'

'But I could check out in the morning.'

'Yes, but you've already paid Derek and I'm meeting him outside the Playboy Club on my way home. If I didn't turn up to get my share of the loot he'd be round here later tonight.'

'You're very cautious.'

'Not really; I hadn't thought it through until you brought the subject up. Derek looks after that side of things.'

'Have you done this before?'

'No,' I lied.

'So why are you doing it tonight and with me?'

'Some of the other girls at the club had arrangements with Derek and they told me about them. It sounded exciting and the money was excellent.'

I am often asked by tricks how I started out as a prostitute and I try as far as possible to tell them whatever it is they want to hear. Sometimes I relate a sorry tale about how in 1961 I met a pseudo-upper class boy who claimed to be writing a book about drugs. He told me he wanted to watch my reactions to smoking grass and knocking back pills since this would help him with his research. What he really wanted to do was get me hooked and then turn me out, since despite a public-school education all he really aspired to being was a pimp. Sometimes I tell the truth. I arrived in London at the age of sixteen and saw an advert in a newspaper for dancers to audition at General Gordon's Cabaret Club. I got the job and between my show routines I earned extra cash by sitting at tables with men from the audience. I found it funny when I was offered money to sleep with guys I found attractive and subsequently transformed such pleasurable diversions into a profitable career. Sometimes I just say whatever pops into my head, but more often than not I later realise these transient life stories are lifted from movies I've seen. I very rarely claim that I've never turned a trick before, because in most situations it just doesn't sound convincing. However with Peter it just flowed on naturally from being asked about the safety of hotel visits.

'Is the money important?' Peter asked.

'If I'd met you before this arrangement was made, I'd have wanted to bed you anyway.' The words I uttered were essentially meaningless since I'd repeated them so many times, but I still flung them out with absolute conviction.

'Would the money be important if you didn't find me attractive?'

'Of course.'

'Why?'

'I've got debts. I fell out with my father over some trifles and he cut off my allowance.'

'What was the argument about?'

'My ambition to become an actress; he thought I was stage-struck and that this made both me and my family look cheap.'

'What does your father do?'

'He's a merchant banker.'

'He works in London?'

'Naturally, he works in the City.'

'Which bank is he with?'

'It's a private bank. I won't tell you the name. I'm discreet and I've no wish to embarrass my father.'

'Are you taking drama lessons?'

'Yes.'

'Have you appeared in anything?'

'Not really; I've got an Equity card and I've done quite a bit of work as a film extra but nothing substantial has come up yet.'

As we spoke Peter put his right hand on my left breast. I brushed my lips against his mouth, a quick kiss. After that I got up and took off my uniform. As far as possible I always tried to avoid having sex in my Bunny gear because it was a drag when it got damaged by an over-excited punter. Being high class I reversed the normal procedures of pavement pounders and charged extra if I kept my clothes on. Once I was naked I lay down upon the bed and Peter got on top of me. There was nothing subtle about what happened next and it was all over in a few minutes. I was fitted with a coil and so I allowed Peter to come inside me. After his orgasm, Peter rolled over and fell asleep with his trousers around his ankles and his shoes still on. I slid the shoes off his feet and eased his pants over his ankles. I hung his clothes over a chair and placed his brogues on the floor beside them. I didn't attempt to take off Peter's shirt, I simply pulled the bed sheets up over him.

As I made the trick comfortable, I thought of all the nights on which I'd missed out on tucking Lloyd up in bed. The years had flown by and at this time my son was already eight. I wondered then and I still wonder now how he was getting along. In the early 70s I went back to the adoption agency in an attempt to learn something of Lloyd's fate, but the social workers there never told me very much. They said Lloyd was happy and growing up in a stable family environment. I wanted to believe them but my eyes as well as my heart provided me with the evidence that I couldn't.

The social worker I was dealing with got me to visit the hospital where Lloyd was born in an attempt to confront my feelings about him. I didn't find doing this very helpful.

I left Peter snoring on his lonely hotel bed and picked up my earnings from Derek. I was back in Ladbroke Grove and fixing up within 30 minutes of leaving Park Lane. I'd taken a taxi home, I always did. I liked the safety and comfort of being driven around town. I'd earned considerable sums of money over the years and aside from drugs it was easy to fritter away on taxis, fashionable clothes, expensive cosmetics, high-class food and other beautiful things. I've never saved: when I have more money than I can spend on myself I buy presents for my family and friends. In the early 60s, before I got into smack, I'd even paid for my youngest brother to having riding lessons and bought him a pony. I wanted him to have the things I never had. When I have money to burn I never have any difficulties spending it. Other people's luxuries have at times been essentials to me. My parents were always horrified by the way I spent my money, but then they never knew how I made it! I've known poverty and I've known affluence, so wealth means nothing to me. You can't take money with you when you die, so I figure you might as well spend it if you've got some in your pocket.

THE ECLIPSE AND RE-EMERGENCE OF THE OEDIPUS COMPLEX

INT. NIGHT. BASEMENT FLAT AT 104 CAMBRIDGE GARDENS, LONDON W10.

One partially seen 'dream' speaker. Five unseen speakers.

An image not intended to be instantly recognisable appears as a horizon, before the credits, filling the width of the screen. It is the brightly lit abdomen of a man moving rhythmically during sleep. After one minute the title of the film appears over this image, after another minute the title disappears. All is still except for this abstracted stomach moving double time to the rhythm of human repose. Twenty minutes of this footage will be shot but it will run at double speed, so that after ten minutes of screen time the camera tilts upwards and the image disappears. The screen is a brightly lit bare wall for almost a minute, then a new image appears as a jump cut: the same man is sleeping on his stomach with his head to one side. He is viewed horizontally from a low level. This shot is mainly of the head and upper part of the body. After 30 seconds a subtitle appears: 'The Perfection Of Suicide Lies In Ambiguity'. The subtitle disappears. After a pause a second subtitle appears: 'The cinema too must be destroyed'. After another pause this subtitle disappears. This sequence of the same two appearing and disappearing subtitles is repeated for roughly eight and a half minutes. At almost nineteen and a half minutes into the film the sleeping man opens his eyes very widely and this image is frozen on the screen for the final thirty seconds, with the end credits rolled over these two glazed eyes. The screen then goes blank: the film has finished. The soundtrack for the first nineteen and a half minutes consists of the dialogue reproduced below, beneath which the sound of a life support machine bleeping is just audible. When the image freezes there is only the continuous tone of this machine indicating a patient is dead. A recording of a panting man and/or a panting animal will also be faded in and out of the first nineteen and a half minutes of the film.

Voice 1 (*estuary monotone*): The cinematic spectacle has its rules, which are framed to ensure satisfactory products are placed in multiplexes and video stores. However, it is dissatisfaction that characterises my line of flight. The function of narrative cinema is to present a false coherence as a substitute for the sovereign activity that is so blatantly absent where the bourgeois ideology of 'realism' still reigns. To demystify documentary cinema it is necessary to expose and thus dissolve its presupposed form. Cinema must become theatre and movie audiences wily actors who consciously understand their role in the realisations of all works. The men and women who gather together for late-night public screenings of martial arts films, talking over the dialogue and cheering during the fights, understand this.

Voice 2: Jillian O'Sullivan, aged 35, died on 2 December 1979 at 104 Cambridge Gardens, London W10. From the post-mortem report made by Dr Sean North after a visual inspection of the body:

> A well nourished woman. 5 feet 6 inches in height, looking considerably older than her stated age. There is a healing injection mark on the front of the left wrist: this is of several days' duration. No evidence of fresh injection marks. There are multiple old scars of the veins on the fronts of both elbows and some scarring over the wrists including some horizontal scarring over the proximal part of the right wrist.

Voice 3 (*Irish lilt*): I first met Jilly when she was introduced to me in Henekey's Pub in Portobello Road, as wanting to go to Spain and being prepared to share gas expenses. I had an old car. I was going to Ibiza. Nobody much in London knew about Ibiza in '62, but Jilly liked what she heard and decided to come all the way. My wife, Moira, got an introduction through Jilly to a job as a hostess at, I think, Gordon's. She worked there for about a month, maybe two months, while we saved bread to go back to Spain. Jilly was much more professional and highly paid than Moira, who simply talked to clients at tables. Jilly was one of the glittering club girls who would go elsewhere with clients after Gordon's closed; where they went or what they did, I have no idea. We had a small baby, and Moira came home immediately the club closed; I'd pick her up outside. Moira found the job a helluva strain; girls were obliged to persuade clients to buy ever more champagne, and then had to drink it with them so that they ended up sozzled night after night.

Voice 1: My mother liked undubbed new wave films because they helped her improve her French, but this was not her only reason for an interest in Godard and Resnais, since such directors simultaneously provided a fashion template for London's proto-mods, and my mother –

alongside other girls on the scene – cut her hair short like Jean Seberg. My mother wore wigs when she was working as a showgirl and hostess in Soho clubs like Gordon's and Kennedy's. Her hair was never the same two nights running.

Voice 2: Both gangsters and businessmen use the same psychological techniques to project an image of wealth and accomplishment, and their methods are something Jilly quickly assimilated. One photograph from Jilly's fashion portfolio shows her looking tough and very beat; she's heavily made up with her hair pulled back from her face and she is wearing a tight white short-sleeved T-shirt. At first glance this picture looks like it could date from the early 60s; however, Jilly is wearing large Paco Rabanne-style earrings that didn't become fashionable until 1966. In another photograph she has donned a wig, a backless and sleeveless black top and heavily flared black trousers; today this image makes her look like a refugee from the future. This is a photograph from the 60s of someone who might have passed as still fashionable five years later on. In a third photograph, Jilly is siting on a chair transforming herself from a 'Swinging London dolly bird' into a 'hippie chick': her hair (or rather her wig) is long and straight; she's wearing a hat that's almost floppy, a loose-fitting top and a short dress patterned with large checks.

Voice 4 (*slight Scots lilt*): In the 60s I became involved with many of the underground movements that were happening during this period, especially those that evolved in and around the Notting Hill Gate area, for example Defence, who combated police racism, Sigma, Alex Trocchi's forum for cultural revolution, SOMA, who fought for the legalisation of pot, RAAS, the black power organisation led by Michael X, London Free School and the Free University. During the summers of '63, '64 and '65 I became a member of the Living Theatre and witnessed the birth of street theatre and the first Notting Hill carnival. I then travelled overland to India, where unfortunately in 1968 I was seriously injured in a car crash. Although I had been experimenting for more than seven years with various types of drugs I had always felt in control. However, after this accident I became heavily addicted to opiates.

Voice 2: *Cain's Weekly* 15 June 1968:

Charming, vivacious and full of joie de vivre is Jilly O'Sullivan from London, who is on holiday in India and enjoying every bit of it. Jilly is a versatile person; she has modelled extensively in Europe and has been designing clothes under the name of Marteau Et Clyde and has appeared (as an extra) in many films, the latest being *If*. Having a natural flair for clothes, she says: 'Indian fabrics are so rich and colourful with such a vast variety and, if designed with a keen eye, have a wide scope on the European market.' Her message to the young fashion-conscious is – 'You are a woman, don't forget it. In this adventuresome year, let's have a change, go armed with your own personal flair for fashions, your own ideas and go alone.' To stress the point, Jilly models here some of her flattering outfits which she has designed from our lovely Indian textiles – 'they're so heady and ready for fun in the tropics.'

Voice 3: I was squatting in Tottenham Court Road when I re-met Jilly in 1975 and, learning that she was in serious trouble, arranged for her and her boyfriend Giordano to move into an empty flat. I actually took them there and helped Giordano break and enter. The trouble Jilly was in at that time may have been to do with a dope bust which cops in Ladbroke Grove agreed not to prosecute on certain conditions. I know Jilly told me a terrible tale about months, maybe years, of police corruption and her exploitation by one particular detective and his cronies, but whether this was in '75 or much earlier, I can't remember.

Voice 2: Part of the lure of both India and heroin for many hippies was as an escape from the misery of the 'rat race', although such escape was illusory since capitalism operated on a global scale; likewise, to those trafficking in it, smack was simply another cash crop. When Jilly died at the end of the 70s, British council estates were awash with cheap skag, 'Thatcher's cure for unemployment' as a graffiti slogan of that later era had it; and it was this mass and lumpen use of heroin that took off in the 60s which led to British media hysteria about opiates. When smack use was largely restricted to a self-styled professional and bohemian elite there were fewer signs of moral panic. The bourgeoisie finds the idea of the proletariat appropriating aspects of its decadence or its hedonism absolutely horrifying. A distinction needs to be drawn here between the British and American moral panics over drugs. Given that extensive international trafficking in opium was part and parcel of the economic bedrock of the British Empire – hence 'Perfidious Albion's' eighteenth-century opium wars against China – and that in the early part of the twentieth century Britain was the major world producer of morphine, opium becoming a controlled substance under First World War defence of the realm legislation was largely a side-effect of American panics about it. British drug hysteria in the early part of the twentieth century found its focus in Sigmund Freud's drug of choice, cocaine. The moral panic over heroin didn't begin in England until the 60s, as the fashionableness of this particular pain-killer spread from bohemia into the beatnik subculture, and from there into other youth cults.

Voice 5 (*light estuary accent*): The downstairs flat at Tottenham Court Road was open for spiritual sessions known as 'satsang' at lunch times, and I remember going a few times on my days off. The flat was next door to a porn cinema. There were only two flats because Jilly's lower-floor flat was on the first floor. You opened the front door and went straight up a flight of stairs, so it was probably directly above the porn cinema. I was very happy there and still look back on that time as one of the high spots of my life – it really was a brilliant time and a lot of that was down to the endlessly entertaining company of Jilly and Giordano and the rapport we all had. I remember listening a lot at the time to a Santana album called *Caravanserai* which for me epitomised that time at Tottenham Court Road. It has a very spacey, druggy, floaty feel to it and that's how we were. I think the key to understanding Jilly, especially in the last part of her life, is in the split between her two lives – the life as a premie (an initiate of the Church of Celestial Awakening) and the life as a junkie, which was really her previous life but one she couldn't ever quite get away from. I also think she probably found the life as a premie a bit too safe or whatever compared to what she'd been used to. It wasn't particularly tame to be a premie in those days, but she would have missed her friends like Alex Trocchi too much if she'd cut off from them completely.

Voice 4: Oh Lord and marvel at your wondrous creation – ten years later I begin to SEE. 1967 flashback of India In-dia. Delhi – finding the space man on a piece of paper in the street. I make India alone – Giordano in Goa with Mary. Subud Lady pays my airfare there. I cut and colour my hair one more time. 1977: is this the year the Subud Lady prophesied for Giordano? Resolutions. Always remember HOLY NAME. No smoking during take off. Lower my voice an octave – lately it has become too shrill – get back Jilly to where you belong. Disciple means disciple – devotee of the Lord. Try to avoid excesses, at least during Lent.

Voice 2: Jilly is the cover model on *Cain's Weekly* dated 13 July 1968, and there are spreads of clothes Jilly has designed in various editions of this magazine. Jilly's cover shot is a classic of its kind: she has one arm up over the side of her face and her left foot forwards. Jilly's legs are bare and her feet are unshod. There is an abstract design of smallish ovals in various colours around Jilly and these bring to mind pills, accentuating the appearance she has of being drugged, while a strap-line beside her reads: 'Another lovely paper pattern'. Capturing as ever the spirit of the age, Jilly is wearing what might be a genuine Paco Rabanne plastic and metal chain-mail dress; but for some unfathomable reason an extraordinarily inappropriate short see-through green half-shift is worn over the top of this, with matching light-green shorts under the skirt.

Voice 4: Dream location Tottenham Court Road. Going out – Drew pulls me into Mary's apartment. Garrett in Holloway happy to see me, it's Jackie's old room but Susan is there. Everything on the surface pretty together. Susan for some reason doesn't want me there. Garrett pretty uptight because he loves me and doesn't understand her reaction. I am angry because she isn't honest with me. I shake her physically. The outside image of me is Jilly, the inner Mary. Upstairs Samson cries – I wake up to that actuality. The dream seemed important to record. Is the pull back to junk/motherhood something I left behind?

Voice 2: Jilly's uncle Dinny McCarthy was a well-known figure in London's criminal demi-monde; he had his fingers in various protection rackets. For legal purposes, Dinny described himself a bookie's runner, and he lost an eye in a fight over protection pitches at the Derby. Rather more endearingly, Jilly's cousin Ziggy 'the Panther' Williams appears as Scotch Sigmund in the autobiography of the old-style heavy Eric Stone. After flashing up the name Paul Sutherland, Stone gives an account of Williams losing heavily in a Notting Hill spieler and then slipping out with his criminal accomplice Geoff 'the Eskimo' Rochester to do a quick robbery. Upon their return Williams and Rochester negotiated the price of a jewel with the governor of the spieler before resuming their places at the game. Recently Williams has been having a spat with another of his one-time burglary partners, Paul 'the Panty Thief' Sutherland. Sutherland's 1995 autobiography *Lusty Larcenist* incensed Williams because in it the Panty Thief claimed sole credit for stealing movie star Elizabeth Taylor's jewels when she was filming at Elstree. In the late 1990s and using a spokesman called Arthur Glynn, Williams ran a campaign to get the public to demand his arrest for this 1960 burglary. Williams asserted there had been a cover-up and that the Old Bill wouldn't charge him with stealing Taylor's jewels because he'd paid corrupt cops £12,000 for information that enabled him to secure the haul. Jilly, incidentally, was named after Ziggy the Panther's mother, her aunt Jilly Williams née McCarthy.

Voice 4: Good Friday morning dream. I can't keep my eyes off the bright flames of white light, they seem to envelop me with their lore – truly this is a soul of a saint. I am awoken by the sound of a baby crying. I recognise that the cry is of my brother who is heartbroken because mother has left her physical body. The whole light is obviously the real mother. Mother, wherever you are, I am so happy that I came through you. Dear God thank you.

Voice 1: A gifted impostor creates the impression that those they're fooling know pretty much all there is to know about them, but cannily avoids providing any concrete details about their background which might potentially provide a means of catching them out. The impostor allows the fantasies of their new acquaintances to fill the gaps in the anti-narrative that is their own life. The life histories of our parents tend to operate in a similar fashion: because mum and dad have always been around we imagine we know all about them. However, try pressing for details and you'll often find there are very few specifics that can be pinned down about the lives of someone's parents. Parents are always and already impostors, and learning to be a parent is often a difficult task for someone who has more usually considered him or herself to be the child of their child's grandparents.

Voice 4: Early Easter Sunday morning about two o'clock. I awake to the soft voice of someone calling, 'Jilly, Jilly, wake up and meditate.' The voice is so full of sweetness. Next I visualise, in cameo, David. I see only his head and shoulders, he's wearing that blue/green/white sweatshirt, his hair is flowing and he's wearing a half-mysterious smile. His vibration makes me get out of bed and pulls me to the veranda; I look out and see the moon is exactly in half. Oh Lord, what are you trying to tell me? Is this meant to be my better half? Or is it just one more of your tests? The vision was so beautiful that it totally satisfied me. How long is it since I've had this experience? The last time I believe was when Giordano was in India but any time I wanted him I could see, touch, hear him, be with him via this astral travelling.

Voice 2: By 1942 the war-time rationing system in London was brought to breaking point by the Blitz, and criminality became an accepted part of life even among those who valued that most perishable of commodities, their own respectability. The black market, bribery, forged coupons and ration books were about the only thing that made existence bearable for the vast majority of Londoners during the second inter-imperialist war and its aftermath. It was in this situation that 'villainy' in England became American-ised; that is to say in terms of media punditry it was transformed from being done in an ad hoc fashion to occurring under the guiding hand of organised crime bosses. Such journalistic manipulations are rather different to the everyday reality of the way criminal activity was carried on, since with regard to this there are more continuities than discontinuities between the early and middle parts of the twentieth century. The main difference in the immediate post-war era was that men like Jack Spot and Billy Hill relished the publicity that accompanied their attempts to style themselves kings of the underworld. Mostly this was a matter of image and developing cordial relationships with favoured crime reporters, with Hill enjoying a special relationship with journalist Duncan Webb and Spot modelling himself on American movie gangsters by dressing in expensive but conservative handmade suits and being seen in fashionable clubs.

In the 60s, the Kray Twins took such exercises in public relations a stage further by setting up photo opportunities at which they were snapped in the company of celebrities, and while the Krays could be nasty, their influence and the purely economic level of their success have been vastly overestimated. Spot and the Krays were ultimately straw men, and even the movies on which these British gangsters modelled themselves were an outgrowth of American police propaganda that built various relatively unimportant and archaic Chicago criminals into major figures of public menace, so that the state could appear all the more powerful when it crushed them. Without this process of Americanisation, which required the connivance of Fleet Street, there would have been no Swinging London. Rock culture is, of course, merely one of the many ways in which 'gangster' flash was both spread and commoditised.

Voice 4: I put an orange felt tip on yellow paper. Feeling out, trying one more time to catch this fleeting high – consciousness, what's that? The red in the shooter, pumping pushing to get that so-wanted high. Eating Canary figs. I think of you. FOR-MEN-TERRA.

Voice 1: At the very moment Freud theorised the unconscious, his fantastic notions were rendered obsolete. Men and women were already assembling in the black womb of cinemas and their collectively realised and suppressed desires were being projected onto silver screens. Nearly fifty years later, Warhol demonstrated his understanding of the essential falsity of 'realism' when he made *Empire*, eight hours of the transition from day to night around the Empire State Building. There is necessarily a certain sadism in recognising that everything which aspires to the mantle of documentary must necessarily fall behind its own premises, and that only fiction can signify beyond erasure. I once came across a mythological account of Warhol's *Sleep* in which it was claimed he shot forty minutes of footage and looped it to make up the eight-hour length of the average night's sleep. If we happily accept the simultaneous truth and falsity of this legend, Warhol's meditations on the night side of human life illustrate very well the dialectical thrust of the old Illuminist dictum that truth can only manifest itself through falsehood.

Of all the dissonant realities brought together here, the smashing of Warholian beauty against Debord's iconoclastic sublime is not yet the most reprehensible. Indeed, these monstrous acts of palingenesis must necessarily constitute an invisible resurrection of *On the Passage of a Few People Through a Rather Brief Period of Time*. Likewise, for me any cinematic realisation of Bataille will inevitably be grounded in a conjunction of terror and exploitation. And it remains more than merely possible that by placing a photograph of the Empire State Building – albeit out of camera shot – above the bed on which I lie asleep, I am also making a virtually imperceptible and heavily solarised version of *Empire*. For me to be filmed asleep in the room in which my mother died was always and already a fiction. The conceit that every individual life is a journey through a valley of tears ranks as an even greater banality than the use of sleep as a metaphor for the transition from life to death. Clichés work, and I am remaking cinema in the way I wish to remake the world, correcting the faults of older filmmakers and simultaneously demonstrating my indifference to any and all so-called works of 'genius' by self-consciously using the cultural heritage of humanity for partisan propaganda purposes. Cinema becomes theatre and there is a much-needed shift of emphasis away from cultural com-modities and on to the human relationships from which such products emerge.

Voice 4: Thursday I thought I wouldn't make it so in defiance the rebel in me bought ten fags and smoked them one after the other while I watched 'Jilly' catching the tube back home. Piccadilly – junkies galore. I realise how much you've changed me. Change for the real. True change and something deep inside whispers I love you and want you to be with me. My heart listens to grace. It can take you anywhere, anytime, even when you're wrapped in a nicotine haze.

Voice 6 (*Midwest American accent*): I actually found out about Jilly's heroin issues when we were flying to a Church of Celestial Awakening event in Florida, from the UK, in the fall of 1979. She told me that she had been using heroin and she was in withdrawal and ill, and asked me to help her. We shared a motel room for the week-long event. She felt strongly that she wanted to stop using heroin and was on her way to the Church of Celestial Awakening event to reinforce herself spiritually so that she could succeed. Jilly was very ill throughout the event but enjoyed it tremendous-ly. She communicated with many Church of Celestial Awakening friends about what she was going through with heroin and about her resolve to change. She said it had always been difficult to be in recovery and that she definitely wanted to kick heroin. Jilly was very brave and strong in enduring the physical pain involved with withdrawal. I admired her for her strength and perseverance in overcom-ing this adversity.

Jilly was involved with Garrett in this period, and she told me that he had been a factor in her starting to use again. She said she had known him in the old days when she was with Giordano, and he had only been a friend. Being in London apparently presented her with the temptation to use, because of association with old heroin buddies, including Garrett, I suppose. I didn't know any of the people Jilly knew who were involved in drugs, but met Garrett once or twice at Jilly's flat in London, in Bayswater, I think. Jilly had become romantically/sexually involved with Garrett, and was connected with him also because of heroin.

We often went to Church of Celestial Awakening meetings together, and that was the reason I found Jilly the night she died. I was supposed to meet Jilly to go to a meeting, and she didn't turn up. This was unlike her so I decided to go around to her flat, assuming she had been delayed and would still be there. When I got there, the door was open and all the lights were on. I remember she had a ground-floor flat, situated in the back of a house or block. Jilly was lying on her stomach with her head to the side, and I don't think she was clothed, but she had a sheet partially draping her body.

Voice 5: The flat in Cambridge Gardens. I'm pretty sure there were steps down to the front door. Anyway, it was definitely a basement flat. The door of the room Jilly lived and slept in was to the right of the passageway – I think it was just a bedsitting room with a kitchen and bathroom. I can vaguely remember a galley-type kitchen. The bathroom I can't remember at all. The room – you went through the door and the window was to your left. The fireplace was opposite the door and there was a double bed to the right of the door. It was a fairly large room. It wasn't furnished or decorated in any style I can particularly remember, but it was comfortable and quite cosy and warm. There were pictures of Guru Rampa on the mantelpiece, but Jilly would have had those wherever she lived from '72 onwards.

Voice 2: 104 is at the shabby end of Cambridge Gardens, the west end of the street closest to Wormwood Scrubs prison. Today, from the front of the house, one can see the Westway, and the studio flat Jilly died in would sell for more than £250,000, which even taking inflation into account is a huge price hike from its 1979 value. During the brief period of time Jilly lived at 104, the property had an air of criminality about it, having been associated for many years with smugglers, gangsters, alcoholics and the generally low-down and desperate. The house is just a few minutes' walk from the two addresses at which Jilly is known to have lived in Bassett Road in the 60s. It is also just around the corner from 10 Rillington Place, where Reginald Christie committed some particularly notorious sex murders in the 40s and 50s. This neighbourhood was made for the wretched dignity of the petty bourgeoisie, and its gentrification in the 1990s brought about the return of the sedentary population for whom it was built but by whom it was so rarely occupied.

Voice 1: After my mother died, her diary was retrieved from the back basement flat at 104 Cambridge Gardens, and the last entry indicates that her use of heroin had been ongoing. In March 1979, my mother recorded that she wanted to write a poem for me on my birthday, though the last thing she actually wrote was dedicated to her smack-dealing boyfriend Garrett.

Voice 4: You lie there, legs straddled, an easy lay. Like some 'gloomy fucker' (your words). For hours you have put me through mental torture. Because I desired you. Sure, I wanted love anyway I could. But you denied me both fuck & fix. And then, dropping a Tuinal, like an over-the-hill whore you became an easy lay.

Voice 2: Jillian O'Sullivan, aged 35, died on 2 December 1979 at 104 Cambridge Gardens, London W10. From the report compiled by coroner's officer PC Paul Wade: 'The deceased woman was separated from her husband who now lives in Hong Kong' (this is untrue) 'and residing at the above address alone' (this is untrue). 'There is a long history of addiction to drugs' (this is correct) 'but well in the past' (this is untrue). 'No recent indications of this at all' (this is untrue). 'She was found dead in bed at 6 p.m. on Sunday 3rd December 1979 by a friend' (this last statement is factually correct).

Voice 1: What usually makes documentaries so easy to understand is the arbitrary limitation of their subject matter. They describe the atomisation of social functions and the isolation of their products. One can in contrast envisage the baroque complexity of a moment which is not resolved into a work, a moment whose movement indissolubly contains facts and values and whose meaning does not yet appear. The journey I'm undertaking, an ongoing drift through the London of my childhood and youth, is a search for this confused totality as it manifested itself at the moment of my mother's death. I don't know how my mother died, about the only thing I am certain of is that the authorities failed to investigate her death adequately. Many traditional African cultures don't view an individual as dead until they have passed from living memory. In *Symbolic Exchange and Death* Baudrillard described cemeteries as the first ghettos, but enough of such nostalgia ... The writing was already on the wall: 'To those who are about to die, we salute you!'

11. DOWN IN FLAMES

When I began to get completely fucked up on drugs I thought that being a junkie was the coolest thing in the world. Fifteen years have passed since then so now the times have changed and I've changed too. London is no longer swinging. Last night I caught the tube home from Piccadilly and I clocked hundreds of junkies swarming around me. There is an army of addicts now, so many more than when I started shooting smack way back when. In the pre-psychedelic 60s using opiates seemed like the ultimate reality trip, and the brothers and sisters who walked in the shadow of the needle appeared to trudge stealthily through this world in states of existential grace. In the beat era to be an outcast was to be beautiful. We really and truly believed we were an exclusive sect of the damned. My heroes of that time had all been junkies, everyone from Charlie Parker to William Burroughs. In England at least the 60s was a good time to be a junkie: the living was easy, with legal scripts readily available. In the 70s we were to be awoken from this long cool nod-out with the rudest of jolts. That said, when I returned to London from India in the summer of 1969 my romantic opium dreams had yet to come crashing down around me, and when someone from my circle was consumed by metaphysical flames these appeared to be fanned by the most personal of demons.

I didn't know it then, but by 1969 I was already a victim of post-hippie burn-out. By the time the 70s really began unfolding I was cursing my dependence on junk, since as a direct result of the corruption that was rife in the Metropolitan Police I was experiencing my own version of hell on earth. In August 1969 I appeared on a float in the Notting Hill carnival. I was dressed in a swimsuit with a Miss World sash resplendent on my chest. There was a giant papier-mâché needle sticking out of my arm. I'm not sure now if I was trying to make a political or a philosophical statement; I just know that at that moment I was happy to be hooked. Russ Henderson, who'd lived downstairs from me in the basement of 24 Bassett Road back in the day, was not impressed. He'd had the first steel band on the streets of London and played a leading role in reviving the Notting Hill carnival. Russ did not like the stuff I was involving myself in or those who kept me company on the float.

A day or two after the carnival I went with Giordano to visit one of our friends who was in hospital having an abortion. Although the cops had been unable to do anything during the carnival I'd heard on the grapevine that they were pissed off about my appearance as a junkie queen, and that it might be a good idea if I got out of town while things cooled down. The friend who was having the termination was called Meg Maud, and she was one of my few acquaintances of that time who wasn't using. I knew that at some indeterminate date in the past Giordano had enjoyed a fling with her. Since Meg was younger than me this almost certainly meant that Giordano had been carrying on with her behind my back. The fact that Giordano had affairs certainly wasn't news to me but that didn't mean I wasn't pissed off about it. Meg had recently moved out of London. We knew Meg and her boyfriend Tom were in town because the male partner in this couple couldn't have looked after a pet rock, let alone his infant son Michael. After dropping Meg off at the hospital in Paddington he'd driven straight over to the Gate and left the child with friends of mine before proceeding to get high. It was these mutual acquaintances who told me Tom was in town. I'd stolen chocolates and flowers for Meg on the way to the infirmary and we found her in a ward filled with lonely girls whose eyes revealed a potent mixture of self-hate and sorrow. It was way past Meg's discharge time but Tom was nowhere to be seen. There was nothing unusual about this situation, so it was mentioned in passing rather than meriting discussion.

'You should have seen the cops when I went past on the float with this giant needle sticking out of my arm,' I told Meg in an attempt to cheer her up. 'They were completely gutted but there was fuck-all they could do about it there and then. After all, they didn't want a riot on their hands.'

'You can't believe what I had to go through to get this termination,' Meg told me. 'Tom was adamant that he didn't want another child. If it hadn't been for him pushing me so hard to get rid of it, then I wouldn't have been able to eat all the shit I had to take from the shrinks. The interviews they put me through about my state of mental health! It's an unbelievable hassle getting a legal abortion.'

'Forget about that,' Giordano put in. 'I've got all sorts of goodies with me. Once we've sprung you, we'll all get so cranked you won't be able to remember your name, let alone what you've just been through.'

'Have they got any food in here?' I asked. 'I'm famished.'

'Eat the chocolates you brought,' Meg suggested. 'I couldn't touch them right now.'

'I'm not going to chow on the things I brought for you. I'll find something once we get out of here.'

'When do you think Tom is gonna turn up?' Giordano enquired.

'I told you, he should have been here more than three hours ago.'

'Don't worry about that, he'll just be nodding out somewhere; he'll be up to fetch us all when he gets his shit together,' I put in.

'Fetch us all?' Meg echoed.

'We've got to duck out of town for a few days,' Giordano explained, 'so we're going to Bristol to stay with you.'

'Has Tom agreed to this?' Meg demanded.

'Yes,' I lied. 'We saw him this morning when we were all scoring at 75a Cambridge Gardens.'

'Tom was round there?'

'Yeah.'

'Did he have Michael with him?'

'No, he left Michael with Sabrina; don't worry about the baby, he'll be fine,' I answered.

Giordano stayed with Meg while I took off, saying I needed to find some food. I fixed up in a toilet and wouldn't have minded nodding out there and then, but instead, with a superhuman effort, I forced myself off the loo seat and took up my watching station at the hospital entrance. Tom Jeeves spotted me as he entered the hospital and he woke me up. After shaking me a couple of times, he handed me his baby son. I didn't mind this since I love children and Michael is a cute kid.

'Jilly, what a stroke of luck! You can handle the brat for me. I can't cope with other people's children, let alone my own. By the way, what are you doing here?'

'Giordano and I thought we'd visit Meg.'

'That's nice.'

'She's a little upset by what she's been through.'

'She's highly emotional and obstinately refuses to shoot smack, which would help stabilise her moods.'

'Meg asked if Giordano and I would go back to Bristol with you.'

'She should have waited until I got here to ask me what I thought about that.'

'She doesn't think she'd be able to cope with looking after Michael on her own straight away; if we don't come with you then you'll have to do some serious child care.'

'In that case you're welcome to a little break with us.'

Everything was set and before long we were all heading out of London. I was sitting in the front passenger seat beside Tom. Giordano was in the back of the car, attempting to charm Meg, but his style was severely cramped by the fact that Michael was bawling on her lap. Nonetheless I got pissed off about the compliments Giordano was constantly paying Meg. I began to stroke Tom's leg and since he didn't remove my hand, I unzipped his flies and jerked him off. I don't think Giordano or Meg noticed. Their attention was focused on Michael, who was extremely distraught.

'Your ability to cope with Michael is improving,' Meg told Tom after the baby had calmed down. 'Usually when he's as upset as he just got you'd stop the car and throw us out. What's changed?'

Tom didn't reply.

'I need a shot,' Giordano announced.

'No dice, not in front of the baby you don't,' I snapped back.

Giordano would have had no qualms about getting high there and then in the car, but I had his works in my bag, so what happened was largely down to me.

'Stop the fucking car and I'll get high by the roadside,' Giordano snapped at Jeeves.

After some arguing back and forth, Tom agreed he'd stop at the next pub we came to. This suited me since Meg would have to stay in the motor with Michael; there was no way a publican was going to allow a child inside his establishment, and it was too wet and windy to sit outside with the baby. I wanted to have it out with Giordano over the way he was flattering Meg, and a pit-stop would provide me with ample opportunity to attend to this. Tom was up for having a drink and getting something to eat, so it was only Meg who objected to this collective plan and she found herself outvoted three to one. Fortunately the place at which we stopped, the Jolly Farmers, was a large and crowded pub, so I was able to engage Giordano in a full-on row while Jeeves went to get the drinks.

'Give me my fucking gear, you whore!' Giordano roared.

'Not until you bleedin' well apologise for trying to chat up Meg. I saw you turn on the charm, you smooth bastard!'

'Look, we need a place to stay to get away from the cops and I've got to keep Meg sweet. Now give me my fucking works, you slut.'

'Not until you say you're sorry.'

Giordano didn't bother to answer, grabbing my handbag instead. However I had a firm hold of the strap, so his hand was caught in mid-air and it wasn't difficult for me to bend my head and bite it hard enough to cause blood to flow.

'*Merde!*' Giordano hollered.

Unfortunately at that moment from the corner of my eye I saw Tom returning with the drinks. I was momentarily distracted and Giordano used this as an opportunity to get my bag away from me. I tried to follow him but found Jeeves blocking my path. Since Giordano had disappeared into the gents', there was no way I could prevent him from getting his shot, and that was the end of the little leverage I had over my obstinate boyfriend. I accepted the pint Jeeves presented to me and it had been empty for a very long time when Giordano finally returned. I didn't need to ask what had happened, since I knew he'd nodded out in the toilets. It was a relief to have my boyfriend back because Tom had been busy pulling moves on me. He obviously hadn't understood why I'd jerked him off in the car, and was unduly optimistic about his chances of getting me to crawl under our table to plate him as he sat supping a pint. Giordano returned my bag to me and I figured I'd shoot some skag to calm my jangled nerves, so I slunk off to the bogs, where I fell asleep in the cubicle in which I took my hit. Upon rejoining my companions I found a pint awaiting me but I had no real interest in consuming it. Giordano and I were happy to nod out some more, while Tom wanted to delay our return to the car in the hope of enticing me to give him some oral action. My drink sat untouched in front of me as I went with a heroin buzz. Eventually last orders were called and we had to go back to the motor, where we found Meg fuming.

'I'm freezing and so is Michael,' Meg complained. 'What the hell have you been doing?'

'We nodded out,' Giordano confessed. 'I'm sorry.'

Maud laughed. Years later she confessed to me that Giordano mixed charm and helplessness so well that she'd forgive him just about anything. We got into Bristol about midnight. Tom decided to go to a late-night film screening of *Midnight Cowboy* at a local cinema and wanted me to accompany him. When I declined this offer he went alone. Giordano dropped some acid and, since Meg wanted to go to bed, we decided to see what action we could find on the streets. The area in which Meg and Tom were living was distastefully suburban, so we made our way to St Pauls. I figured that if we could find an all-night café then there'd be punters around interested in buying some of the large stash of acid Giordano and I had brought with us. We got as far as ordering a couple of cups of tea in a greasy spoon but were thrown off the premises for causing a disturbance. I'd got back on Giordano's case about Meg and he didn't like it. I told the guy behind the counter that we'd been having a ding-dong all the way down from London and he needn't worry himself about our little disagreement. He wasn't impressed and said that if we didn't leave immediately he'd call the cops.

'Jesus Christ, woman, can't you leave it alone? I don't fancy Meg, I just want to keep her sweet while we're lying low at her pad.'

'Bullshit!'

'I'd rather kill myself than betray you!' As Giordano said this I could tell by the tone of his voice he was about to make one of his characteristically dramatic gestures.

It was about three o'clock in the morning but there was plenty of traffic around. The cars out on the streets included more than enough kerb crawlers to force everyone who was driving through the city to travel at a snail's pace. Giordano threw himself down on the road in front of a Ford Cortina that was moving at around twenty miles an hour. The driver braked hard and the vehicle stopped not much more than an inch from Giordano's prostrate body. Moments later a panda car careered around the corner and ploughed into the back of the stationary Cortina. The two cops manning the squad car jumped out and I was off and running immediately. I didn't want to give the rozzers an opportunity to see me properly as I made my escape.

'Run!' I shouted at Giordano, who was still lying on the ground.

I didn't hang around and I got to Meg's place a couple of hours before Giordano returned.

'Shit!' was the first thing Giordano said after getting in. 'Shit, shit, shit!'

I was relieved to hear Giordano using English since when he was really agitated he swore in French.

'What happened?' Meg asked.

'Didn't Jilly tell you?'

'She told me about her escape from the law. I don't know what happened to you.'

'When Jilly shouted I got up and the Old Bill had a good look at me as I did so. I had to run like fuck to get away from them. I ended up hiding in a garden shed for some time. I heard some coppers talking about the incident as I waited in the dark for them to go away. The fuzz are hopping mad about what happened and they've got an accurate description of me. More than that, they know Jilly and I are from London because of the conversation we had in the café. They've got patrols out looking for us.'

'What are you going to do?' Meg asked.

'We need to get back to London,' I told her.

'They've got guys at the station keeping a look-out for us,' Giordano put in.

'If Tom were here he could drive us home,' I said.

'What?' Giordano roared. 'Tom isn't about? Is that right?'

'Yes.'

'In that case we've got to figure out some other way to get away from here.'

'Like what?'

'Where's Tom's motor?'

'He took it with him.'

'Let's steal some wheels. I saw a nice Rover in the driveway next door.'

'No, no, no!' Meg wailed. 'You can't go stealing a car from my neighbours. You'll bring a whole heap of trouble down on everyone including yourself.'

In the end, to placate Meg we agreed to wait a couple of hours and if Jeeves wasn't back for breakfast, we'd figure out a way of getting home that didn't involve vehicle theft. Tom stayed out all night. In the morning Meg was able to leave Michael with a neighbour, so once we'd rounded up one of her male friends we were all set to put the plan I'd formulated into action. I wanted to sneak on to a London-bound train but wasn't going to attempt this without Meg doing some reconnaissance first. Giordano and I waited in a town-centre café while our friends went off to check whether the coast was clear at the railway station. When they returned they reported that uniformed cops who seemed to be looking out for us were standing guard on the platform from which the London train departed. This called for a diversion, and my scheme for dealing with the filth was simplicity itself. Meg and her friend would walk ahead of us into the station, where they were to fake an intense domestic argument, and while the law's attention was momentarily distracted, Giordano and I would sneak on to the waiting train.

I told Giordano to hang well behind me, since if the cops nabbed me the consequences were probably less serious than if they got him. The circumstances dictated that we separate before attempting to get into a carriage, since there was no point in creating a situation in which the Old Bill had an opportunity to nick both of us. At first everything went well and I couldn't help grinning when I saw Meg bop her friend over the head with her handbag. I sauntered casually along the platform and on to the train as the rozzers focused their attention on these decoys. Giordano was not so lucky: despite the fact the fuzz were having words with Meg, this didn't prevent them from clocking him. My boyfriend broke into a run with a copper in hot pursuit and I watched helplessly as he legged it out of the station. The train took me safely back to London and it wasn't until darkness had fallen that I discovered what had happened to Giordano. He found me back at our 58 Bassett Road bedsit, listening to *The Hangman's Beautiful Daughter* by the Incredible String Band.

'I had to run like hell to get away from the filth.' Giordano was eager to recount his story when at last he rejoined me. 'It was lucky you made an arrangement with Meg about what to do if things went wrong, so as agreed we rendezvoused in the café. We had terrible trouble getting back to her house. There were cops everywhere and they were looking for me. There was a patrol stationed close to Meg's home. We ended up knocking on the door of a house with a car parked in the drive and Meg told the man who answered she'd just got out of hospital and wasn't feeling well. She said she was terribly sorry but could he give her a lift home? The geezer was very nice and invited us in. We had a cup of tea and then he took us in his car to Meg's place. I had to slide down low in my seat and hope the law didn't see me. I guess I was lucky they were looking for a man travelling on foot. Tom had returned to the house by then, so he had to drive me to Bath and it was only from there that I was able to catch a train to London.'

'Are you sure that's the full story?' I demanded as I chose a fresh record, Dylan's *Highway 61 Revisited*.

'What do you mean?'

'Well, I got home hours before you, so are you sure there isn't something you left out of your tale, such as having sex with Meg? After all, you never told me what happened to her friend.'

'He had to go to work. Nothing happened between me and Meg; after all, Tom was in when we finally made it back to their place.'

'Are you sure?'

'You're crazy!'

'Giordano,' I laughed, 'we're all crazy!'

Giordano chuckled too and soon afterwards we were having sex on our bed. I'd put a fresh platter on the turntable, since *Their Satanic Majesties Request* by the Rolling Stones seemed more appropriate than Bob Dylan. Later that night as we chilled to Van Morrison's *Astral Weeks*, one of our neighbours told me that the Mets had been around looking for me, and upon being told I'd gone to Paris with my boyfriend they seemed to lose interest. It was months before I had any further problems with the law.

Recalling this incident brought to mind another occasion when I made love to Giordano, this time in California in the mid-70s. Full moon in Sagittarius. We were doing it in the kitchen when our west-coast wildcatting was interrupted by our hosts, who, having just come home from work, didn't want us performing in front of them. We had *Led Zeppelin II* blasting out from the hi-fi in the lounge and our friends didn't like that either, so they took it off and put on Joni Mitchell's *Blue*. I sang along to my favourite track, 'Carey'. Giordano and I had spent time together under the Matala moon back in 1967. The summer before we went to India we'd joined a hippie commune that resided in the Matala beach caves. We did our first clean-up from smack there, but found ourselves skagged up again within days of returning to northern Europe. I like Mitchell's song since it reminds me of happy times, even if she's a little too judgemental about the freak scene in Crete. Maybe her take on the Greek islands was soured by the relationship she sings about in this number. The consensus among both fans and critics is that the lyric is about James Taylor. I don't have an opinion on this matter, I just like the tune and Mitchell's invocation of the Matala moon.

As I warbled through the Mitchell track Giordano told me to shut up, since my singing, which isn't good, was spoiling his enjoyment of the song. Giordano and I are cosmic twins but we drive each other crazy, which I guess is why we no longer live together. More than a year has passed now since I last made love to him. These days we only have sex if we meet in America. I wish he was somewhere close to me in London instead of living in a Church of Celestial Awakening ashram in the south of France. Things are no longer like they were in the early 70s when I was in England and Giordano was in India. Eight years ago I could still feel him and touch him whenever I wanted by traversing the astral plane. These days the effort of getting my soul to leave my body is so great that I can't sustain the separation of my spirit from my corporeal body.

12. LOVE CHILD

They say heroin kills pain and love heals emotional wounds. This isn't true and I ought to know. As I have already mentioned, when I returned to London from India in 1969 I'd been addicted to opiates for several years and I had so much more than a regular lover in Giordano. I may have had stand-up rows day and night with Giordano but we were nonetheless soul mates. We watched each other like hawks and probed each other for weaknesses precisely because we loved one another to bits. Our love was intense but despite this there wasn't a single day on which I didn't think of my lost son Lloyd. Some of the people I spoke to about Lloyd attributed my feelings of guilt to my Catholic background but I knew they were wrong. I'm happy that I come from a large Irish family, and it's obvious when you think about it that my personal background was shaped by the broader culture that surrounded me as I grew up in Greenock. Scotland is a benighted land and the marked sado-masochistic tendencies that its people have sublimated into various forms of religious mania are ultimately a product of Calvinism. The Scottish national character is leavened with guilt and this is something that transcends the sectarian divide. I've spent time in France, Italy and Spain and the all-pervasive sense of culpability and doom that has been rotting the soul of Scotland for centuries just doesn't exist on the other side of the English Channel. I feel guilty that I've let Lloyd down but I'm also very angry about the way my son was stolen from me.

I flitted across to Spain when Lloyd's adoption papers were supposed to be signed, but after I returned to London the Krays and their henchmen forced me to do the wrong thing. From the moment my son was taken from me I've wanted him back, but by 1970 it was seven years since I'd last done anything more than talk about being reunited with Lloyd. After my return from India, I knew it was time to swing back into action on this front. I was living in Bassett Road but I didn't want to use my own address when dealing with social workers, so I went to see Ruth Forster, who I knew from my days at number 24 and who'd been resident in one of the two basement flats at my old address for years and years. Ruth was a Jewish refugee from Nazism, a card-carrying member of the Communist Party and always willing to provide help when it was needed. She was very happy for me to use her address while I made enquiries about Lloyd. She understood that because of my involvement in various scams that supported my habit, I liked to shield myself from the prying eyes of the authorities. That was also why I used false names and dates of birth whenever it was feasible to do so.

To an extent I abused Ruth's hospitality, since for me the early 70s were a period of full-blown kleptomania and I would stash suitcases filled with stolen goods in the homes of various friends. Ruth's pad was located conveniently close to mine, so she provided the main storage space for the spoils of my dipping and shoplifting sprees. Ruth let me use her telephone, so I called the London Children's Adoption Agency from her flat and told them I was suicidal because they'd taken away my son. My plan was to act as if I'd totally lost the plot and, once I'd conned the social workers into thinking I might top myself, to use their fears as leverage to gain access to Lloyd. The story wasn't so far-fetched, since I had once slashed my wrists when I felt totally unable to deal with the pain of losing Lloyd, but that was in the days before I'd got into smack. Ruth was through in the kitchen when I made my first call, and after I got off the phone she told me I'd overdone the theatrics. I was able to reassure her I seemed to have gauged it about right, since I had an appointment to see a social worker called Mrs Haling at the adoption agency in two weeks' time.

'Let me begin,' Mrs Haling told me from across a desk a fortnight later, 'by reading the note I have about you. It says you're very depressed because after giving your son Lloyd up for adoption eight years ago you still haven't started a family of your own, and unless you find a man who'll marry you soon you're thinking of taking your own life . . .'

'That's not quite right,' I put in. 'You see, I'm very guilty about having had Lloyd adopted, and I know that because of my failure to look after my son I'm no longer able to conceive. God is punishing me for my sins and I do feel very guilty about what I did. Since I lost Lloyd I haven't been able to form a steady relationship with a man, and it would be very wrong of me to attempt to do so now because I couldn't get married to someone knowing that I'd be preventing them from having kids.'

'Are you sure you can't conceive a child? After all you did give birth to a son in 1962.'

'I told you, I'm being punished by God. There is no way I could get pregnant now.'

'Are you sure of that?'

'Of course I'm sure. God told me that I am a sinner, and because of my failure to look after my son, I'll never be able to conceive another child.'

'Have you tried to get pregnant?'

'No, there would be no point. God won't let me have another child until I make things up to Lloyd.'

'Have you had sex with a man since Lloyd was born?'

'Don't be ridiculous.'

'I'm not prying. I'm just trying to find out why you believe you can't conceive a child.'

'I've told you, I'm being punished by God.'

'So what have you been doing since Lloyd was born?'

'I left England, I've been abroad, I've just recently returned from India.'

'How did you support yourself?'

'I lived in ashrams where I'd help out with the cooking and cleaning in return for my keep.'

'Were you doing anything besides domestic labour?'

'I spent as much time as possible meditating and pursuing other spiritual practices.'

'Was it these interests that took you to India?'

'I felt totally unable to face life in England without Lloyd. I've only returned because during the course of my spiritual studies God spoke to me and told me I must make things up to Lloyd if I'm ever to live the life of an ordinary woman.'

'You're 26 now. Do you think you could have looked after Lloyd when you were eighteen?'

'It would have been difficult but I would have done the best I could.'

'What's happened to Lloyd's father, Matt Bradley?'

'He's married now,' I lied. 'He's got a baby daughter. I was very annoyed when I came back from India and found he'd started a family with a girl from a very similar background to my own.'

'Why didn't he marry you? If he'd done that you could have brought up Lloyd together.'

'We were going to get married but his parents objected to me because I came from a working-class family. Matt's mother and father are working-class too but his dad worked hard and made enough money to send his two boys to public school. They weren't going to let me marry Matt after forking out for his private education. Matt's elder brother George got a girl pregnant when she was seventeen but they were allowed to marry because Felicity's father was a commander in the Air Force. George is an even worse snob than his parents: I met him once and he is completely ashamed of the fact that his father is working-class. Of course, he hated me for that reason too.'

'How does Matt feel about what happened to Lloyd?'

'He feels very guilty about it. When I was pregnant and after Lloyd was born, Matt was adamant he didn't want a child. He thought he was a genius and he used to tell me that great men and especially great artists could never have anything to do with children. Matt was at art school and back then he was also planning to write a book about drugs.'

'What does he do now?'

'His wife supports him.'

'Did he write his book?'

'No.'

'Does he still paint?'

'No, Matt's a dreamer, he'll never achieve anything.'

'How do you feel about him?'

'I hate him! I hate him! I hate him! He made me give away my baby!'

'I think you need to get your feelings in perspective.'

'I want to know how Lloyd is getting along.'

'Do you want to see Lloyd?'

'I'd give my right arm to be able to see Lloyd and tell him I love him. Would it be possible for me to see Lloyd?'

'It's out of the question! How do you think Lloyd's new parents would feel if you suddenly turned up to see him? They'd be worried you are planning to take him away again. All the children placed by this agency go to wonderful families: we vet them very carefully. Don't you think that Lloyd was better off with a wonderful family?'

'I couldn't say, because no one ever told me anything about the people Lloyd went to, I don't know the first thing about them.'

'Well, young lady, I really don't feel you appreciate all the things the London Children's Adoption Agency has done for your son. I can assure you that all the families we send children to are vetted and they are wonderful, absolutely wonderful.'

'Could you tell me something about the wonderful family Lloyd went to?'

'Well, we don't keep detailed records of the families, but they are all wonderful. Let me have a look. Ah, yes. Lloyd's adoptive father worked as an assistant to a scrap metal dealer at the time of the adoption and he was a member of a darts team attached to a local pub. It says here that he is a wonderful man, a pillar of the community. Look at this: Lloyd's adoptive mother and father had been married for eight years at the time he became a part of their family. An extremely stable set-up, wonderful, wonderful. And there's a note here saying Lloyd's adoptive mother is very fond of children. Yes, a perfect set-up for Lloyd. Wonderful, absolutely wonderful!'

'Could you tell me anything else about Lloyd's family?'

'We don't have anything else in our records.'

'You must have the names of Lloyd's new parents in the file.'

'That, my dear, is confidential. I've told you more than enough to prove that Lloyd is being brought up by a couple who are far more capable as parents than you could have ever been. If you won't admit that Lloyd's new parents have done a far better job of bringing him up than you'd have managed, then I'm going to end this interview right now, and what you've just heard will be the last news you ever have of Lloyd.'

'Does that mean that if I say Lloyd's new parents have done a better job of bringing him up than I could have managed, you'll contact them to find out how he's getting along now?'

'I didn't say that, it would be most irregular. I've told you Lloyd is getting along very well. What else do you need to know?'

'But unless you make enquiries I'm not going to get any more news about Lloyd. I want to know he's OK. You don't seem to have a clue about what's happened to him over the past eight years.'

'He's bound to be doing fine; the family who adopted him are wonderful. All the families we place children with are wonderful.'

'He could have died in a car crash; he might have been horribly injured in a sporting accident. I want to know that he's alive and healthy.'

'You have a morbid imagination, my dear. Of course Lloyd is alive and healthy. After all, we placed him with a wonderful family. He will be growing up into a fine Christian man.'

'Will you contact Lloyd's new parents to find out how he's doing?'

'First you'll have to tell me you don't want to upset them, and that means suppressing any desire you have to see Lloyd, and secondly you'll have to admit that they've done a better job of bringing him up than you could have done when you were eighteen.'

'OK.'

'OK what? If you want me to find out how Lloyd is you'll have to repeat what I just told you.'

'I don't want to upset Lloyd's new parents, and since me gaining access to him would upset them, I don't want to see him.'

'And?'

'I know Lloyd's new parents have done a better job of bringing him up than I would have managed if I hadn't had him adopted.'

'Wonderful. Wonderful. I'm glad that now we've talked to each other you're beginning to see a bit of sense. How are you finding this counselling session?'

'Wonderful, I'm finding it very useful. It is helping me place everything in a proper perspective.'

It seemed Mrs Haling was incapable of recognising mock praise, no matter how blatant it became, and so my recourse to irony enabled me to humour her while remaining true to myself.

'Jilly, it strikes me that you are a very unhappy girl, and I wonder if you've ever seen a therapist?'

'Yes, I've seen R.D. Laing a few times.'

'Was it about the baby?'

'No, it was about something else.'

'What?'

'Well, every time I swallow a piece of food, I think I'm going to choke.'

'You really are very disturbed, aren't you?'

'Yes.'

'Are you schizophrenic?'

'No.'

'Are you sure about that?'

'Yes.'

'What about your other personalities? I'll call them Martha, Mary, Alexis and June for the sake of convenience. Are they also sure you're not schizophrenic?'

'I don't suffer from split-personality syndrome.'

'Answer yes or no! Are Martha, Mary, Alexis and June sure they're not schizophrenic?'

'Yes.'

'That's better, we can't solve your problems until you own up to them. Now, could you talk to R.D. Laing about Lloyd?'

'No, we see each other about other things.'

'In that case you'll have to come here to see me. I'll go through everything with you from the beginning and we'll sort it all out. Once you realise that Martha, Mary, Alexis and June are merely figments of your imagination everything can be resolved. I'll have you happily married and raising a family before you're 30.'

'But God is punishing me, I can't bear children.'

'We'll go through everything from the beginning and then we'll see what can be done about that. Do you go to church?'

'No.'

'It says in your notes that you were brought up as a Catholic. Do you attend the Roman mass?'

'No. God is everywhere and I am a temple to God.'

'No wonder you're having difficulties; you're a mere hair's-breadth away from succumbing to a heresy even worse than that adhered to by your parents. I want you to go to church this Sunday, and once you're open to God about being a sinner you'll find he's on your side.'

'Really?'

'Yes, really! All you need to do is go to a Protestant church. It is, however, essential that you avoid ashrams and all the left-footer nonsense you grew up with, since that will only lead you astray. Now, will you go to church this Sunday for me and see what happens?'

'OK.'

'Wonderful.'

The session went on interminably in this fashion and I had ample opportunity to fake suicidal tendencies. When I left I didn't know whether to laugh or cry. Mrs Haling had certainly bought my act: she thought I was crazy. If I got some solid news of Lloyd then enduring Haling's nonsense would make it more than worthwhile. I wanted Lloyd back and I hoped to find out something that might lead me to him. Unfortunately at that juncture there didn't seem much chance of the adoption agency putting me and Lloyd back together, regardless or not of whether I was feigning madness. I continued to see Mrs Haling for more than a year, and although I found the sessions inordinately depressing, I only stopped attending when I found myself in such deep shit with the cops that all my energies became focused on attempting to save my own skin. Winding back the clock, my second counselling session was much like the first and the third was equally repetitious. I was going into the adoption agency in Knightsbridge once a week, and at the fourth session I was told by Mrs Haling that she had good news for me.

'We've contacted Lloyd's new parents and they tell us he is a very normal and happy eight-year-old. He has a younger sister who is also adopted, and is growing up in a happy household amid much merriment and laughter.'

There was a handwritten note concerning Lloyd and his new parents on Mrs Haling's desk. Although it was upside down I was able to read it surreptitiously during the course of the session. The memo was short and easy to memorise: 'Lloyd's adoptive father died a few years ago. His adoptive mother has been in and out of hospital since her husband's death. Although his adoptive grandparents live a considerable distance from his home they have been assisting with his care, as have various neighbours.' It isn't only junkies who bullshit: Mrs Haling was clearly a past master of this art. The note made me feel depressed about the things Lloyd was going through. However, it also gave me hope. If things were proving rough for Lloyd, perhaps the adoption agency would conclude that returning him to me would be the best solution. I'd made it clear that I wanted him back and they could see I was serious about this. That said, if I'd known the score about my son's circumstances from the off I'd have presented a more sober front when I initially re-entered the portals of the London Children's Adoption Agency. The only things I've had to remember Lloyd by for the past seventeen years are a handful of photographs of him as a baby. I got a set done at a photographic studio and my favourite is one of him in my arms. I'm writing all this up nearly a decade after I went back to the adoption agency, and Lloyd will be eighteen in three months, which means that for the first time in his life he'll be legally entitled to find out who I am. I'm hoping that he'll come back to me then. On Lloyd's birthday I always write a poem for him and I hope one day soon he'll be able to read the seventeen verses I already have stacked up waiting for his return.

13. THE MYSTERIES OF LOVE-MAKING SOLVED

Bill Burroughs was a difficult guy to get to know. He used to call in at Trocchi's pad and when we greeted him he blanked everyone except our host. Burroughs was there to see Alex and that seemed to be that. Burroughs was our number-one literary hero and our inability to befriend him became a frequent topic of conversation. Some of the junkies, hangers-on and two-time losers who befriended Trocchi considered Burroughs arrogant, whereas others thought he was shy. I noticed a gender split on these positions, which led me to suggest that Bill's haughtiness covered a deep-seated insecurity and that underneath it all he was probably a regular sweetie. I never was much of a feminist, and often let down my women friends by adopting stances that accommodated the opinions of the guys around us. I have always been too fond of men. A girl who was new to our circle suggested one night that Burroughs was a misogynist. Alex dismissed this assertion and insisted that what Burroughs had told interviewers like Daniel Odier about women was a cultivated pose. Indeed Bill's woman-hating routine was Swiftian satire that revealed the base realities of our world, and this of course meant that anyone who denounced him as a woman-hater was too stupid to be part of our scene. The lass who'd raised the matter was ejected from Trocchi's apartment and never darkened his doorstep again.

William Burroughs was certainly a controversial figure. In the early 60s the British authorities considered him to be the last word in filth. I had to go to Paris to get copies of *The Naked Lunch* and *The Ticket That Exploded* and then smuggle them home. Fortunately this wasn't particularly inconvenient for me, since I was making regular and rather lucrative trips to the continent. I'd go across to Paris in a car, and after spending time there would proceed to Spain. Indeed these jaunts sometimes took me as far as Gibraltar and then across to Morocco. Back then I was still a teenager and unfamiliar with anything much stronger than grass, pills and champagne. I drank a lot of champagne – it was an integral part of my job as a club hostess – but I smoked even more grass. I started off scoring blow in Frank Critchlow's *El Rio Café*, and pretty quickly became involved in shifting huge quantities of dope around Europe. There was a racial split to such activities in the early 60s, since the West Indian dealers had grass whereas the white dealers sold hash. It was all pretty innocuous, and aside from pot, I did a less lucrative sideline in smuggling books that the ignorant British authorities had condemned as pornographic. It was in Spain that I first tried opium; I smoked it to begin with and it was quite a while before I moved on to injecting morphine and heroin. My admiration for Burroughs was one of several factors which led me to trying hard drugs when I was offered them. I'd just turned twenty when I toked on my first opium cigarette in the summer of 1964. At that time I only knew of Bill and Alex because I'd perused their masterpieces of modern literature, but even to a casual reader it was obvious that *Naked Lunch* and *Cain's Book* could not have been written by someone who'd never had a heroin habit. If it hadn't been for smack then the work that Bill and Alex produced might have been no more arresting than the novels of Irving Wallace or A.J. Cronin. Burroughs was my hero, and after I'd got involved with Trocchi I was desperate to find a way of getting him to speak to me. I seized my chance at Alex's pad one evening when an intense young man called Clyde Hughes tried to pick me up.

Clyde was a gawky and alienated engineering student with intellectual pretensions, exactly the type Burroughs was sexually attracted to. Hughes simply didn't have the things I like in a man, including but not limited to the copious amounts of money that all too often help me overcome other obstacles to physical intimacy. Alex had told me Bill was going to be there later that night, so I flirted just enough to keep Hughes interested in our conversation. I had to stifle a laugh when Clyde asked me if I'd like to go back to his drum to see the layouts he'd roughed up for a new underground publication.

'Can't you just give me a copy when it's printed?'

'Baby,' the boy shot back, 'the stuff I'm doing is so hot there probably isn't a printer in London who'll touch it.'

'What about the home counties?'

'Who knows? What I'm saying is that if you wanna avoid disappointment and be sure of seeing the spreads I've got on the likes of Spanish film director Jess Franco and beatnik kingpin Allen Ginsberg then you gotta come back to my pad. It'll be a groove, I got plenty of way-out sounds and some really soft lighting . . .'

'If I'm gonna look at art work then I'll need decent illumination.'

'Of course, of course. But once you've seen the spreads we can dim the lights and enjoy a trip with some of the freakiest records known to man. I bought the new Soft Machine album this afternoon and I ain't had time to listen to it yet.'

'So where . . .' Then I noticed Bill Burroughs walk into the room and so did my companion. Hughes made a bolt for him and I travelled in Clyde's wake.

'Mr Burroughs, I'm Clyde Hughes from *Macabre Magazine* and I must have an interview with you.'

'What publication did you say you were from?'

'You've never heard of *Macabre Magazine*?'

'No.'

'I sent you a letter some time ago soliciting a contribution.'

'Young man, you remind me of an adolescent Arab I once knew who'd do literally anything for a dollar.'

'Mr Burroughs, I'm not a rent boy.'

'Kiki had a lovely ass.'

'Are you propositioning me?'

'I used to pay the rent boys in Tangier to have sex with each other; all I did was watch.'

'Although I'd pretty much die to get an interview with you, I'm afraid I'm a ladies' man.'

'You don't look like a transvestite to me. Are you wearing frilly knickers underneath your pants?'

'I like balling chicks.'

'Do you know what men do with each other sexually when they get it on?'

'I know, but I don't know Biblically.'

'Listen, Clyde,' I put in, seizing the opportunity that Bill's sexual interest in this jerk presented to me, 'I'd love to see you get it on with another man; if you'd let Bill and I watch you having some gay rumpy-pumpy then it would get me so steamed up I'd pretty much have to make you my man.'

'Really?' I'd piqued Clyde's interest. 'Would it make you want to fuck my brains out?'

'Yeah, baby!' I said as I touched Clyde's arm.

'Could you, could you,' Hughes stammered, 'could you teach me how to do it? I'm not that experienced.'

'Virgins really turn me on,' I whispered as I squeezed Clyde's crotch. 'They make me feel in control and I love wearing the trousers when I make love to a man.'

'Don't miss your chance to grope this classy lady, Clyde,' Bill cajoled. 'She wants to eat you up but first you have to thrill her by going with another man.'

'No offence implied, Mr Burroughs, because I think you're a genius, but I just don't find you sexually attractive.'

'I've taken too much heroin tonight to indulge in anything more than mere voyeurism. All I want to do is watch you having sex with another boy who is as pretty as you. Afterwards we can do an interview for your magazine.'

'That sounds good,' Hughes admitted.

'I'll get a nice skinny guy for you, Clyde,' I said reassuringly. 'I'll have him made up to look like a girl and I'll put him in my wig and dress. There is a friend of mine here who can give you a great blow job. It won't be any different from having sex with a chick.'

'I don't know, I don't know what it's like,' Clyde stuttered.

'I'd give you an interview afterwards.' Burroughs was repeating himself.

'Is the guy you've got in mind for me enchanting?' Hughes asked me.

'You see Greek George over there?' I pointed.

'How do you know he'd have sex with me?'

'He will as a favour for me and Bill. He's a huge fan of Bill's novels.' I didn't bother adding that he was also a junkie who'd do anything with anybody for the readies with which to buy smack.

'In that case have him made up, and if I get an erection once I'm with him then I guess we could do it.'

'You'll get a stiffy.'

'How do you know?'

'I know.'

Now that everything was in place for some outrageously kinky voyeuristic action, Bill reverted to his silent routine. I shouted across to George, and once he realised what I was procuring him to do, he was eager to perform in front of his literary idol. I took the Greek through to the main bedroom and found Trocchi's wife Lyn nodding out on the double bed. She was positioned over to one side, so she wasn't going to cause any problems in terms of George and Clyde making out on the mattress. Lyn had thrown off her baby-doll nightie and I decided to dress the Greek in that, rather than my own as yet uncreased gear. I was still attending to George's eye make-up when Bill and Clyde came into the room.

'My, he sure looks winsome,' Bill cackled. 'You've fixed him up real nice, Jilly. What a fool I've been, thinking he was too old and ugly for me. You're a lucky boy, Clyde, our friend Georgie here is a complete cutie.'

'This is my lucky day,' Hughes enthused. 'An interview with Bill Burroughs in the first issue of *Macabre Magazine* is going to leave all the beatniks I know back in Margate sick with envy.'

'Did you get Alex?' I asked Bill.

'He's nodded out,' Burroughs told me.

'What about Pete the Plank?'

'He's not interested,' Burroughs sniggered. 'A pathetic heterosexual who only goes with men if he's desperate for drug money. I've had him a few times, of course.'

Once I'd fixed my wig on the Greek's head we were ready to go. I got Clyde to sit down beside George, and instantly the Greek's hands were wandering all over his body, unbuttoning clothes and exposing flesh. The only downer was that every time George tried to kiss Clyde on the mouth the engineering student would turn his head away. Burroughs sat back in an easy chair to watch and while he was at it got his works out so that he could shoot up. Needles puncturing flesh was the kind of penetration the beat writer liked best. Lyn lay motionless on the other side of the bed. In her heroin haze she was dead to the world. The Greek got Hughes's cock out and I realised that my help was required after George had been caressing Clyde's still-flaccid manhood for several minutes. It was time for me to repeat some of the tall tales of sexual hijinks I'd heard from our man Trocchi.

'When Trocchi lived in Paris in the 50s, Alex and his friend Guy Debord knew a female dwarf who worked as a

prostitute,' I announced. 'They'd invite gay friends over to
Guy's flat and they'd get the actress Jean Seberg to let these
friends of Dorothy into the apartment at the appointed
time. Shortly before the guests were due to arrive Alex and
Guy would get it on with the dwarf. The positions varied,
but the first time Burroughs walked in on them the girl was
lying on her side with Debord fucking her up the arse as
Trocchi was licking her clit. Since the dwarf was short and
Alex's legs were dangling off the bed, Bill was able to kneel
down on the mattress, and Guy gave him a blow job while
the dwarf continued to receive her double dose of pleasure.'

Like the sexual exploits recorded in Trocchi's porn
novels, this story was unexpurgated bollocks. Although
Alex and Bill had both been in Paris in the 50s they hadn't
known each other then: they'd first met at the 1962
Edinburgh Festival. Likewise, if Trocchi had attempted to
engineer a scene of this type it would have concluded with
Debord denouncing Bill as a bourgeois imbecile rather than
getting it on with him. However, Burroughs wasn't about to
question the veracity of this fantasy since he was too busy
getting his jollies while simultaneously fixing up. In any case
my speech was having the effect both Bill and I desired,
since Clyde's member was no longer limp. George got off
the bed and on to his knees before proceeding to suck the
student's erect cock. I couldn't see much since the Greek
was positioning himself to provide Burroughs with the best
possible view of this oral action. I just kept talking, and I
watched a big grin spread across Bill's face after he'd shot
up. Burroughs was high on both heroin and hormonal
excitements. Opiates affect the individual sexual appetite in
different ways. Bill wasn't jaded when it came to sex; it was
just that, like Alex, his kick involved degradation. That said,
Clyde was delighted to have the almost undivided attention
of a literary outlaw he hero-worshipped.

'In Paris Alex became great friends with Jean-Paul Sartre
and many other famous French intellectuals,' I continued.
'Sartre would be invited with his pals, including Trocchi, to

the very plushest brothels. These were not the places you'll have heard about in Pigalle but discreet joints located in the most respectable neighbourhoods. When they went to these whorehouses the men of letters would be lined up and the girls would take their pick of the brain-boxes and pay them for sex. Alex has particularly fond memories of one girl called Josephine who paid him a thousand francs just to talk about neo-Platonist philosophy as she gave him a blow job.'

As I said this Hughes started making noises that alerted me to the fact he was coming. The Greek pulled his head back. The grin that was already spread across Burroughs's mug widened. I couldn't see what was happening but I know Clyde spunked into George's face, because when the Greek turned around I could see he was splattered with sperm.

'Let George fuck you up the ass, my boy, and after that I'll grant you an interview,' the beat novelist croaked in his excitement.

What impressed me then as now is that Bill made no attempt to jerk off. He was happy just to watch. Hughes spread himself across the bed and the Greek had to give him a playful slap to let him know that giving the unconscious Lyn Trocchi a furtive grope was not allowed. When that sort of thing went on Alex liked to be around and conscious enough to enjoy it. As George proceeded to buck above Clyde the voyeuristic Burroughs was transfixed. My role in the proceedings had been pretty much played out. The Greek didn't require me to repeat Trocchi's tall tales of sexual adventure in order to get his rocks off. Now that Clyde had become acclimatised to the rhythms of arse shagging it was an irrelevance whether or not he'd have enjoyed a further fictive episode from Alex's virtually non-existent love life. Trocchi was, as anyone who knows him will vouch, almost unbelievably monogamous after he met Lyn. Alex was married to heroin and therefore not really interested in sex. As for Burroughs, I felt that the ice between me and my literary idol had been broken, that we could and would speak on subsequent occasions. For the time being it was enough that Burroughs savoured the scene I'd set up for him. There was a tremble in Bill's hands and a broad smile on his lips as George and Clyde's coupling came to a climax. The Greek rolled off his ride and slumped on the bed, totally spent.

'OK, young man, let's find somewhere nice and quiet to do this interview you were so desperate to secure,' Burroughs boomed at his young fan.

As Hughes rose and proceeded to dress, Lyn Trocchi stirred. Waking when someone she was sharing a bed with got up was probably an ingrained reflex.

'If you're going I hope you had a good time.' Lyn didn't open her eyes and was clearly under the misapprehension she was with a trick. 'Don't forget you agreed to pay me 50 bucks. I want you to leave the cash on the bedside table.'

With that Mrs Trocchi fell back into her heroin slumber. Lyn, like Alex, struck me as being fundamentally asexual. Turning tricks was an instrumental activity designed solely to raise money with which she might buy drugs; it was anything but erotic. I found it impossible to imagine Lyn and Alex having sex. It was easier for me to conjure up fantasy images of my own conception, and not simply because I'd witnessed my parents having it off when I was a child. That said, Lyn and Alex must have had sex at least twice in order to produce their handsome sons Mark and Nick. Alex liked women, but he clearly preferred getting them fucked up on drugs to any kind of physical intimacy. Trocchi got a kick out of watching a beautiful woman like Lyn spiralling downwards through endless cycles of degradation. And when Lyn did die Alex was mortified, and it seemed to me that he'd been killed either with or before her. Trocchi no longer simply took drugs; he had become heroin. Alex was dead and didn't yet know it. I liked and admired Trocchi, he was a visionary who'd written two brilliant novels, but when it came to his relationships with other people he could be a complete cunt. Alex regularly claimed his behaviour was the prerogative of a great man and he genuinely believed in his own greatness. Friendships like the one I had with Alex weren't necessarily good for me, but without them I'd have died of boredom. People who claim there is nothing glamorous about heroin or having produced a classic work of modernist literature lack imagination.

14. BLACK POWER IN A HONKY TOWN

Garrett was always the man who supplied Trocchi's dope to other dealers, except in the instance of Michael X. Sometimes Michael collected a stash from Observatory Gardens, but more often than not after I returned from India it was a case of me couriering it to the Black House in Holloway Road. The Black House was an incredible warren of buildings that were being shoddily converted into a community centre. The guys doing the construction work were black power activists, mainly kids who Michael fired up. It was a crazy scene, because Michael got these young boys off the street and then turned them on to anything from pot through to smack and proceeded to rap about how the white man had been on their backs for too long and they had to fight back. The Black House was always filled with dark-skinned men and light-skinned women. Garrett would not have been acceptable in such a setting, and the fact that I was had more to do with my gender than my Irish-cum-Scottish background. Michael informed his followers that I was cool because I was a Black Celt. De Freitas told these acolytes that my ancestors came from Africa, but after many generations of living in Europe, the Irish and Scots had ended up with pale skins. Some of Michael's supporters bought this line, but those who called me a white bitch clearly didn't, and it was generally the latter type who came on strongest as regards attempts to seduce me. Michael knew Garrett well and they liked each other, but theirs was a friendship tempered with realism, and it really wasn't cool for light-skinned men to hang out at the Black House; even Nigel Samuels, who bankrolled the place, was wary about entering it.

The Black House shut up shop in the autumn of 1970 and Michael left the UK the following February in order to avoid the legal repercussions of an incident that had taken place at his defunct Black Muslim Centre. This was the roughing up of a businessman called Marvin Brown who Michael believed had ripped off one of his supporters. Brown was enticed to the Black House, where he was pushed around and punched. A spiked slave collar was then placed on his neck and he was paraded about in front of a laughing audience of black power activists and pale-skinned hookers. Since there were sharpened spikes on the inside of the collar, sudden movement had the potential to puncture the skin on Brown's neck, although, unlike colonial plantation owners, de Freitas was always extremely careful about the ways in which he made use of this instrument of torture. I wasn't around when Michael put the frighteners on Brown, but I did witness the slave collar being used on a prior occasion. This was when Michael wanted to punish a speed freak called Richard Owen, who'd ripped off one of his associates. Owen had been lured to the Black House with the promise of drugs. The basic elements of an appropriate psychodrama predicated on the knowledge that Owen was impotent had been worked out in advance. I was already in Michael's office, and *Psychedelic Shack* by the Temptations was blasting out on a hi-fi when this victim arrived.

'Richard, my good man.' De Freitas sounded as if he was greeting a long lost friend, although this was actually the first time he'd ever met Owen. 'I hear you're a chap who likes to have a good time. There are a lot of willing girls here and I want you to take your pick of them.'

'Hey man,' Owen almost swaggered, 'that's right kind of you but I prefer jacking up a bit of speed. When you take the quantity of drugs I do on a regular basis, it kind of suppresses your desire for a love life.'

'Richard.' Michael was adopting a slightly peeved tone. 'I was told you were a man's man. Now if you won't pick a girl, I'm gonna choose one for ya.'

'I understood I'd get a great speed deal here,' Owen protested.

'I'm not some honky would-be hip capitalist, which means I place pleasure before profit. Once I'm satisfied that you appreciate my hospitality, I'll happily do business with you.'

'Speed is my pleasure, the thrill of the hit my orgasm.'

'A man with only one vice is a man who can't be trusted. He will sacrifice everything and everyone to his mono-maniacal pursuit of this singular obsession. If we're to do business you must first prove to me that you enjoy more than one pleasure. Pick a girl.'

'I'm not interested in girls.'

'Are you a faggot?'

'No.'

'In that case pick a girl.'

'I can't.'

'OK, I'll choose one for you. Rose.' De Freitas snapped his fingers as he said the name.

Rose stepped forwards, quickly undid Owen's belt, and seconds later his pants and trousers were around his ankles. The speed freak looked down at his flaccid member and everybody else laughed. Rose hauled up her dress and bent over Michael's desk. She wasn't wearing any knickers.

'Give it to me, big boy! I'm just creaming myself thinking of your hot cock shooting gallons of white spunk into my juicy hole.'

'Go on,' de Freitas encouraged, 'give her one.'

'I can't . . .'

'Are you a virgin?' Michael enquired. 'Do you want me to show you what to do?'

'I can't . . .'

'It's easy,' de Freitas insisted. 'I'll show you.'

Michael stepped daintily around his desk, dropped his pants, and within seconds of him penetrating the mystery that was Rose, she let loose with the first of many orgasmic shrieks. This wasn't sex, it was pure theatre. De Freitas kept up his humping for a very long time. Rose either feigned or actually had dozens of orgasms. She was screaming her head off. The men witnessing this performance applauded, while the women present looked on in admiration.

'Right on, brother!'

'I want you to take me next, Michael,' a girl with the fingers of her right hand working their way between her legs wailed.

'I'm not taking any of you other girls right now,' de Freitas announced majestically as he humped. 'I've got a lot of business to attend to today. I'm just showing this honky virgin how to make it with a woman. I'm buttering Rose's bun for him and once it's good and greased, I want to see what he can do with it.'

Owen attempted to pull his pants up, and this was the psychological break Michael had been holding out for before he allowed himself the luxury of coming. As Michael shot his wad, a couple of the teenagers present pulled Owen's hands away from the waistband of his jeans and the pants plunged back down around his ankles. The two black activists kept a firm grasp on the speed freak's wrists, as de Freitas wiped spunk from his cock with a tissue and then casually pulled up and fastened his trousers.

'Friend,' Michael announced, 'it appears you are suffering from a sexual problem. I've just shown you what to do and you still don't have an erection. What have you got to say for yourself?'

'I'm impotent.'

'Well, Rose is waiting for more fun. My brothers and I have work to attend to, we can't see to her needs. What do you propose to do?'

'I don't know.'

'If you can't use your prick then you'll have to use your tongue.'

'But you've just come inside her.'

'So what?'

Rose sat up on Michael's desk and spread her legs. Owen was pushed onto his knees immediately in front of her, his bare butt sticking out behind him.

'What are you waiting for?' de Freitas demanded. 'I told you to lubricate her beef curtains!'

The two teenagers who'd previously restrained the speed freak removed their belts and began flicking them against his arse, while a third black activist grabbed Owen by the hair and shoved his face into Rose's twat. At that moment Owen decided it was in his own best interests to do what Michael wanted, and he got licking.

'God, this is so boring!' Rose announced. 'This guy is useless. His technique is completely lacking, he's just a clumsy oaf. He couldn't satisfy a nymphomaniac who'd been stranded on a desert island and hadn't encountered another human being for the best part of a decade. This slob doesn't know how to eat out a woman. He'd have difficulties licking up the remains of a plate of custard.'

Owen was made to perform for around ten minutes, and when he was pulled away he asked if he could go to the toilet.

'Hitch up his jeans,' de Freitas told his henchmen. 'He can piss in his pants.'

'I don't want to wet myself,' Owen panted.

'You'll piss in your pants when I tell you, or else you'll get a fist in your face.'

'Piss in your pants! Piss in your pants!' the assembled male teenagers chorused.

The chanting went on for some time. Eventually Owen was punched on the nose. After he'd been hit, he wet himself amidst much laughter and jeering. Michael's teenage disciples then formed a circle around Owen and pushed him back and forth between each other. Finally the man for whose benefit this show was being put on entered the room.

'You ripped me off, Owen,' Charlie Smith announced. 'You abused me just like your forefathers abused my forefathers. I gave you a key to my flat and cut you in on my dealing; you stabbed me in the back by ripping off my stash.'

'I never took it,' Owen sobbed.

'Don't lie to me, scumsucker!' Smith screamed as he slammed his open palm against Owen's face.

'I think,' de Freitas announced, 'this white boy needs to learn about how his forefathers treated our forefathers. Bring out the slave collar.'

The slave collar was then placed around Owen's neck. While the speed freak was made to parade up and down in his sodden clothes, the function of this restraint was explained to him at great length. Michael had lots of figures about the number of slaves who'd died on different plantations due to the use of the implement, and he intercut these statistics with graphic descriptions of the injuries sustained by those who'd been tortured to death with the slave collar. Slave owners were named and white racism denounced. Eventually the collar was removed.

'Right,' de Freitas proclaimed as he jabbed a finger into Owen's chest, 'I want you to see Charlie right about the gear that went missing. If the matter isn't sorted out by tomorrow night, I'll send my boys out after you. Before you leave I want you to go through to the bathroom and clean yourself up. I'll put a couple of quid on the desk for you, so you can go and get some new jeans since you've made a right mess of the pair you're wearing. I don't want to hear about you ripping off one my brothers again. Let's shake on it, boy.'

Owen trembled as he shook Michael's hand. He was quivering so much he found it difficult to pick up the money that was laid out on the desk for him. When at last he'd accomplished this simple task, he was shown through to a bathroom where he was left to sort himself out. That was the last I ever saw of the speed freak. I heard he left London, although there were also unsubstantiated rumours he'd been murdered. What struck me most about Michael's psychodrama was its similarity to the odd bits of violence I'd seen meted out by the Kray and Richardson gangs back in the 60s. The overriding influence on all these performances seemed to be Hollywood gangster movies. The Old Bill used identical techniques to put the frighteners on those they pulled in. The element of humiliation was integral to these rituals, since an individual must necessarily be dehumanised as they are abused if street theatre of this type is to achieve the desired result. There can be no doubt that de Freitas was a very angry man, and while I don't want to excuse his excesses, I think they at least become comprehensible when placed in this light. Michael was a hustler and a conman, but he knew racism first-hand and he was sincere when it came to his demands for black power. Anyone who suggests that Michael's politics amounted to nothing but a hustle clearly has an axe to grind.

Michael's tragic history after he left England is well known, but it is nevertheless worth providing a sketch of it here. I was horrified when Michael went to the gallows in Port of Spain on 16 May 1975. After fleeing London to avoid being tried for assaulting Marvin Brown, de Freitas returned to his native Trinidad, and it was there in 1972 that he was sentenced to death for murder. His execution was very much the culmination of a show trial organized around a confession provided by the star witness, Adolphus Parmassar. Alongside Michael, also convicted for the murder of Gale Benson and Joe Skerrit were Stanley Abbott, Samuel Brown and Edward Chadee. Of the others implicated by Parmassar in his confession, Steven Yeates had died while swimming in the sea before anyone had been arrested, and a man known as Kidigo, who'd worked with Benson's boyfriend (the black power activist Hakim Jamal), managed to avoid extradition from the United States. While forensic evidence shows that Gale Benson was forced into a shallow grave, hacked at with a cutlass and buried while still alive – with Skerrit meeting a similar fate – the convictions are nevertheless unsound because they were based on a confession. It is impossible to say exactly who was responsible for the murders at Michael's black power commune at 43 Christina Gardens, Arima.

Although it seems likely that some of those working with Michael at the time of these slayings were involved in the killings, establishing precisely who played what part in the homicidal acts isn't possible on the basis of the available evidence. Confessions are always based on the person testifying telling those listening what they expect to hear. A tale will not be treated as a confession unless it meets certain narrative expectations, which is why confessions are notoriously unreliable despite their extensive use in so-called courts of justice. A confession implies repentance; it is simultaneously a plea for clemency, and as such it can never be disinterested or objective. Michael maintained he was innocent, and while I know he could when the occasion demanded it be nasty, I don't for a minute believe he was a murderer. His trial and execution were a self-conscious travesty of justice on the part of the Trinidadian authorities, who clearly had it in for him. Michael employed violence with surgical precision to achieve predetermined ends. He was too cool and calculating to kill. I could see that when I witnessed him putting the frighteners on Richard Owen. While the treatment dished out to Owen was intended to be degrading, Michael was actually very careful to ensure that the man he was punishing suffered no long-term physical harm. Once the slave collar was placed around Owen's neck, Michael treated the man with kid gloves, since he was intent on inflicting psychological and not physical pain.

15. THE DAY I MET GOD

The early 70s was not a good time for me. I couldn't live with Giordano, and after he left me to return to India, I found I couldn't live without him either. That said, I simultaneously understood that if Giordano failed to head East then I'd probably lose him forever. Michele Prigent, from Paris, Giordano's oldest girlfriend, had killed herself, and there was a real danger he would be forced to follow in her footsteps. Michele had initiated Giordano into the arts of love when she was seventeen and he was still fourteen. Prigent had an older married lover who saw to her material needs, but it was Giordano who even at that time held a more significant place in her heart. After Michele had taken Giordano's virginity, she made a pact with the boy who had become both her lover and her protégé. They were to embark on a spiritual quest and if they failed to achieve something significant by the time they were 33, the age at which Jesus died, then they would commit suicide. They even swore blood oaths to this effect. It was Michele who first took Giordano off to India in 1966, although by this time he had run through one wife and many other lovers. Michele spent many years in India seeking enlightenment, but without any sign of a breakthrough.

Prigent reached the age of 33 on 30 November 1969, and at the beginning of that month she'd returned from India to Europe to see her family and friends one last time. After spending several weeks in France, Michele arrived in London at the end of November and quickly tracked Giordano down. I'd got to know Prigent when we were all in Goa in the summer of '68, and during that time we'd become close. Michele spent her last full day alive taking the air on Hampstead Heath with both Giordano and me. After it got dark we went to a café and then an Indian restaurant. Finally we returned to Bassett Road and all went to bed together. In the past when I'd done threesomes I'd been paid handsomely for my troubles. In this instance it was a matter of love, and lucre didn't enter into it. Michele had never had sex with a woman before, but she seemed to enjoy it every bit as much as she relished Giordano's testosterone-soaked carnality. On the morning of Michele's 33rd birthday I stayed in bed and Giordano walked her up to the toilets at Notting Hill tube station. He left Michele with more than enough heroin on which to overdose and returned to Bassett Road, where he got into the bed in which I was already nodding out. The authorities treated Prigent's death as an accident, but Giordano and I knew it was suicide.

After Michele's death, Giordano and I attempted to get on with our lives. Our heroin haze was punctuated by a steady stream of arguments, and we both knew we were living in denial. This state of affairs couldn't continue forever, and things came to a head on Giordano's 31st birthday. By March 1970, Giordano had but two years to live unless he found spiritual salvation. Since Michele was now dead, he felt honour-bound to see through his pact with her. It was under these circumstances that we agreed he must return immediately to India. I had no doubts about the fact that Giordano was the love of my life, but at this time there was no point trying to keep him by my side; not only did we require a separation, but he desperately needed the knowledge that would allow him to live. After we'd seen through a few scams, Giordano was able to fly off from Heathrow. I accompanied him to the airport at the beginning of April 1970, just three weeks after his 31st birthday. The period that followed was testing for both of us. Giordano sold his passport and gave away his possessions; for many months he wandered ill-clad through the Himalayas and on a number of occasions was nearly killed by the cold. I was always well dressed and made-up, which helped my sense of self-esteem and ensured I remained able to make good money from a better class of man. Nevertheless, in many ways I was becoming desperate and careless. I did stupid things, and one of them was breaking off relations with Alex Trocchi in 1971.

It came about in this way: I'd left Alex's flat in Observatory Gardens with a big consignment of smack that he wanted me to take to a dealer in east London. Normally this would have been Garrett's job, but for reasons I would only discover years later, Garrett did not appear that day. I was supposed to deliver this mega package and then go back to Trocchi's to make my usual round of rock stars and their low-life friends. However, I didn't make it to east London since I was picked up by the cops as I approached the steps that led down to Notting Hill tube station. I put this down to more than bad luck, since I'd told Trocchi I'd catch the tube from High Street Kensington, but he'd said I should walk up to Notting Hill since I'd get to Mile End far quicker if I took the central line, which is what Garrett always did. Although Trocchi has been used and abused as an asset by bent cops, I was wrong to conclude he'd informed on me. Years later in 1975 Garrett told me that he'd been the person who'd set me up, and he'd felt bad about it ever since. Garrett owed PC Lever some serious favours because this notoriously sadistic cop had overlooked both his peripheral involvement in a couple of murders and equally significantly the very central role he played in a great deal of drug dealing. As soon as Garrett admitted this to me, I went round to see Trocchi, who was inordinately pleased that I'd called, and we became thick once again. However, right now I want to go back and deal with the events of 1971, when I had my first face-to-face encounter with Lever.

'You know, girlie,' PC Lever sneered once he had me safely stashed in a Ladbroke Grove police interview room, 'you aren't necessarily in any trouble at all. If you help me then I will help you.'

'How?'

'If you're nice to me and pleasant with my friends, then I'll omit to place the full facts of your case before the court.'

'You'd weigh off the evidence?'

'Reginald will do it, but right now he's dirty and I want you to lick him clean.' As he said it, Lever undid his flies and exposed himself to me.

That was the first time I went down on Lever but certainly not the last. Giving this bastard head was one of the biggest mistakes of my life. It would have been better to go to jail, because once a bent copper has a hold on you it becomes impossible to pay the bastard off. Initially I thought everything was going well. I'd visit the cop shop once a week and provide Lever with his jollies, and after that we'd talk through my charge. Since Lever was adamant that he shouldn't lose too many cases before the local beak, I was told that when I appeared before the Magistrate's Court I was to demand a jury trial. Eventually a date was set for my appearance at the Old Bailey. The line of defence Lever instructed me to adopt was somewhat baroque, and if he hadn't sorted me out with a lawyer I might well have had trouble finding a brief willing to accept it. I was to pretend to be a naïve young mother who'd been cynically exploited by a drug dealer who'd approached me using the name Professor Thom Geoffries. The cover story with which Lever provided me was that I met Geoffries while I was out shopping and that he'd asked me to deliver some packages to his brother. I innocently agreed to this without even knowing what the packages contained, although the professor had created the impression that it was the fruit of secret medical research. To make this claim appear a tad more convincing, I was told to borrow a small baby from one of my junkie friends and take him to court with me. In the meantime, the substance I'd been apprehended with had unfortunately disappeared before being tested at a police laboratory to determine whether it was actually heroin. Therefore no one could say with any certainty what it was I'd been in the process of transporting when I was arrested. As for the mysterious Professor Geoffries and his brother Jeremy, the addresses I had for them turned out to be recently vacated squats, and it remained unclear exactly who had been domiciled in these derelict buildings.

Back in the early 70s I was still innocent enough to believe I was off the hook once my trial came to a successful conclusion. Since I was making good money as a hostess, cutting loose from Alex Trocchi's drug dealing wasn't something that created any immediate financial hardships. I found a new connection in Notting Hill and with the addition of some cash I was able to swap my drug script for somewhat impure but nevertheless to me preferable street heroin. Unfortunately, Lever was soon on my case and he made it his business to arrest me in possession of a wide array of illegal drugs. This bent cop was extremely angry with me for dropping out of sight as soon as he'd successfully steered me through to a not guilty verdict at the Bailey. The next time he took me up to the interview room he slapped me about a bit, and when I went down on him he yanked out tufts of my hair. Lever also showed me a file he'd compiled about me and insisted that unless I did exactly what he said, then I'd be banged up for certain. Later on he called in several of his colleagues and I was forced to have sex with all of them, while Lever and his cronies punched and insulted me.

'You think you're high-class, girlie?' Lever hissed. 'Well, let me tell you something, a slut is a slut is a slut, and even if you've worked at fancy joints like Gordon's, you're still no better than the whores who parade around our streets.'

'You fucking slag,' another cop who'd just raped me goaded, 'you're no better than a piece of shit. You're slime, you're garbage, you're just a subhuman piece of junkie filth. I bet you'd fuck anything that moves and enjoy it. You're fucking lucky to have sex with upstanding white men like us, and you're probably cranked up too high to appreciate the fact.'

Several of my friends accidentally overdosed during this period, and I was saved from a similar fate when Hetty's daughter Samantha found me lying on the floor of an Oxford Gardens bedsit foaming at the mouth. Samantha, who was twelve back then, ran to fetch her mother, and Hetty kept me awake until the worst effects of the overdose had worn off. At the time I'd half wanted to die, since besides regularly slapping me around, Lever had me selling drugs on his behalf and informing on other addicts. We've now reached the fag end of the 70s, and the drug racket in west London remains in the grip of bent cops, although organised crime is currently vying with them for this prize. That said, it remains the case that any dealer who isn't giving the right officers a big whack of their profits finds themselves busted and the bulk of their confiscated stash recycled through sanctioned outlets, of which I am far from being a solitary example. PC Lever is unbelievably vindictive, and for years I've felt like I had no option but to turn up for his regular sessions of assault, rape and humiliation. Obviously it left me feeling sick to the guts that while a few of Lever's mates in the drug squad got sent down for their shady practices, he remained apparently untouchable despite his completely unsavoury reputation among wide swathes of the community he is supposed to be policing. Although I'd have rather seen Lever jailed, I certainly didn't feel sorry for Norman Pilcher when in the autumn of 1973 Justice Melford Stevenson handed him a four-year stretch, and during the summing up this detective was told: 'You poisoned the wells of criminal justice and set about it deliberately . . . and not the least grave aspect of what you have done is to provide material for crooks, cranks and do-gooders who unite to attack the police whenever opportunity occurs . . .' Of course, contrary to Melford Stevenson's apparent beliefs, the overwhelming majority of bent coppers get away with their disreputable activities.

What makes Pilcher unusual is not what he did but the fact that he was finally handed a custodial sentence after spending years terrorising those he took a personal dislike to, including John Lennon of the Beatles and Brian Jones of the Rolling Stones. Of course, Pilcher would never have been sent down if he hadn't been caught up in a feud between his own boss Victor Kelaher and the cops working with Customs and Excise. The Old Bill are a law unto themselves and there's not much someone who is victimised by these uniformed thugs can do about it, as Frank Critchlow, the owner of the Mangrove Restaurant, can confirm. I had straight friends who caught a glimpse of what I was going through, and they urged me to expose the pigs who were abusing me. While those who doled out this advice meant well, their views were misplaced. They really had no idea of how badly society treats junkies and prostitutes. I was never going to get an even break, and it would have been madness to think I could be anything other than the folk devil I'd become in the eyes of the uniformed sadists who had it in for me. Although I'm discreet in my activities as a call-girl and a drug user, my word would never be believed against that of a copper like Lever. Rape leaves few traces but it is not a victimless crime, and it is for precisely this reason that so many Old Bill have a real penchant for it.

PC Lever and his friends revelled in the humiliation I felt when I was forced to have sex with them, and it was clear enough to me that I was trapped in an escalating spiral of violence. The more Lever and his chums slapped me around, the more they felt able to treat me as subhuman and thus increase the severity of their assaults. Lever is evil, and I soon learned he had a major reputation for handing out beatings to many of those he arrested. He was probably the most hated man in Notting Hill, and given that his uniform provided him with almost unlimited opportunities to express his virulent racism, it is not surprising that feelings about him ran particularly high in the West Indian community. As I've made clear, the intensity of the mistreatment I was suffering at the hands of PC Lever was forever increasing, and as I slipped into a state of depression brought on by this I sought relief by further involving myself in dipping and cheque-book frauds. The additional money I made from these sources of income I lavished on luxuries in an attempt to make myself feel better. However, what I really needed was the practical support of a friend, since the rewards of the petty crimes in which I was indulging were not really worth the risks they entailed. Eventually I discovered from a casual acquaintance that Giordano was staying at Sri Aurobindo's ashram in Pondicherry, and a few months before his 33rd birthday I wrote him a letter telling him I was strung out and needed him in London to help me. In December 1971 Giordano wrote back saying he'd return to Europe if I'd cover the airfare. I bought an open one-way ticket so that all Giordano had to do in India was hustle a new passport with money I wired over.

However, as January turned into February I began to lose hope of ever seeing Giordano again, and a new plan formed in my mind. One of my junkie buddies, Carl Bristol, felt things were getting too heavy around the Grove and he'd decided to head back to his native Nottingham. I elected to go with him since it seemed like a good way of evading Lever and his chums. Carl's parents owned a hotel and we were able to make use of one of the rooms. Bristol had plenty of connections in the town, and for a few weeks we were happily forging drug scripts and making good money from selling on most of the uppers and downers we fraudulently obtained. Although all good things must eventually come to an end, our big mistake was to get lazy and go back to the same chemists too frequently with scripts in different names. In short, we were nicked and booked in for an appearance at the local Magistrate's Court. Meanwhile, Giordano had managed to acquire a new passport from the French Embassy, and the delay to his reappearance in my life was simply due to this process having been drawn out and fraught with difficulties. As he was at last hurrying to catch a plane to London, Giordano was stopped by a young man dressed in a saffron robe who addressed him as follows: 'The age of darkness is almost over. How can darkness prevail when the very Light of Existence is here with us now? The last time this world was lit up, God sent His Son, but this time the Father Himself has come in all His Glory.'

Giordano told me that without the slightest hesitation he replied, 'I'm sorry, I'm in a rush to get to London, I don't have time for this now and in less than a week I will be dead.'

After Giordano stepped off the plane at Heathrow and had battled his way through customs and immigration, he was approached by another young man dressed in a saffron robe who addressed him in exactly the same manner: 'The age of darkness is almost over. How can darkness prevail when the very Light of Existence is here with us now? The last time this world was lit up, God sent His Son, but this time the Father Himself has come in all His Glory.'

Giordano replied, 'This is amazing, I have just arrived from India and the last person who spoke to me there addressed me with exactly the words you've just used. Unfortunately I have urgent business to attend to and in three days' time I will be dead.'

Giordano then made his way to the address in Notting Hill where I'd told him I was living, only to discover I'd moved on and the new tenant didn't know where I could be found. Fortunately, I'd also sent Giordano a current address for my friend Hetty, and she was able to inform him that I was being held under lock and key in Nottingham with a court appearance looming. Hetty had tricks to turn that evening, so Giordano sought out other friends and spent the night in London with them. The next morning he took a train to Nottingham and as soon as he'd alighted from the carriage he was stopped by a young man dressed in a saffron robe who addressed him in a now familiar manner: 'The age of darkness is almost over. How can darkness prevail when the very Light of Existence is here with us now? The last time this world was lit up, God sent His Son, but this time the Father Himself has come in all His Glory.'

Giordano told me his response was: 'This is too much; I have just travelled across the world and everywhere I go I am told the same thing. I made a pact with a friend in which we agreed to commit suicide if we had not achieved something by the time we were 33. Tomorrow I will reach that turning point in my life, and as yet my quest for spiritual enlightenment remains unrealised. Perhaps you have the answer, since to have received this message three times in my present circumstances leads me to think it must come directly from God. I have business in this city; where can I find you once I've attended to it?'

'God will not wait for your earthly affairs to be put in order,' the young man replied. 'You must come with me now.'

'I don't want the philosophy of enlightenment, I want the experience.'

'God will not disappoint you.'

'I have spent long years in India and all the Holy Men I met disappointed me. They told me they could give me the Light, and yet I always knew they were faking it. During one initiation ceremony I opened my eyes and discovered that the Master I was prepared to abase myself before was shining a torch in my face.'

'Guru Rampa will not disappoint you.'

'Who is Guru Rampa?'

'God.'

'So why does God call himself Guru Rampa?'

'Guru Rampa is modest; He makes no great claims for Himself. He says merely that He enables each of His disciples to find the Light within themselves. However, once Guru Rampa has enabled you to see the Light you will know without a shadow of a doubt that He is God. Guru Rampa does not claim to be God. It is His disciples who have discovered this Truth for themselves.'

'When can I meet God?'

'You must be patient, my friend, I cannot lead you directly to God; it is crucial that when you go to him you go in complete Faith. If you genuinely seek God then come with me now to a meeting in Leicester. If after that you are still interested, you can meet Guru Rampa and he will provide the vibration that will remove the veils from your eyes.'

'Unless I achieve something by tomorrow at the very latest then I am as good as dead.'

'All the more reason to put yourself directly into the hands of God.'

'What about my business in Nottingham? I've travelled halfway around the world to attend to it.'

'It can wait; God cannot wait.'

'Can I grab an hour or two in Nottingham before going with you to Leicester?'

'No. If secular matters are of greater concern to you than Eternal Truths then you are not yet ready for God.'

'OK, I'll go with you to Leicester.'

After attending the Church of Celestial Awakening meeting in Leicester, Giordano was taken directly to London, where Guru Rampa gave him the Light. It was a miracle, since at the last possible moment Giordano had snatched victory from the jaws of defeat. He achieved a sense of spiritual oneness for the first time ever the day before his 33rd birthday. Giordano busied himself with the Church of Celestial Awakening while I, not yet knowing he was back in England, got myself sorted out in Nottingham. When I came up before the beak I'd been held inside for so long that I was immediately released. I returned to Notting Hill, where I'd planned to crash with Hetty. She told me

Giordano was in town and within hours of being informed of his arrival, we were together once again. Giordano and I hopped from squat to squat around Ladbroke Grove, and for many months I succeeded in staying one step ahead of PC Lever. Giordano had cleaned up in India but being back with me meant that he started to shoot smack again. Nevertheless, the Church of Celestial Awakening gave us hope and we attended many of its London get-togethers. I had to wait, but when Guru Rampa finally returned to London in the late summer of 1972, I was more than ready to receive the Light. For the first time in my life I felt centred; instead of a bottomless yearning I was temporarily calm and at peace with myself.

Here I mention merely how I felt after encountering God for the first time during this my present life. To adequately describe the Infinite lies way beyond my puny capacities, and so I will not even attempt to portray Rampa in all His Glory as the Supreme Being. When I tell people about this they often think I am crazy, but to be crazy for God is the sanest thing a mortal can be. I know this is true because I have seen Him in all His Magnificence. I can add little more other than that Rampa told me it was my spiritual task to meditate so that I might experience His Presence as an ongoing reality. Unfortunately, for the past seven years I've only felt truly centred when I've shared physical space with God in the guise of His earthly manifestation as Guru Rampa. Indeed, I had to meditate for a full five years merely to locate my heart chakra. It's been a long hard struggle, and there have been times when I've turned my back on God because using heroin is so much easier than the hard road to enlightened self-knowledge offered by Rampa. Sometimes I think I'll never learn Rampa's lessons, but whenever I speak to him he insists that I must keep struggling with my demons and that when my Faith in Him becomes absolute I'll succeed in giving up drugs. When I'm away from Rampa's physical presence I invariably find myself overwhelmed by a terrific loneliness, and this is when my craving for smack really kicks in. Sometimes when this happens I stand up and do a laughing meditation, chuckling as hard as I can out from my belly and into the rest of my body with my hands on my hips, and that is often a great help. With Rampa's guidance I will eventually overcome my addictions. He is All Wise, and while I've frequently let Him down over the years, he nevertheless forgives me.

Life was better too with Giordano back at my side, especially since both of us knew that the death sentence which had been hanging over his head for the past eighteen years was at last lifted. I had good and bad times with Giordano over the summer of '72. Some weeks we did nothing but shoot smack and speed, and although we never actually stopped taking drugs there were nevertheless periods when we were really focused on God. That November, the Church of Celestial Awakening chartered a jumbo jet to take hundreds of disciples from London to an ashram just outside Bombay, where we were able to rocket ahead on our spiritual trajectories in the Divine presence of His Grace Guru Rampa. During those wonderful weeks in India at the tail end of 1972, Giordano made a far greater impression among the Elect than I did. So by the time I returned to London in the middle of December, Giordano had accepted an invitation to travel to Texas with Rampa and His Inner Circle. It was after they arrived in the States that Rampa asked Giordano to set up a mission for him in Hong Kong. Rampa provided Giordano with a one-way plane ticket to this British colony and I didn't see my love again until the summer of 1975.

To my great misfortune, in January 1973 PC Lever caught up with me again. I was hauled off to his interview room where I was raped and given the worst beating of my life. I don't know how many men fucked me but I was taken by more than I was able to count. While the coppers took their pleasure, I was kicked and punched. Finally I was turned on to my stomach and, while Lever sodomised me, he ordered one of his cronies to break my right arm. When

I got out of hospital I returned to Greenock to recuperate at my parents' tenement. I had no one else to turn to and nowhere left to go. I told my family I'd been in a car crash. I was too ashamed to tell them the truth. My father was ill with cancer and he died the following year. My mother was going senile but a couple of my brothers were still living at home and they cared for me as I recovered. For the next two years I commuted down to London from Scotland. I was afraid to base myself full-time somewhere Lever might catch up with me. When I was in London I usually stayed with friends of Giordano's who had a squat in Hither Green. At that time I preferred to be in south-east London, which was well away from Lever's Notting Hill stomping ground. However, I would on occasion spend time in the West End, most usually to meet johns. These were hard times, but not so much harder than those that would follow.

TAPE TRANSCRIPTION: SESSION 73 WITH R.D. LAING

R .D. Laing: This is Ronnie Laing having a talk with Jilly O'Sullivan on the 12th of May 1976, and I'm paying Jilly to help me work through some of my sexual-cum-psychoanalytic fantasies. My current thing is Patty Hearst, which Jilly handles very well despite the radical ways in which the role-playing during our sex sessions has changed over the years. Patty, in session 72 you said that producing your autobiography was taking longer and proving harder than you'd at first envisaged.

Jilly O'Sullivan: I've just done the first draft of a sample chapter. It took a couple of weeks for my agent and the ghost-writer's agent to agree on the terms of us writing the book together. So Sissy has done a synopsis of my notes, and we did an interview last week, and that's the sample chapter, which is about my first night in the broom cupboard. We did a two-hour interview, and she found that I didn't relax and go into enough detail until towards the end of the tape. Consequently the beginning and middle of the chapter isn't as detailed as the end, and she'd like another interview, which we're doing on Friday. She sent me the draft, which I got this morning, and I can see exactly what she means.

R.D. Laing: Did you listen back to the tape of the interview?

Jilly O'Sullivan: I didn't have the tape. Sissy kept it so that she could transcribe it. So what I suggested was that we do the next interview at night-time in the dark. That would help me recall more detail about what I was feeling in the broom cupboard.

R.D. Laing: Do you like Sissy?

Jilly O'Sullivan: Yes. I've known her for some time. She's a professional journalist and we first met when I was awaiting trial, and she did an interview with me. I hit it off with Sissy straight away. We became friends, so she got to know not just the story of me and the SLA, but my whole life history in quite an intimate way. After I came out of jail we socialised quite a lot. So when I realised that I wasn't able to write the book myself, that it was too difficult to go so deeply into my emotions, and that I wasn't used to writing either, I thought Sissy would be the best person to employ as a ghost-writer. Sissy said she'd be happy to do it, and we agreed not to discuss money, we'd leave it up to our agents to sort out the terms.

R.D. Laing: So what is the split?

Jilly O'Sullivan: The split is 55 to 45 in my favour up to a million dollars, after which it becomes 60 to 40 in my favour. That is only for the book and any serial rights. On film and television rights there will be no split at all, I get the money. My agent did tell me that the norm for ghost-writing is 50–50, and she wanted to see if she could get 60–40, but Sissy has a good agent. So we ended up with a 55 to 45 deal which I'm happy with. Once the sample chapter is finished next week, it goes to my agent and she'll take it to various editors. I think she's taking it to five different publishers and she wants them to bid for it. Until that happens I have no idea what my financial situation is going to be. It could be anything between one hundred thousand to one million dollars for the advance.

R.D. Laing: That's the advance, but it will become a bestseller?

Jilly O'Sullivan: Yes, but obviously it will take at least a year and a half before royalties start coming in. The advance will be split anyway: money for signing, money for delivery of manuscript, and money on publication.

R.D. Laing: And you have to recoup the advance before you get royalties?

Jilly O'Sullivan: I'm not sure, that depends on the deal my agent does. I'm really having to watch my money until I know what the advance will be on the book. However, I don't feel any regrets at having left my family. It's been a relief. I can be a lot more honest in this autobiography than the first one I did. It wasn't that I felt happy about being dishonest, it was just that there were certain things I couldn't say before because my family can't stand its self-image being compromised. So I'm feeling good about this break with my family. The first autobiography was done to satisfy my father. He fixed everything up with the ghost-writer, then got me to agree to do it. He wasn't happy when I said I wanted to do another autobiography, especially given that my initial plan was to write it myself.

R.D. Laing: What about Cinque? How do you feel about him?

Jilly O'Sullivan: Well, the rest of the SLA told me that his wife had put him down for years and years and years. So maybe he liked women who put him down, but that wasn't the kind of woman I was or am. Maybe he ended the relationship with his wife and discovered he'd made a mistake, because he liked being put down. I think after the kidnap we started our relationship with too many outside pressures and strains. It was OK when we were in the broom cupboard together, it was like being in a womb isolated from the rest of the world, but the minute we came out of the cupboard there were too many outside stresses on us for our relationship to work.

R.D. Laing: You seem very confused about this relationship.

Jilly O'Sullivan: I didn't know where our relationship was going when Cinque died. I thought I did, but I'm very insecure about it now. I've been so thrown since I've been doing these sessions with you. Just now, as I was talking about it to you, I suddenly felt really depressed about Cinque. I just don't know what to think.

R.D. Laing: My feeling is that Cinque was fairly unstable and therefore you're putting some things on him that don't correspond to his feelings. But that's not really the whole of the problem we need to deal with. The real question is how you can get the degree of fulfilment in your relationships that you really want, and whether you can recapture the degree of intensity you felt in your relationship with Cinque in a future relationship. (*pause*) I think you need to find love. Your desire to be loved by a man is overwhelming. That's wonderful, but it's mixed in with an inferiority complex, and by a constant fear that you're not going to get what you want.

Jilly O'Sullivan: Yes, in any relationship I've had with any man I've loved I've experienced rejection.

R.D. Laing: We need to look closely at fear and rejection because they are terribly powerful emotions, and we need to get you to the point where you don't have these lurking fears any longer, where above all what's been confronted is whether these fears you suffer have any justification. I'll elaborate here. If you've got great anxieties about not being loved, it could be that you tend to be a bit cloying, and nobody will like that. Now the cloyingness is sometimes difficult to avoid because your pain is intense, so you will tend to go to the person you love for reassurance, and because you're cloying they won't give you the reassurance you crave, which increases your feelings of pain and insecurity. There is a difficulty here. (*long pause*) We can't resolve this matter theoretically merely by talking about it as we are now; you have to connect with your own feelings, and speak while you're in the state of emotional turmoil that these fears bring on, which will make what we're talking about seem very real. It's only then that we can unearth the deeper roots of this problem and deal with them. (*pause*) The best thing for me to do now is invite you to talk about how you would like to be loved by a man, and to pick out episodes where this pain of fearing you might not be loved has been particularly intense.

Jilly O'Sullivan: The way I'd like to be loved would be to not have any fear, to be able to be myself without having to worry that any of my actions might jeopardise the relationship or turn the man off me. (*pause*) Can I have a cigarette?

R.D. Laing: Yes, you can, let me get you an ashtray. (*pause*)

Jilly O'Sullivan: I'd like there to be an equal partnership, where just as I am happy to love someone despite their faults this would be reciprocated. I'd like to know that if I was going through a crisis or if I was ill, the man I loved would be there and would be supportive, just as I would be if it was the other way round. I'd like to be able to talk quite freely, and for the other person to feel they could be frank with me. (*pause*) I'd like to have the security of knowing I could be myself, and that my man was always honest with me.

R.D. Laing: I'd like you to tell me instances where you've found this hasn't happened.

Jilly O'Sullivan: Well, with Cinque and the SLA, there was always this mistrust because it was assumed that at least one person in the group was an infiltrator from the CIA. So there was this assumption that careless talk cost lives and that we couldn't be ourselves, we had to remake ourselves as revolutionaries. I know that Cinque knew this upset me. I didn't feel that I could say to Cinque what I felt about him, because he'd have seen it as cloying. There was also this real fear that at least one of the group had been programmed to go berserk when they heard certain trigger words, so there was a reluctance to use anything but conventional and clichéd language within the group. (*pause*)

R.D. Laing: The things that happen in a terrorist cell aren't necessarily totally different to what happens in everyday life, but the sense of paranoia many ordinary people feel is heightened in urban guerrilla groups. Since you are paranoid, I want to help you overcome this paranoia, but I can't do that by saying don't be paranoid, because that just makes you more paranoid. There's a difference between my acceptance of you, and the general refusal by most people to accept you as you really are. Most people's acceptance levels of what they don't like are extremely low. I'm exceptional in that I've had many years of training and experience in treating unloved individuals as if they are loveable. What you need to do is pretend that you aren't paranoid without this hurting you or driving you completely bats. The fact that you are somewhat unpleasant and won't be accepted warts and all by your friends and family will take a bit of getting used to. It will also mean that you'll have to conduct your relationships on a somewhat superficial level, as a kind of sado-masochistic role playing.

Jilly O'Sullivan: I know. Cinque used to complain I never showed my real emotions, but when I did give expression to a naked feeling he freaked. It was a no-win situation; no matter what I did, it was wrong. I was frightened to ask Cinque what happened when he was taken into the psychiatric ward the last time he was in prison. I was afraid to ask what the doctors had done to him, and what the CIA offered him in return for becoming a double agent. I know it was a perfectly reasonable thing to ask, after all Cinque talked about it in his sleep, but we had to keep up this sham that he was a totally committed revolutionary who'd remade himself in the image of the people. Cinque was so persistent in his insistence that he was a revolutionary, that he actually came to believe it, at least consciously. What I'd have liked Cinque to say was that he believed in the revolution, but he'd sold out to the CIA. I don't know, maybe he planned to double-cross them. However, he'd never admit he'd done a deal to get out of jail. That was what I wanted him to tell me, but I was never going to get it.

R.D. Laing: I think we're getting closer to the feeling state in you that matters. When you say that you didn't mind that he'd done a deal to get out of jail, but he wouldn't admit it, then we're very close to your fundamental dilemma.

Jilly O'Sullivan: Yes, because he always said that I was made by the elite white establishment. He insisted that I could never break the mould of my background. I just wanted to ball and for us to break free from our pasts by being totally honest with each other. (*pause*)

R.D. Laing: You are in a state of deep neediness, and we have to look closely at this. We must accept your neediness as a given, while acknowledging that most other people would not accept this consciously, let alone on other levels. In other words, we have to say that you are who you are, and then we can see where we go from here. Our job is not to work on who you fundamentally are; we must accept that despite knowing that most people who understand what you're really like want nothing at all to do with you. You are both physically and emotionally unattractive, but there is nothing we can do about that.

Jilly O'Sullivan: I did make a point of not asking Cinque for reassurance.

R.D. Laing: Practically speaking that put you at an advantage, but it simultaneously placed you in a position where you didn't get the reassurance you wanted.

Jilly O'Sullivan: That's right.

R.D. Laing: You had a difficult childhood and adolescence. For long periods you haven't been getting what you need, affection. I'd like you to talk about this.

Jilly O'Sullivan: Funnily enough that's something I've been thinking about because of the work I've been doing on my autobiography. Having done dozens of interviews with the ghost-writer, I now realise I'm going to have to delve even more deeply into the bad sides of my character in order to produce something really funky. I think the root of these problems is that I have no memories of my father or my mother being loving to each other.

R.D. Laing: Do you have any memories of them being loving to you?

Jilly O'Sullivan: Not really.

R.D. Laing: So when you were a child who was loving to you?

Jilly O'Sullivan: My grandmother.

R.D. Laing: How loving was she?

Jilly O'Sullivan: She was very loving. She made me feel like I was a special person in her life. She was physically very affectionate. I have vivid memories of sitting on her lap. She had really big breasts. I'd look down between them when she was reading me a story, I loved that. She would take a lot of time to read to me and to teach me things. She used to talk to me all the time. She was the person I felt most secure with. I can never remember either my mother or my father making me feel secure about their love for me. So I used to try and make life difficult for my parents.

R.D. Laing: How?

Jilly O'Sullivan: It was a feeling I had, I can't remember any specific instances. (*pause*) One Sunday when I was seven and my mother and father disappeared into the bathroom, I knocked on the door and got no response from them. Then I got this ladder and put it against the outside wall, climbed up and looked through the window. My parents were making love and I felt a terrible sense of shock. I jumped off the ladder and shouted 'Mommy' over and over again.

R.D. Laing: I see.

Jilly O'Sullivan: Then I went and hid behind a chair in their bedroom. My parents tried to get me to come out from behind the chair. I can't remember what they said, but I remember feeling angry. My feelings about what I'd seen were rather mixed.

R.D. Laing: You said you were shocked at what you saw. What did you see?

Jilly O'Sullivan: I can't remember very clearly; they were on the floor and daddy was on top of mommy. It was all very quick. A moment after I'd looked in the window, I jumped down and ran away. I remember my feeling of shock. I can't remember what my mommy actually said to me afterwards.

R.D. Laing: The nature of the shock you felt when you saw them does in fact have some content. To try and reconstruct what the content might have been is quite important. (*pause*) It sometimes happens that when a young child sees a couple making love, especially when they are her own parents, that if the mother is underneath she feels the mother is being attacked. In which case you get a feeling of protectiveness in the child, and a belief that her daddy is a nasty man who hurts her mother. Or the child might think that her parents were cuddling, in which case you can get feelings of jealousy and abandonment.

Jilly O'Sullivan: I felt abandoned.

R.D. Laing: It is important to determine whether this was what you actually felt.

Jilly O'Sullivan: It was a feeling of jealousy. I didn't think she'd been attacked. That's why I wanted to give her a hard time. Over the years, as my mommy's drinking and drug problems got worse, I used to feel sorry for my daddy. I disliked it when they got physically violent towards each other, I hated that, but I almost understood why he hit her, because she was so vile. She was a foul creature when she was drunk. I felt more secure with my daddy and his love for me than with my mommy. I never felt secure with my mommy. She used to say she loved me but I never felt it, I never believed it. I have a sort of love-hate for my mother.

R.D. Laing: I'd like to get more of a feel for that love-hate, and I'd like to separate the love from the hate.

Jilly O'Sullivan: When she wasn't drunk, when she was sober, she was a very (*long pause*) loving person. The moment she started to drink, I could see the change coming over her. She would become extremely critical. I can remember her calling me names. She was very insulting, I hated her.

R.D. Laing: How was she insulting?

Jilly O'Sullivan: She'd usually start by dissing my grandmother; she was very jealous of my relationship with my grandmother. She also had an absolute fixation with her daddy, so she'd rave about how she didn't like her mommy because her mommy hadn't been nice to her daddy. She'd rant about how wonderful her father was, and how awful her mother had been. Then she'd scream about what a liar my daddy was, and how unfaithful he was to her. After that she'd move on to how terrible I was, and how I was just like my daddy.

R.D. Laing: So what did your father say to you about your mother?

Jilly O'Sullivan: He'd say she was a drunk and he'd make derogatory remarks about her. I didn't like that either. I didn't like my mommy insulting my daddy, or my daddy putting down my mommy.

R.D. Laing: You didn't like the sense of disharmony between your mother and father being strengthened or reinforced?

Jilly O'Sullivan: When I was with my mommy I wanted to be with my daddy, and when I was with my daddy I wanted to be with my mommy, and when I was with both of them, I didn't want to be with either of them. They never really loved me. (*long pause*) Since Cinque died, I've felt that there is a part of me missing. When Cinque was alive I felt whole, I felt good. We could talk, not about everything, but about a lot of things. We talked about the revolution all the time. We talked about strategy and tactics. What we never talked about was ourselves. We were in tune with each other's moods when we were physically together. Being with Cinque wasn't always wonderfully good, but we seemed to be in tune. I never felt the need when I was with him to ask if he loved me. It was just when he'd say one thing, then something completely contradictory immediately afterwards, that I'd get really upset and I didn't feel in tune with him at all.

16. THE CONMAN WHO TURNED ON THE WORLD

The underground scene back in the 60s, and especially the early 60s, was very small. It was easy to get to know everyone. One person led to another, but there were also chance encounters. Just two months after Lloyd was born I was drinking in the Kensington Park Hotel and fell into conversation with the guys who were the first major Euro pot smugglers. The number one in this operation I shall call Marco Polo; he's living in the United States now but we stay in touch. I last saw Marco in California a year and a half ago. In the early 60s Marco was running dope around Europe hidden inside the panelling of various vans; by the mid-60s he was using yachts and had the biggest operation outside the Middle East until his lieutenants were busted in London. After this Tommy Graham took over as *numero uno* hash hustler. When Graham and my former flatmate Matt Bradley were busted in Lorrach, Howard Marks used this as his opportunity to leapfrog over those higher up in the organisation, including Charlie Radcliffe. Graham used to get the dope air-freighted in using Pakistani diplomatic cover, and then employed convoys of cars to move it around Europe.

It was through Marco Polo and the other men running that first big dope scam in Europe that I met Giordano in Spain in 1964. The same people would pop up everywhere: it didn't matter whether you were in London, Paris, Ibiza or India, they were always there with you. Michael Hollingshead was one of those faces, and he springs to mind because of his front – he even called his autobiography *The Man Who Turned On The World*. The people who created the counterculture came out of the beatnik movement, and they'd learned how to hustle in order to survive the rat race that confronted them in the late 50s and early 60s. These boppers were creative in a way that later drug impresarios could never be. They invented the scams that men like Howard Marks later took over. One need only cite the example of the Marks rock PA scam, where he'd seal dope into the amplification used by rock groups before shipping it around the world. This was hardly a new idea, since years before Marks did his PA smuggling one of Marco Polo's lieutenants, who happened to be a minor British artist, was sealing dope inside his large fibreglass sculptures. These would be sent around the world, supposedly for exhibition, but actually they'd be smashed open once they reached their destination so that the hash could be retrieved once it had passed safely through customs. These men valued invisibility and anonymity, which is why I won't name those who have neither died nor deliberately sought publicity. Their scams are less well known than those of Howard Marks precisely because they were carried off more successfully. Press coverage is generally treated as a sign of failure in the drug trade.

Howard Marks is a raconteur; he is very pleasant company but he is not my idea of a good dope smuggler, because he likes being noticed. Marks is a clever man and good fun, but his excessive conviviality makes him unsuited to being the grey eminence behind a harmless but nevertheless illegal trade. In sharp contrast to this Tommy Graham provides a perfect fit for what I view as the archetypal drug dealer. After the authorities rumbled Graham as a major player, he simply adopted a false identity and carried on regardless. Rock on Tommy! When Howard Marks self-consciously performed a vanishing act, it resulted in his picture being carried on the front pages of assorted British tabloids alongside the suggestion that he worked for British intelligence and was probably the victim of a Mafia kidnapping. Howard may have been on bail and ducking out of a court appearance but when he went absent without leave his primary consideration was to ensure his disappearance would make him more visible. Marks loves melodramatics. He wants to be a rock star and he deserves to be one.

It was Tommy Graham who introduced me to Howard Marks as well as Charlie Radcliffe. That said, while Tommy was applying himself to mastering the hash trade I was already actively involved. Under Marco Polo's influence my smuggling activities began in the early 60s. Marco loved me like a sister and has always looked after me when I've been down on my luck. He was disappointed when I got into smack and warned me that lying and hustling like a junkie would lead me into serious trouble. Marco has told me I could do better for myself, but nonetheless whenever I need his help he does all he can for me. Marco insists hash and acid expand consciousness whereas heroin arrests emotional development. I know what he thinks, although he's never laid a heavy trip about this on me. I know he's right, but after losing Lloyd I needed a painkiller, and all the trouble Marco has gone to on my behalf can't keep me away from heroin and the stupid hustles in which I'm sometimes tempted to engage.

Michael de Freitas introduced me to Alex Trocchi a few months after I'd first tried smoking opium in Spain in the summer of 1964, and it was Scotch Alex who towards the end of 1965 took me along to Pont Street, where Michael

Hollingshead had just set up his World Psychedelic Centre. Hollingshead's London headquarters was a luxury flat in Belgravia, and this conman made much of the fact that he was the first person to provide acid guru Tim Leary with LSD. Hollingshead was charming, and I soon discovered his forte was parting wealthy fools from their money, usually under the guise of providing support for some wonderfully philanthropic project. Ultimately the beneficiary of such financial aid was always Hollingshead himself. In the early 70s I finally got to meet Tim Leary when he was on the run from the US authorities in Switzerland, and by then I'd learned that he was an even better hustler than Hollingshead but less shrewd as a judge of other people's honesty, or rather lack thereof. My current love met Leary when the latter was hiding out with exiled Black Panthers in Algeria, and for a while this countercultural icon told people Garrett was his guru mainly because he'd become sexually obsessed by Carmen Jones, with whom I now vie for our smack-dealing pimp's favours. I don't think Leary ever sussed out that Carmen was a high-class call-girl who was being pimped by Garrett. But then I'd have never guessed that it was Garrett who'd informed on me until he confessed to setting me up for a fall with PC Lever. It was just as much of a surprise to me when I really got it together with Garrett a few months ago. In the early 70s Garrett was Leary's man in London, and like Hollingshead before him he exploited this situation to solicit donations and other favours from the credulous.

Backtracking, although LSD was still legal in the spring of 1966, Hollingshead made a tactical mistake when he spiked various undercover cops who were attempting to infiltrate his scene. Shortly afterwards Mike found himself the subject of a probe by the yellow press and this was followed by a dope bust. Hollingshead made another error when he decided to get high on acid before conducting his own court defence, and for the heinous crime of coming to believe his own bullshit copped a 21-month sentence. I didn't see Hollingshead again until 1972, because after doing his prison time he moved on to the United States via Norway and finally landed up in Nepal just after I arrived back in London from India. Hollingshead, like me, is a British national, and despite our officially recorded involvement with the drug culture it is easy enough to get a visa for the States. We simply lie about our convictions on the application form, since no one ever seems to check them.

When I ran into Hollingshead again in 1972 he'd been organising an LSD cult on a remote Scottish island, but the set-up had encountered problems and he was back in London. Mike's latest con had inevitably freaked out his landlord, which turned out to be the Church of Scotland, and he was now organising his scam religion from a squatted former gas works in Kentish Town. We both knew a former jockey-cum-smack dealer who operated out of a basement flat in Cambridge Gardens, and once Mike was back in London it was inevitable that our paths would cross via one of our many drug connections. Hollingshead needed some pretty girls to work with and I was perfect for the part. A wealthy man called Taddeo Gaddi had expressed an interest in Mike's drug cult, but it was apparent to Hollingshead that this potential benefactor was more interested in sex than consciousness expansion. Mike's solution was to provide the mark with a little of what he desired and the promise of a lot more to come. All I had to do was call in at the Polytantric Church in Kentish Town, and while Gaddi was present create the impression of my sexual availability once I was under the influence of drugs. Mike told me when and where to appear and assured me that if we were successful I was in line for ten per cent of whatever Taddeo donated to the cause. It wasn't difficult to find the Polytantric Church, so having located it sooner than I expected I sat on a wall a few hundred yards away from the building and read Henry Miller's *Tropic Of Cancer* to avoid arriving too early. When I finally knocked on the door a young hippie boy let me in and showed me through to Hollingshead's office.

'Hello, stranger,' I said.

'Jilly, it's been a long time,' Mike replied. 'I haven't seen you since the Pont Street days.'

'Fabulous times, man, fabulous.'

'1966.'

'Yeah, that's right.'

'Do you remember how you'd always refuse to make love to me until we got high?'

'How could I forget it?'

'What was that all about?'

'Mike, I don't want to sound rude but even way back then you weren't exactly the best looking guy in the world. You're bald, you're overweight and you've got broken veins in your face from drinking too much when you were younger. But underneath all that I know you're beautiful, even if I can only see your radiant soul when I'm high.'

'Jilly, before we go on I must introduce you to Taddeo.'

'Hi!' I said.

'Hi,' Gaddi echoed.

'Are you related to Mike?' I asked.

'No.'

'You look a little like him.'

'Would you like to make love to us?' Hollingshead enquired.

'No, no,' I laughed.

'You used to say just the same in Pont Street, but after we'd dropped acid you'd make it with me and any other man who was around.'

'I remember that first time we did it so very well.'

'Do you?'

'Of course I do.'

'Then tell me about it.'

'When the trip came on I was in the bedroom with another girl called Vicki Barrett. Somehow we got the idea that the light hanging above the bed was the sun and we took our clothes off to enjoy its warmth and get a tan. Then you came into the room with another man called Pete. Vicki called you over and I just lay on the bed next to her as the pair of you made love to each other. Vicki screamed obscenities in my ear as she reached her first climax and I pulled you on top of me and got you to shoot off inside me. When you sprayed your sperm into me it felt great and it was only afterwards that I noticed Pete was by this time making love to Vicki. Then you and Pete swapped places. I came again and again; until then I'd never have believed it was possible to have so many orgasms in a single afternoon.'

'Do you want to do it again?'

'If you've got some acid we could drop it, but I won't make any promises about what I may or may not be up for once I'm tripping.'

'What do you think, Taddeo?' Mike asked as he turned to his guest.

'She'll be gagging for it.'

'You're an optimist,' I put in, 'and I like happy-go-lucky men.'

'OK then,' Hollingshead announced, 'let's trip.'

We each took a blotter, and since Gaddi had only done a handful of trips and Mike and I had done hundreds apiece, we were very clearly in control of the situation. To give himself a bit of edge Hollingshead took some speed with his acid. The hallucinations I had were mild. Looking at the room was like gazing into a beautiful mandala. There was a bit of movement here and there plus some distortion in my field of visual perception, but the smack I'd taken before I'd headed to north London smoothed out the trip. Mike and I gave it about an hour before starting to manoeuvre Taddeo into some three-way fucking. What I did wasn't exactly subtle, but it had worked well enough for me in the past when I'd been confronted by shy guys like Taddeo. I took my clothes off and began to dance.

'Fellow creatures,' I giggled, 'I want you to move your bodies to the music of the spheres.'

'You what?' Mike asked.

'The music, don't you hear the music?'

'That's the sound of nine million people daily all making love.' Hollingshead was a big fan of west-coast rock, and I knew this reply more or less approximated the title of a track by a Californian band called the Seeds.

'Yeah, let's get it on and make Kentish Town a world centre of sexual energy!' I shot back.

'Taddeo, are you up for a threesome?' Mike enquired.

'Taddeo, Taddeo, where are you?' I chanted.

When Gaddi gave no reply I moved over to the corner in which our mark was standing and pulled down his pants. He didn't seem to notice as I got down on my knees and began to play with his limp manhood. I wasn't wearing any clothes, so taking me from behind didn't present Hollingshead with any problems. After a few strokes Mike shot off. I had Taddeo's member in my hand and it was still flaccid.

'To know the difference between sex and death it is necessary to pass over to the other side!' Mike screamed in his ecstasy.

'Right on, brother!' Gaddi responded, although my by now frantic tuggings had failed to bring on so much as the first stirrings of an erection. Everything was resolved when Taddeo added, 'Get away from me, woman, so that Michael can give me a blow job.'

I moved out of the way and immediately had to stifle a laugh, because the minute Hollingshead touched him, Gaddi got it up. Like most straight men Mike considered it a great kick to watch two girls going at it like rabbits, but guys were really not his thing. However, a mark is a mark, and since Hollingshead wanted Gaddi's money he had to provide the promise of something in return. Mike was gagging as he placed his lips around Taddeo's throbbing gristle, and his face became even more contorted after his mouth was filled with the mark's hot spunk. I found a copy of the then brand spanking new Lou Reed platter *Transformer* and spun it, an appropriate choice given the many hymns it contained to sexual decadence. It was a fabulous

album, with tracks like *Vicious* and *I'm So Free* being every
bit as good as the best-known cut, *Walk On The Wild Side*,
which was a hit single.

'Michael, you've been transformed into a skeleton.' Gaddi
enunciated these words as though they were a mantra.

Hollingshead was attempting to spit Taddeo's come from
his mouth and appeared less than happy that he was failing
miserably. He'd obviously swallowed some of the white
stuff. To cover up for my friend I figured I'd better say
something.

'Have you made it with a man before?'

'No, and now I know what was wrong with my love-
making: I went for the second sex. Getting it on with a guy
is the ultimate reality trip.'

'If you find oral stimulating, how do you think you'll like
giving and taking it up the arse?' I enquired.

'That's it, that's it. Michael, I want you to come over here
so that you can stretch my sphincter with your fuck stick.'

'What about I get one of the guys from the commune to
attend to you?' Hollingshead was stalling.

'But they won't be tripping.'

'Sure they will be, everyone in the Polytantric Church
ingests acid day and night.'

'How old would these guys be?'

'Depends which one, but mid-twenties is about average.'

'And what about their arms?'

'Their arms?'

'Yes, do any of them have eight arms?'

'Depends how you look at them.'

'And big biceps?'

'Sure, those are on the whole absolutely enormous.'

'Mmmmmmm . . .'

'I'll go and get one and you can see what you think.'

'No, no, I want you here with me. Send the girl to fetch
me a hunk.'

'Jilly, go and ask one of the better-hung guys if they'll
come in here and do something for the Church.'

'Sure.'

So I got dressed, went out and sent the first guy I found off to do his bit for Mike's new psychedelic religion. Although I was expecting payment in cash for my services, in this hope I was to be disappointed. Once Hollingshead had secured a several thousand pound donation from Gaddi to cover the costs of some elaborate full moon trips at key ley line intersections around the British Isles, he took the money and ran. Initially Mike headed for Manhattan, where he'd hoped to wrest custody of an eleven-year-old daughter from his former wife Sophie. Later on I heard he was in Bolivia organising lucrative cocaine shipments back into the overdeveloped world. I'm not the only person Hollingshead owed money when he split and if he ever comes back to London it will inevitably entail him facing a few angry showdowns. Mike was charming, but at the end of the day there are rip-offs and rip-offs. The world would be a better place if there was at least honour among thieves.

It should go without saying that since the mid-60s I have been involved in endless LSD shenanigans. Giordano was rather too fond of spiking people but there are so many stories about unsuspecting individuals being tricked into ingesting acid that recording further instances of this is not really worthwhile. Giordano also picked up a nice little con from Barbet Schroeder's first film, *More*, which we went to see because Pink Floyd provided the soundtrack. The main characters in this movie are addicted to smack and attempt to clean up by taking LSD in Ibiza. It doesn't work for them, which didn't surprise Giordano or me because we've always taken a lot of acid alongside our regular fixes of smack. Nevertheless, Giordano would often get judgemental non-junkie friends off his back by telling them he'd overcome his smack habit by taking regular doses of acid. This was, of course, a bare faced lie, but a lot of people were taken in by the line because they knew we regularly tripped out. Likewise, Giordano made his claims on this score sound even more convincing by stressing that LSD had also been used as an experimental cure for alcoholism.

17. FROM DRUGS TO RUGS AND BACK AGAIN

In the early part of 1975 I reached an agreement with Giordano and he came to an accord with Guru Rampa. The Church of Celestial Awakening's Hong Kong operation was flourishing and Giordano was to leave it in the capable hands of other initiates and return to Europe after spending a few months starting up a new Enlightenment Centre in Tokyo. There was inevitably a minor downside to these changes. Giordano had set up his own business in Hong Kong called Eastern Traders. Officially Eastern Traders exported oriental rugs to Europe, North America and the Antipodes. In reality this trade in rare carpets was a cover for drug running. Giordano made money from selling rugs but he made a lot more from smuggling drugs. Most of Giordano's profits had been ploughed back into the Church. Guru Rampa had been told no more than the Hong Kong authorities about the real nature of Giordano's business ventures, but since He was Divine, our conclusion was that He knew and approved of this piece of Heavenly Deception. Once Giordano returned to Europe, overseeing his thriving drugs empire would have necessitated him commuting back to Hong Kong, and since neither of us wanted this, he decided to place Eastern Traders in other trusted hands. Guru Rampa would still receive money from Eastern Traders, but Giordano wouldn't be seeing a penny more from the enterprise he'd set up. We were going to live together again in London and to this end I secured a large bedsit in Bassett Road. This was a move which I soon came to realise had been a major lapse of judgement.

I'd developed drug connections in south-east London and I had plenty more in Greenock and Glasgow, but once I was back in west London familiar faces from my subterranean past in the Grove began turning up like proverbial bad pennies. Garrett walked by as I arrived, suitcase in my hand, at my new flat. I invited him in and he turned me on. Giordano and I had agreed that when we got back together our relationship would be open, so I didn't feel bad about having sex with Garrett there and then. After we'd fucked and shot up, Garrett announced he'd been crazy about me for years and this somehow led on to a confession that he'd been the person who grassed me up to PC Lever. I told him I'd wrongly blamed Trocchi for dropping me in the shit with the pigs. Garrett replied that he was still working with Scotch Alex and suggested that we go around to Observatory Gardens straight away. I agreed to this, since I fancied putting a touch of glamour back into my life. Trocchi greeted me warmly and immediately offered to cut me in on various drug deals.

'Jilly,' Scotch Alex enthused, 'a lot of the celebrities still ask about you, they miss your style. They rated you for class and never for a minute guessed that you were on the game. The girl working for me now looks like a groupie and everyone knows she'd suck the last fix from your arm. It's as if she'd walked straight out of *Cain's Book*. The slags that preceded her were just the same. They all came from thoroughly bourgeois backgrounds but get mistaken for proles. Junkie rock stars have unlimited access to girls like this. Your father may have been a docker but since you've worked hard on your manners and deportment, all the marks imagine that you are a genuine bit of posh. They like the way you dress, too, and the care you take over your make-up. I need you working alongside me if I'm to maintain my place in the illegal drug market. I understand why you left so suddenly. I'd have cut you off if I'd thought you were a grass. So let bygones be bygones. We'll do well together. The younger girls getting into smack these days aren't of your standard. They revel in their junkie image as if they were men, whereas you are so much more discreet.'

I accepted Trocchi's offer and the three years during which I'd broken off relations with him melted away as if they were no more than a dream. I lived in my new Bassett Road pad for ten days before Giordano arrived home and moved in. During that time I reforged most of my old hustling connections. That said, several of my former acquaintances had died, generally in the most sordid of circumstances, while others had disappeared into the twin wastelands of twelve step programmes and the suburbs. In the instances of those who'd croaked, the cops didn't look very closely into the circumstances surrounding their deaths. PC Lever and his cronies didn't want the nice little earners they had going disrupted in any way and dead men tell no tales, especially when there isn't so much as an inquest into the circumstances surrounding their demise.

So when a dealer of my acquaintance called Bashful Bob Sylvester had given up the ghost in 1974, his death was officially attributed to natural causes despite the fact that he was found drowned in a bath with his throat slit. Another dealer called Charlie Taylor, who'd been sweetening Lever with hefty payouts, was gunned down outside Paddington railway station. Officially the cause of Taylor's death was heart failure, and passers-by who believed they'd heard shots were assured the noise was only that of a car backfiring. The blood that had been splashed around was explained away as coming from a cut that had opened up on Charlie's forehead because he'd fallen heavily while suffering the coronary. However, the bent cops running the local drug rackets were rarely very happy about one of their licensed traders meeting an untimely end, and so one unlikely death officially attributed to natural causes was inevitably followed by others. What the coroner listed as an official cause of death meant less than nothing amongst the drug fraternity, and so never impeded Lever's insistence upon retribution being seen to be done. Indeed, all my acquaintances knew that the Old Bill made whatever arrangements they wanted among themselves when investigating cases, so the facts placed before a coroner rarely bore much relationship to what had actually gone down when it came to deaths within the drug scene.

Giordano was tired from his flight when I met him at the airport. I had gear on me so he took a hit in a toilet and nodded out on the tube back into town. It was just like the old days as we walked the short distance from Ladbroke Grove tube to our Bassett Road home. When we got there Lever was waiting for me. He'd been told that I was around. Lever informed me he had a few things to do but that I was to be up at the cop shop in an hour. Giordano went to bed and I took another hit before going out to endure yet another prolonged session of sexual assault.

'You can't stay away from me, can you?' Lever sneered as he showed me into an interview room. 'Take your clothes off and lie down on the desk.'

It turned out to be a pretty standard bout of sexual humiliation. I had to pull a train. The constable took me first then four of his detective colleagues also had their evil way with me. I was slapped about a bit and insulted but received no major injuries. Lever told me to bring him money. He knew I could earn it and didn't care how. He also informed me I was to get involved with the Westbourne Project, since the best pair of eyes and ears he had inside this drug-addict self-help initiative had just been busted by a rookie cop who hadn't yet learned how things were done around the Grove. It had been suggested to the rookie that he weigh off the evidence, and after he'd failed to do so, much to his bemusement he'd found himself suspended on full pay while being investigated for various corrupt practices.

When I got home I burst into tears, but Giordano was exhausted and my sobbing failed to wake him. I wasn't going to cry myself to sleep. Instead, I took a hit and immediately felt on top of everything. The next day I talked to Giordano about what had happened. I'd agreed to come off the game once we got back together, but the easiest way to deal with Lever's demands for money was to go and turn a few tricks. Giordano reluctantly agreed to this. I still had my little black address book and used a pay-phone to contact various long-term johns. Those I was able to reach were still interested, so I set up a series of assignations. I also resolved to go and get myself some hostess work.

After leaving the phone booth, I shifted my butt along Portobello Road to the Westbourne Project offices. The people running the place looked like weekend hippies and held all the qualifications needed by the most strait-laced social worker, degrees and other stuff. None of this fazed me. I'd had a trick in the 60s who'd been a philosophy student at UCL. When Gerald Stubbington was doing his PhD he used to take me into the UCL philosophy department in Gordon Square, and back then I got well in with the faculty. In the early 60s Gordon Square was still Bloomsbury, and the heir to the 'radical' traditions of Bentham and Mill. Many of the philosophers working there had achieved celebrity status. A. J. Ayer was on the Brains Trust, Stuart Hampshire wrote for *Encounter* and Bernard Williams was widely believed to be the cleverest man in England. These figures were perceived then to be engaged with everything 'advanced' in culture. They had all the 'taste' and 'discernment' of the haute bourgeoisie. They were public school and Oxford but their morality was unconventional, with a frisson of scandal. They also found a pretty girl like me irresistible, particularly as my own take on morality was rather more sophisticated than their own. The plastic hippies who were employed as social workers at the Westbourne Project were impressed by my faked academic credentials, since I knew enough about Gordon Square to fool them into thinking I'd gained a degree there in 1963 and then successfully completed an MPhil in 1966. I told those who were interested that my post-graduate dissertation was on sense perception, with my focus very much being the ways in which perceiving is connected to knowing. This made quite an impression among the Project workers, since several of them had studied philosophy but only to degree level, and at redbrick universities rather than at a prestigious department like the one they were conned into believing was my alma mater. Ultimately my new friends were more interested in gossip about Ayer and Hampshire than serious philosophical debate, and this enabled me to play to my strengths.

I explained to the do-gooders running the Westbourne Project that I wanted to help those still attempting to overcome their addictions. My cover story was that I'd begun experimenting with drugs in the early 60s but had always felt in control of what I was doing. Unfortunately, after being involved in a serious car crash in India in 1968 I'd become addicted to opiates, and it was not until returning to England and undergoing a cure in 1972 that I'd been able to lead a normal life once again, that is to say one free from drugs. I also made much of my involvement with various countercultural projects in the 60s, ranging from the Notting Hill Free School to Defence. My personal connections to figures like Alex Trocchi and Michael X, who was very much in the news at that time due to his recent hanging, greatly impressed the hippie social workers I was bamboozling. I claimed I'd gone to India after I'd completed my studies in 1966 and stayed there until 1970. It wasn't difficult to convince those running the Westbourne Project that while I was in India I'd attempted to duplicate some of the projects I'd been involved with in London. The most successful of these was the still flourishing Bombay Free School. I claimed that initially this project was conceived and brought into existence by two close colleagues and myself. We'd simply rented a large rambling house in Garneshpuri (a small village several miles from Bombay) and filled it up with orphans and vagrants we'd found on the streets. I confessed a little sheepishly that most of the informal teaching was conducted in English as our knowledge of Hindi was rather limited. We were able to coach some of the brighter pupils in reading, writing and the comprehension of simple mathematical problems. That said, the majority of those we aided were more able to express themselves through music, art and drama.

Ever since I was a small girl I'd loved inventing stories, and I had a smashing time with this one. One of the things I'd learned long ago was that in order to lie successfully the best approach is to mix outrageous fabrications with concrete details from factual material one knows inside out. With regard to this, the eighteen months I'd spent bombed out of my mind in India and my long-term involvement with the counterculture stood me in good stead. Despite the extended periods of time the do-gooders I was spinning this line to spent around drug addicts, they'd yet to consciously understand the extent to which junkies hustle. You couldn't hope for better marks, since they were extremely keen to believe anything I told them. Initially these bozos put me to work as a volunteer counselling drug addicts, and they were very pleased with my progress. Being naturally curious, I found listening to tales of woe and addiction rather absorbing. Obviously a great deal of what I was told was complete horseshit, but since I consumed these yarns as a form of entertainment I rarely attempted to separate fact from fiction.

I was found to be diligent and reliable in my volunteer work, and so it wasn't long before my typing skills were put to use in the Westbourne Project office. I'd stayed on at school until I was sixteen, and although in that final year I trained to be a nursery nurse, I also learned to type. PC Lever was overjoyed when he heard about my office chores and he had me going through files with a fine-tooth comb. Indeed, Lever often got me to work late so I could sneak files out, and he'd browse through them in a nearby pub. Lever's interest in me was greater than ever, and living in Bassett Road became a serious drag because he took to dropping in on me at all hours of the day and night. Giordano couldn't bear watching the brute slap me around and then force me to have sex with him in our bed. If Giordano attempted to go out when Lever called around, he was ordered to stay, since our tormentor enjoyed humiliating us by forcing me to have sex with him in front of my boyfriend. As a consequence of this we decided to move out of Notting Hill, having sussed that Lever would have less opportunity to pull these sick tricks if we didn't live on his beat.

At this point I had a stroke of luck, since through the Westbourne Project I ran into an old friend, Pete Walker, who was running the Gort Squatters Association in Tottenham Court Road. An addict who was looking for a place to live had gone to a Gort Squatters meeting and told me about it. I hadn't seen Pete for several years, since he'd never really approved of my junkie lifestyle, but when I told him about my problems with Lever he immediately cracked a squat for Giordano and me at 30 Tottenham Court Road. Walker was living at 34 Tottenham Court Road with Faye, his wife of that time. Pete took me to the flat that would become my home and Giordano helped him break and enter, which was how we renewed our friendship. Walker was involved in a political struggle to delay the redevelopment of Tottenham Court Road by putting squatters into flats bought from private owners by EMI, who wanted to turn them into office space like that in the vacant Centre Point building, which loomed above these properties.

There was an empty flat above the one Giordano and I occupied, and we moved other members of the Church of

Celestial Awakening into that. Everyone would gather together in my living room and we'd listen to a Hawkwind album called *Space Ritual*, which for me epitomises my time at Tottenham Court Road. *Space Ritual* has a very heavy, druggy, trippy feel to it and that's how we were. Other groups we listened to a lot at Tottenham Court Road included Camel, Quintessence and Gentle Giant. Other than Guru Rampa publications, my reading at that time was far more nostalgic than the sounds I grooved to. I was rereading everything from Colin Wilson's *The Outsider*, through to the anonymously penned French sado-masochistic classic *The Story of O*. When I'd first read these works the soundtrack that had accompanied them was the modern jazz of Miles and Coltrane. Another book I obsessively returned to from the same era was *The Morning of the Magicians* by Louis Pauwels and Jacques Bergier. These latter authors had long been favourites of mine since by opposing the overly rational views of our society, they were able to treat alchemy, the possible extraterrestial origins of mankind, immortality, ESP, higher consciousness, precognition, Atlantis and much else, with an open-mindedness that is always missing from academic works on these subjects.

With plenty of like-minded people living in the Tottenham Court Road squats, we were able to start lunch-time Love Sessions to raise spiritual awareness among office and shop workers in the West End area. We advertised these services in Guru Rampa's weekly paper, *Celestial Times*, and most weekdays we'd have at least a dozen people in our flat between noon and two o'clock to testify about their love for God and His Creations. I missed out on a lot of the early sessions since I'd be going over to Portobello Road to counsel drug addicts at the Westbourne Project. At that time I was still a volunteer, but a vacancy had come up for a paid job as a social worker and Lever insisted I put in for it. It wasn't difficult to get a good application together using my old contact from the UCL philosophy department, Gerald Stubbington, Giordano and Alex Trocchi as my referees.

Lever even put in a good word for me on behalf of the local police and I secured the post without difficulty. Once I had an official position at the Westbourne Project as a social worker I was able to make professional prison visits, and as these became increasingly frequent, the body searches I was subjected to on my way in became more perfunctory. Lever made use of this by getting me to courier drugs to the various individuals he had operating as dealers inside Wormwood Scrubs. I knew all of them from the many years I'd spent scoring smack around Ladbroke Grove.

However, the nine-to-five routine I endured as an employee of the Westbourne Project didn't really suit me, and I was in any case under a lot of pressure because of the double life I was leading. I was using and dealing drugs despite my employer believing I was clean. Likewise, I still had to make regular trips to the Labroke Grove cop shop, where I'd be gang-banged and slapped around by Lever and his mates. My only relief was to spend three or four nights a week in the company of Alex Trocchi, which was something I greatly enjoyed. On the domestic front, Giordano and I were rowing again, although not quite as badly as during the early 70s. Whenever we were together Giordano used smack; he only ever cleaned up when we were apart.

I wasn't feeling well, and initially I put it down to all the pressure I was under to appear respectable enough to hold down my Westbourne Project job. However, after consulting a doctor I discovered I had rectal cancer. I could get treatment on the National Health Service, but that would mean wearing a colostomy bag for the rest of my life. I'd heard about an experimental treatment at the Mayo Clinic in the States, which would enable me to retain full use of my bowels, but it was expensive. Giordano understood how much I wanted to avoid having to wear a colostomy bag and he sorted the money out. It wasn't difficult: he imported a large shipment of Peruvian cocaine into Europe and realised a substantial profit. He'd have made even more money if he hadn't had to borrow dosh from drug-world connections to cover the set-up costs. I was sorted as far as the treatment I wanted went, although the chances of my dying were more than merely an outside possibility. I left London in the spring of 1976 and didn't return again until the spring of 1977. The treatment I underwent was successful, and one of the unplanned side-effects of this was that I stopped taking street drugs when I was in America. This wasn't something that could last, and as soon as I returned to London I was buzzing on speed and nodding out on smack. Giordano came over to the States to see me while I was undergoing the treatment, but when I returned to Europe he took a vow of celibacy and retreated to a Church of Celestial Awakening ashram in the south of France. I was back on my own, and although the US was better for my health, I knew London and London knew me, so I found myself unable to stay away from drugs. I'd take time out in California, Florida and even Bath in the English West Country, but ultimately the lure of London and smack always proved too much of a temptation to resist.

18. THE TIMES CHANGE AND WE CHANGE TOO

I wanted to write about Guru Rampa and how my quest for spiritual illumination has changed everything for me, but before I can get on to that subject I have to deal with what's in my head right now. My problem as I sit here in Cambridge Gardens is that I feel trapped by my previous life, and so it is the issues thrown up by post-hippie burn-out that I must resolve before I can move on to new ways of living. That said, I've always enjoyed watching the local youth, and used them as a barometer of social change. Partly this is because I figure they must be into similar things to Lloyd. Of course, round here Rastafari has been big news for some time now. That's not a bad thing, because Rastafarianism is one of the many ways God manifests Himself in this world of ours, and it provides a pathway to Truth for Afro-Caribbean kids. A lot of white kids like the beat of reggae music, and to a large extent they can also identify with lyrics that address the ways in which it is possible to tear down Babylon. Like the man said, when the rhythm of the music changes the walls of the city shake. I can remember blue beat from back in the day when I was still that mythical beast, a teenager, but reggae, it must be said, is very much a progression from those earlier sounds, and not some tired 60s retread. I hope Lloyd likes dub and toasters, since they provide a great soundtrack for the times we're living through. Another thing Lloyd might be into is punk rock, which I don't like as much as reggae. Punk reminds me of the mod movement in its mass stage of evolution, and musically it is very much rooted in the 60s sounds of groups like the Action and the Creation. People tell me punk appeared very suddenly; all I know is that in the spring of 1976 I went to the States for my cancer treatment, and when I returned to London in the spring of 1977 there were punks everywhere. Most of them seem kind of cute to me but, like Garrett when he's wired on speed, they can turn savage.

Shortly after I'd first moved in with Garrett earlier this year, I guess it was the beginning of July, we went to meet some friends at the Acklam Hall underneath the Westway in the Portobello Road. I'd call Ronnie and Bonnie friends, although Garrett was actually in the process of putting a drug deal together with the male half of this junkie couple. Anyway, Ronnie and Bonnie wanted to see some reggae band, so off we trooped to meet them at the concert. Being archetypal junkies, Ronnie and Bonnie failed to arrive on time; they were nodding out at home. Garrett and I stood drinking bottles of Pils at the back of the main hall and took in the scene. What we were witnessing wasn't a regular music promotion: it had been put on as a Rock Against Racism benefit, which meant that although there was a reggae band topping the bill, the support act was a punk rock group and the audience was overwhelmingly white. The group on stage when we arrived were political zealots; one of their songs was about the social crisis in Italy and the lyrics advocated rebuilding the Trotskyist Fourth International as an alternative to guerrilla warfare and therefore a better way forwards for the working class. What was particularly bizarre about this was not so much the fact that the group appeared to be genuinely working-class, but that kids were dancing to their dirge. The band and their audience were a subcultural mix of punks, skinheads and rockabillies. There was nothing going on that I hadn't seen or heard before, but the specific blend of elements was new to me.

Garrett and I were standing towards the back of the hall because we were as interested in watching the audience as the band. Garrett is an amazing character, in that people who don't know him sometimes imagine he is sleep-walking through his life, when in actuality he's taking everything in and running all the angles through his mind. Talking about what went down afterwards, we put it together like this. The group were not from Notting Hill and they'd brought most of the audience with them, which meant they were either from some other part of London or one of its satellite towns. There were some kids from the Grove in the hall, but they were very much in the minority. A local skinhead attempted to get fresh with a punk girl who knew the band, and she retaliated when he attempted to touch her up by kicking him very hard in the balls. The boy was with four friends who didn't witness this incident, and masculine pride being what it is, when the tear-stained teenager's mates demanded to know who'd given him the beating, he pointed out a male punk. Since honour must be satisfied among the subcultural tribes, the Ladbroke Grove skins attacked the punk who'd been wrongly fingered for the attack. This was a miscalculation on their part, because after surrounding their target and getting in some ineffectual kicks and punches, they found themselves outnumbered as not only other members of the audience turned against them, but the band leaped off stage to join in this fray. The aggressors wisely turned on their heels and fled from the hall, knowing full well that if they stayed they were going to get a serious kicking.

After this incident the punk band got back up on stage and finished their set. They seemed energised by the mild violence I'd just witnessed, and not only did their playing improve, but they even did a couple of encores. There was a short break, during which records were played, and then the headline act came on. The reggae music that began throbbing through the hall was more to my taste than punk rock, and even the kids who'd come for the support group hung around to skank. In some ways it was lucky they stayed, because without them there wouldn't have been much of an audience. However, the reggae band only got as far as playing the second number of their set when all hell broke loose. The local skinheads who'd got the worst of it in the earlier fight had returned mob handed and tooled up with pick-axe handles and other improvised weapons they'd stolen from a local building site. Those at the head of the hundred-strong mob who steamed through the front door made a serious error of judgement, since while the Socialist Workers Party activists who were operating the cash desk were no match for them, a good number of those in the audience were experienced street fighters. Garrett and I were standing by the doors between the entrance and the main hall, and we were pushed towards the overturned pay desk as members of the audience came steaming out of the auditorium to join in the fight. As the few locals who'd made it into the hall beat a hasty retreat amidst kicks and punches, an improvised barricade was thrown up using various pieces of furniture.

Meanwhile, scooterists were grabbing their helmets and piping was torn from walls and broken into weapon-sized lengths. Before long the barricade that had been so hastily thrown together was torn down by the crew who'd just built it, so that a phalanx of those defending the hall could wade into the milling crowd of Ladbroke Grove skins. These shock troops clearly adhered to the dictum that attack is the best form of defence, because they charged outside with their arms viciously windmilling blunt implements down on to the cropped heads of the local skins. Crash helmets were being held by their chin-pieces with the visor up, and manipulated with a skill that betrayed the fact that those wielding them had considerable experience in this style of combat. The punks and rockabillies fighting in this fashion worked in pairs to protect each other's backs, and the local skinheads were clearly unused to dealing with rival gangs who had the ability to defend themselves with what amounted to military precision.

In terms of numbers the rival gangs were evenly matched, but the Ladbroke Grove skins had lost the element of surprise and this was probably the one thing that had been working to their advantage. As fighters it looked like they'd be outclassed by those they'd rather foolishly chosen to attack. In the end this battle wasn't about numbers, since with the doorway to the Acklam Hall acting as a bottleneck, the winning side was going to be the one which had the fiercest of its fighters engaging the enemy. I'd seen plenty of rumbles in my time and had no great desire to witness yet another unfold in its entirety, particularly as anyone in a position to view this clash risked getting hit by one of the many beer bottles that were flying in all directions. Garrett and I beat a tactical retreat into the auditorium, where the reggae band were busy carting their equipment off the stage and into a dressing room. We helped them shift some big amps and speakers, which once we were inside the dressing room were used to barricade its door. All told there were about twenty people packed into the smallish room, a dozen rastas and a few of their women, a punk couple, Garrett and me. Fear pervaded that little room precisely because there was a palpable sense of danger in the air.

'Those people are all violent and crazy!' the reggae band's singer complained. 'Much better to sit safely in here smoking ganja than to fight. Them kids got no sense, they enjoy trouble more than good times.'

'Right on, brother!' the male half of the punk couple concurred. 'We know the other band and they're always getting into brawls. What they like best is beating up Nazis, but when there are no racists around they'll fight anyone, and if they're the only people about then they beat each other up. We like their music, not all the scraps they get into.'

'Them people plum crazy!' one of the rasta women added.

'Them Ladbroke Grove skinheads ain't racists,' the rasta bass player put in. 'I know some of them, they're redskins and like old school reggae music.'

'It's just a gang fight,' the rhythm guitarist observed. 'Same shit all around the world. It's just another Saturday night in Babylon.'

'These anti-racist benefits always end in disaster,' the singer added. 'It's never like this when we do a blues party.'

'So why do the Rock Against Racism shows?' Garrett asked.

'I do them to benefit the rastaman, of course!' the singer laughed. 'Them white Socialist Worker school-teachers say they want reggae band for Rock Against Racism, so I say it cost them £120. They say the punk rock group playing with us pull all the audience and only take £10 to cover costs of petrol to get to the gig. I say if you want reggae band, man, then you pay going rate for reggae band; also I say rasta band have to headline. Our friends don't come to these benefits but it looks good to see the listings in the music press with our name at top of the bill. I talked to the bass player in the punk band and he said he's in Socialist Workers and believes in the cause. That's his problem, man. I play free anytime for Jah, not for the white man. Anti-racist benefits provide the beginnings of our reparations for slavery.'

'Besides,' the guitarist put in, 'we have more expenses than a punk band; they travelled further to get here but they don't need to smoke ganja to get into the right groove. That punk sound is uptight, that's wired music, man, for people who like to pretend they've got a beer bottle rammed up their arsehole when they dance. We smoke good weed to get into a mellow groove. Noise comes cheap while polyrhythmic subtlety costs extra wedge.'

'I like your hustle,' Garrett put in. 'Reminds me of a cat I used to know who went by the name of Michael X.'

'That's a heavy dude, man,' the singer shot back. 'Him fitted up for murder in Trinidad and go to the scaffold.'

'We were involved in the campaign against that particular miscarriage of justice,' I added. 'We both knew Michael from way back when in the 60s.'

'That's the kind of politics I like,' the singer enthused. 'Much better to try to save the life of a man from judicial murder than this Socialist Worker opportunism.'

'Where'd you learn words like opportunism?' Garrett's bullshit detector was working overtime.

'I was a member of a libertarian communist organisation called Big Flame when I was a student at the London School of Economics,' the singer declared.

'Just like Mick Jagger!' Garrett whooped.

I've no idea whether or not the reggae singer was signifying, but that's the type of verbal exchange we got into once Garrett made his Rolling Stones riposte. My boyfriend went on to impress everyone with his 'I'm a healer not a dealer' routine, during which he takes a good twenty minutes to explain that modern man has been stressed out by over-stimulation and that regular shots of smack are the only known cure for this. Garrett's audience found his speech hilarious, and I don't think they realised that he believed passionately in the argument he was putting forward. During the course of this signifying, Garrett got to palm off many of his favourite lines as if they were brand new. Perhaps the catch-phrase that went down best was Garrett's standard reply to junkies who asked for smack on tick, viz: 'no one wants to pay for drugs they've already consumed'.

Joints were passed around amid much laughter, and as Garrett shot the shit everyone seemed to forget that we were sheltering from a riot. We carried on in this way for quite some time, and when things seemed to have calmed down we shifted the speakers with which we'd barricaded the door. Stepping out into the auditorium, it looked like it had been hit by a bomb. Outside the Acklam Hall quite a number of cars had been trashed. The cops tended to stay away from this sort of situation until they were certain things had really cooled off. When they could avoid trouble, the filth invariably did so. They were both gutless and powerful, an extremely obnoxious combination. Nonetheless, Garrett and I figured it was best to get going while the coast was still clear. The incident I'm relating took place months before I went into hiding at 104 Cambridge Gardens, and at that time Garrett and I had a bedsit up in Queensway. Before going there we decided to head around to Oxford Gardens to see if Ronnie and Bonnie were home. Once we'd got them to answer the door, which took some time, Garrett and I shot up with them and then nodded out. We didn't go back to our drum until the following morning. Being with Ronnie and Bonnie was like stepping back into another era, but what had gone down at the Acklam Hall is clearly the reality youths like my seventeen-year-old son Lloyd are having to deal with. Things are heavier now than I've ever known them to be on the Ladbroke Grove smack scene. With various turf wars going on, it seems junkies are more likely to be bumped off than to overdose. The 60s are well and truly over: naked self-interest has destroyed any sense of solidarity there once was on the drug scene, and our little world is an increasingly brutalised place. I'm glad I'm not young any more, and I sincerely hope Lloyd is tough enough to survive this benighted era. Thatcher attaining power is a symptom and not the cause of the things that are wrong with London.

19. THE UNDER-ASSISTANT EAST COAST PROMOTION MAN

I've always criticised my friends when they're judgemental. For most of my life I've been prepared to live and let live. Perhaps what some of the pimps I've met have told me about the overlay is true. What we're most prone to criticising in others is the thing we most hate in ourselves. Being cooped up in this Cambridge Gardens basement flat is making me more critical of my friends, and especially the very few I still get to see. I've always admired Alex Trocchi for writing two great novels, but here I am ruminating on the downsides to his character. I never met Trocchi's father, but my understanding is that Alex was a chip off the old block. Although as a youngish man Alfredo Trocchi worked as both a musician and for the Performing Rights Society, in later life he was unemployed and resorted to a ritual acting out of tasks to create a sense of order in his essentially unstructured and empty life.

Alex satirised this behaviour in his novel *Cain's Book*, and while he used drug addiction rather than a mythological notion of respectability to cover up the voids in his discreetly wretched existence, the wayward son never really escaped the baleful influence of his would-be bourgeois dad. Trocchi was always talking about getting his writing career back on track, but after he fled from the United States in the early 60s to escape narcotic-trafficking charges, he's never done anything very much. For the past couple of decades Alex has used heroin as a way of ordering his days. The routine never changes. It has been pretty much as follows for many years now: in the morning Trocchi collects his government-sponsored drug script, then he attends to a bit of secondhand book-dealing followed by a drink in the Catherine Wheel. After that various illegal drug deals are sorted out, and having secured himself the better part of a grand, Alex spends the afternoon drinking in the Elephant & Castle pub. Evenings are generally whiled away at home, and that's when I most often see Trocchi.

Alex doesn't do much: in fact as time goes by he does less and less; there is an assistant to do everything and a cleaner to take care of his apartment. Years ago, when Alex was desperate for readies or being humiliated by bent cops, he would do street-level drug dealing, but such activity is well behind him now. Were it not for Trocchi's ability to fritter money away he might be wealthy. I'm one of only a handful of people who've sold drugs for Alex over the years. Trocchi says this is because despite his financial and other arrangements with corrupt detectives, he is fearful that his public standing as a writer means that if word of his involvement in this trade really got around then even the bent cops he works alongside would find it difficult to turn a blind eye to such activity. Trocchi doesn't strike me as being genuinely concerned that he might be busted or ripped off; this is simply a rationalisation of his resistance to expanding his minor drugs empire. My view is that he likes the security of remaining at the same level in the drug business, off the street but not so high up the chain of supply that he feels exposed. That said, in contrast to the stability of his drug dealing, Alex changes literary assistants almost as often as other people change their underwear. Perhaps this isn't surprising, since Alex pretty much stopped writing twenty years ago, and the main function of these people is to prop up his ego. After a while the litany against those who didn't and still don't understand him – his parents, his teachers, his peers in Paris, the literary establishment, the counterculture – becomes a little wearing, and a new face is required to provide Trocchi with sympathy. Apparently, if there was just one person who really understood his writing, then Alex would feel it was worth completing a new novel.

I was at Trocchi's last night and there was a new boy present who answered to the name Humphrey Anderson. Alex called him The Hump behind his back. Anderson was very young and earnest. He'd been renting a room from Alex's junkie friend Pete the Plank. It was Pete who'd first brought the Hump over to Trocchi's place in Observatory Gardens. Pete called Anderson the Hump and many other rude names to his face. Despite these provocations the young man had proved obsequious enough to land himself the unpaid post of Trocchi's literary assistant. As I've already made clear, this is a purely honorary role, and all that is actually required of the person who holds it is that they continually flatter their master. Anderson isn't the first of Trocchi's literary henchmen wanting to write the great man's biography, and I'm sure he won't be the last. The Hump has been sorting through Alex's papers and he hangs on to Trocchi's every word, apparently without realising that his idol's pronouncements cannot always be accepted at face value. Trocchi enjoyed watching Anderson sitting open-mouthed as I shot up in front of him. Our host had a hit too, as did Pete the Plank. Now, after Alex has jacked up there is a good time and a bad time to ask him a question. The Hump knew nothing of this, and subjected us all to his incredibly inane patter at a point when he would have made a better impression if he'd remained completely silent.

'So tell me, Alex,' Anderson bubbled, 'when you were at school did you ever involve yourself in mock elections or other political activities?'

'Aye, Humphrey, aye,' Trocchi responded slothfully. 'I think I've told you all about my interest in UFOs.'

'No, Alex, I had no idea you were interested in Unidentified Flying Objects. I'd like to hear about that, because it is something with which the general public is not yet familiar as regards your interest in it.'

'During my last two years at school we were evacuated from Glasgow and sent out to Dumfries in the borders. We were safe from Nazi bombs but there were other dangers. The local papers were full of stories of visitors from beyond the stars arriving in Scotland aboard UFOs.'

'Really!' the Hump exclaimed as he transcribed Trocchi's tall tale into the notebook on his lap.

Pete and I silently pissed ourselves. We'd discussed UFOs with Trocchi many times in the past. The first recorded reports of UFOs occurred in America after World War II. Anyone who believed that Trocchi had seen newspaper reports about this phenomenon while still at school was patently incapable of recognising bullshit as it was being fed to them on a plastic spoon.

'So at this time I was boarding with a Church of Scotland minister, and he didn't like me because he'd overheard a conversation I'd had with my friend Roy Smith in which we'd talked about my great-uncle being short-listed to become the next pope.'

'Was your uncle actually elected pope?' The Hump could barely contain himself.

'Laddie, you're not listening to me. There are enough silly rumours circulating about my life as it is, so I don't want you to go out and spread new ones. I was talking about my great-uncle, my grandfather's brother. My great-uncle, who was a leading progressive cardinal, was quite rightly put forward as a candidate to become the next pope, but to the world's great misfortune he didn't win the election.'

'Alex.' The Hump choked on the name as he said it. 'You're a biographer's dream. I have to write your life story, since it will be my passport to literary fame. To write about a man like you is akin to joining the immortals!'

'Aye,' Trocchi conceded. 'You'd certainly have a number of publishers fighting each other for the honour of putting out your book, which is a gratifying situation for any young writer to find himself in. However, I want you to stop interrupting me, since until you do so I cannot answer your initial question. But by the by, Jilly and Pete are both from Catholic families like me. I want you to tell me honestly whether or not you're an Orangeman.'

The Hump writhed in his seat. He was desperate to hear what else Trocchi had to say, but simultaneously the last thing he wanted to do was own up to his Protestant background. I could see the funny side to these mind games, but they were beginning to get too heavy for my taste. For a moment or two there was silence.

'Humphrey,' the Plank suddenly put in, 'Alex asked you a question, so don't embarrass me by failing to answer. Are you a proddy?'

'I'm a humanist. I thought we were all humanists!' Anderson blurted.

'Don't procrastinate. I want you to tell Alex whether or not you were baptised, and if so the name of the church to which you belong.'

'Like the majority of people in the British Isles I don't have a Catholic family background, but that doesn't mean . . .'

'OK, Hump,' Pete cut in, 'now we've sorted that out please allow Alex to continue with his story.'

'So while I was boarding with this minister I'd sneak out at night and scour the countryside in search of UFOs. I can't claim to have been abducted by aliens, but on numerous occasions I observed their spacecraft and so did my friend Roy Smith. You should try to track Roy down if you can, he might still have the notes we made about our UFO sightings.'

'So what's this got to do with political activities at school?' Anderson asked.

'Shut up!' the Plank snarled.

'I was getting to that,' Trocchi continued. 'You see, also attending the school to which I was evacuated was this complete idiot called Terry Lowther, who'd take mock elections terribly seriously and stand as the Scottish National Party candidate. I remember Lowther giving his speeches and going on for hours about how Scotland had been ruined by Irish immigration. Anyway, after about a week I was so fed up with this nonsense that when Lowther gave his next speech I got some of my pals together and we hid behind some bushes dressed in tinfoil suits to look like aliens. We waited until the Scots nationalist had become so steamed up about the terrible things Catholics were allegedly doing to his country that he had to loosen his tie, and then we emerged from the bushes to hand out leaflets we'd printed up instructing everyone to vote Martian. Of course, we went on to a landslide win within that particular election. Lowther felt crushed and actually gave up on his ambition to become Grand Master of the local Orange Lodge.'

'What do you think of that?' Pete asked.

'Incredible,' the Hump replied. 'It's a fantastic anecdote for my biography of Alex; I'm sure a novelist couldn't improve on it.'

'Think of some way it could be improved,' Pete goaded.

'I don't think it could be improved, particularly as it is a true story, not fiction.'

'Tell me what you'd do with it if you were going to transform it into fiction,' Alex instructed his literary assistant.

'There is one thing I'd change,' Anderson shot back. 'I'd have Lowther standing as a Labour candidate. It would make the appeal of the story broader. People in England don't care two figs about Scottish nationalism.'

'Aye,' Trocchi allowed, 'that's true enough, but Scots nationalism is certainly a motor for reaction on the other side of the border. If it wasn't for bigotry of this stripe no one would have heard of a buffoon like Hugh MacDiarmid.'

The Hump looked as if he was about to say something more but he stopped himself. There was silence for a few minutes, but that moment of peace Trocchi so wanted to enjoy after his hit had already passed. Eventually Alex gave Anderson a small parcel and told him to deliver it to PC Lever at a nearby cop shop. Alex had an ongoing relationship with this corrupt and drug-addled cop. To my inordinate regret, I did too. We all did. If the Hump wasn't careful he was going to end up getting to know this sadist. Alex was irresponsible, as are most of the men I know. I didn't think it was a good idea to get an innocent to deliver heroin to a bent cop, but there was no point in saying anything about it to Trocchi since he did whatever pleased him.

'Let's have a laugh with the Hump when he gets back,' the Plank suggested. 'We could bully him into taking a hit by insisting it's the only way he'll ever attain a proper understanding of *Cain's Book*.'

'The boy's not ready for smack; he'd be frightened by it,' I replied.

'I'm all for giving him a scare!' Pete roared.

'You're both right,' Trocchi put in. 'The Hump's not ready to accept junk mentally, but that doesn't mean he can't take it physically. So I suggest we approach the matter in a subtle fashion. We can explain to him that addiction to heroin isn't just about getting the drug into your blood stream, but that the mentally soothing ritual of preparing and injecting the shot is equally important. Indeed, some junkies will shoot up with warm water if they can't score skag. Therefore to help him understand my work he's to let us shoot him up in this way. At least he'll think he's getting warm water, but we'll prepare a few shots at the same time and switch his placebo for the real thing.'

'Let me give him the hit,' I pleaded, 'and as his blood blooms in the dropper, Pete can explain the sexual connotations of the needle penetrating his silky skin and mind-fuck him about how he's a mere hair's-breadth away from being a rent boy.'

'Jilly,' the Plank guffawed, 'I didn't know you had it in you to be so low-down and nasty.'

'It isn't that nasty; it might make him think before he accepts a second shot.'

'You've got to be cruel to be kind – that's your thinking, is it? But wouldn't it give him even more of a jolt if Alex punctured the vein? We could even pretend we're going to have an orgy after we've had our hits, and see if that freaks the Hump out even more. At least he'll have the excuse that he feels sick; most people do on their first shot.'

'Right, then.' Alex wanted the conversation wrapped up before his literary assistant returned. 'It's all agreed. We'll switch the spikes around and Jilly will turn him on.'

'Can I tell him he's had a real hit?' Pete asked.

'We'll play it by ear,' Trocchi ordered. 'Let's see how he responds to the idea that he's been placed last in a gang-bang line-up for Jilly.'

'Let's tell him it's an initiation rite into the Brotherhood of the Needle: as the senior junkies, you and me are going to shoot our wads inside Jilly and then he has to lick her out.' Every time the Plank opened his mouth he reminded me of PC Lever.

'Whatever . . .'

Then Alex drifted off somewhere else. Sex never held his attention. The only thing that really turned him on was drugs. Trocchi stared into space and I gawked at a spoon that had been abandoned on the floor. I didn't have anything to say to Pete, so we sat in silence until the Hump returned and everyone did their part in the agreed routine. Everyone that is except for me, because I did a double switch with the syringes. Alex got a kick out of turning people into junkies, but I couldn't go along with this. While drugs can give pleasure, the main reason people end up addicted is because they also kill pain. I'd been trying to kick my heroin habit without any long-term success for more than a decade. It was exciting to hang around with a famous writer like Alex, but it would have been better if I'd been able to enjoy his company without shooting up. I wanted the Hump to lead a happier life than I had done. This end was best served if he remained an ignorant fool. I didn't want to be responsible for wising him up to the realities of addiction, or rather the horrors that surround addiction. The Hump was a year or two older than Lloyd, but not so very different in age to my son. I shuddered when I thought of the things PC Lever had done to me, and I'm shocked that Trocchi would expose a complete innocent to such an evil thug. I was determined that Anderson would not be spiked with smack while I was around to prevent it, especially as he'd already unknowingly been exposed to greater danger that evening. Alex, Pete and I ran through the various grooves we'd plotted in the Hump's absence. When the Plank explained how Anderson was to be initiated into the Brotherhood of the Needle, the boy complained he felt sick and needed to go home. I knew the Hump wasn't ill, but Alex and Pete were innocent enough on that score to accept his excuse as unquestionably genuine.

20. NOWHERE TO RUN

Initially the events of recent weeks plunged me back into the past, and now they are returning me to the present. It is almost as if I'd died, and as I slipped from this world into the next my entire life passed before my eyes. However, as I reviewed my passage through this world many of my experiences seemed to hover just beyond my grasp. Right now, as I sit here in Cambridge Gardens, the only thing that seems real to me is my life in London. When I recall biographical incidents that took place outside this great metropolis it feels as if I'm reviewing someone else's existence. I moved to this city more than nineteen years ago, when I was just sixteen; my son Lloyd was born in London a year and a half later. I can recall many incidents from my life outside London, but these episodes appear so one-dimensional to me right now that I've found it impossible to recount most of them at any length. I was born again when I moved to London in the summer of 1960. This city moves and breathes; it has become a monster. The sense of evil I feel around me is all-pervasive; it has penetrated the bricks and mortar of every building in every street of this sprawling town. The poison has welled up from the sewers and hangs in the air like a fog. The Devil no longer wants our souls. God is welcome to them, since Satan gets his jollies reanimating our fleshy bodies. We are the *morti viventi*, and since I am already undead I'm not afraid to die again.

I am getting ahead of myself here, so perhaps I need to set down the events to which I'm alluding in their proper chronological sequence. Please bear with me while I reiterate that my father died five years ago and my mother went senile around the same time. Two of my brothers still live at home, and they look after our mum. They all live together in a council house in Greenock, and there isn't much money to spare since one of my brothers is unemployed and the other does a milk round. I knew the house needed new carpets and I also wanted to get my mother a television, so I decided to pull a scam. I asked around to see if there was anyone new to the scene interested in buying smack, and I was put in touch with a Mr Donaldson from Bermondsey in south London. The man I met appeared naïve, and after providing a genuine sample, I sold him some extremely expensive talcum powder which I'd bagged up so that it looked like skag. If I'd known Mr Donaldson had married into an extended criminal family with the means to find out who I was then I'd have picked a different mark. After paying for my mum's new carpets and giving a sizeable donation to Guru Rampa, I found myself knee-deep in shit with some hardcore London heavies. As a consequence I decided to go into hiding. The word on the street is that at the very least I'm going to receive a severe beating and will have to pay back the money I purloined plus onerous interest. I don't have the wedge, and even if I did there is no guarantee I can buy my way out of trouble.

The west London drug scene was nasty enough with bent coppers running it, but now that organised crime is attempting to move in things have got even heavier. Given this, my opting to hide out with a notorious smack dealer and pimp like Garrett probably wasn't the greatest idea in the world, but then my life has never run on a smooth groove. I was surprised when I finally established a proper relationship with Garrett after so many years of flirtation, but for some months now he has been my live-in lover, and so it seemed logical to do a flit with him when I landed in serious trouble. Garrett organised the rental of this basement flat in Cambridge Gardens, and after I came back from a trip to Florida, we moved into it together two weeks ago.

Florida was good. There was a big Church of Celestial Awakening event with thousands of disciples present. By chance, on the plane over I met up with an old friend called Marianne May, who like me was crossing the Atlantic to be with Guru Rampa. I'd first met Marianne in 1975 through church activities, but more recently I'd lost contact with her. A lot of those currently involved with the Church of Celestial Awakening come from the hippie scene and have histories of drug use, but Marianne is very respectable. She actually works as a lawyer. I told Marianne that I was a drug addict and that I was in recovery. I said I wanted to give up heroin and that seeing Rampa would help me with this. I explained that I was undergoing cold turkey, and Marianne offered to assist me through my withdrawal. Marianne and the many other disciples I saw in Florida were enormously supportive, and I managed to kick although I was very sick the entire time I was there. My plan was to clean up and then after returning to England to hide in the country with friends who didn't use smack. I lasted two days in Leiston on the Suffolk coast before I became so bored with the situation that I returned to London.

I sought out Garrett, but I wouldn't stay with him at our old bedsit in Queensway because everyone knew I'd been living there over the summer; instead I rented a room in a fleabag hotel. While I was there Garrett organised this new place at 104 Cambridge Gardens, and by the time we moved in I was shooting up again. So much for my plan to stay clean! Garrett supplies me with junk and I'm more than able to cover the cost by turning a few tricks. Since no one from the demi-monde is supposed to know where I am, I only see johns at hotels. Marianne and a few other members of the Church of Celestial Awakening know I am here, but other than that I've attempted to keep my whereabouts a secret.

I saw my friend Neola Shott two days ago; she'd seen Giordano in Marseilles, and he told her that when she returned to England she had to find me and help me because I was in serious trouble. News travels fast among the initiates of the Church of Celestial Awakening. Neola came to Guru Rampa from the hippie scene, but she's never been a hard-drug user. Now she's with the Church she's pretty much given up soft drugs too. It was good to see her, and she told me she had a terrible job finding me. She'd eventually got my address by phoning Marianne. Neola had lived upstairs from me in Tottenham Court Road and we'd become very close at that time. After I went to America in 1976 she'd moved to Bath, and I lived with her there for three months at the end of 1977, when I was making another of my abortive attempts to give up skag. It was two years since I'd last seen Neola and we had a lot of catching up to do. Since Neola wanted to stay overnight, around ten in the evening I told her I had to go out for a while as I'd arranged to have a boogie with a friend. I found a phone box and called Garrett, who was at Trocchi's. I told him not to come home that night. I didn't want Neola to know that we are living together, because she'd tell Giordano. If Giordano found out I am with Garrett he'd be straight over from France. I love Giordano but I really don't want my soul mate attempting to save me from myself. After I'd spoken to Garrett I went and turned a couple of tricks. I returned home around two in the morning; Neola was still up and we talked some more. We decided that we'd attend Guru Rampa's solstice celebrations in the States later this month. I gave Neola some money so that she could hit a bucket shop to buy return tickets to Florida for both of us before she went home to Bath. I didn't have any spare sheets, so eventually we both got into my double bed. We slept until ten the next morning, and after chatting to me for a couple more hours, Neola left. It was great to see her, and until she turned up I hadn't realised how much I missed her company.

In sharp contrast to Neola's visit, last night was not a happy occasion. I'd been out to service some johns and I happened to return to the flat at the same time as Garrett. Since we approached our bedsit from the opposite ends of the street, my boyfriend was able to clock that I was being tailed by someone he knew to be a bent detective. Now, if this pig knows where I am there can be no doubt that the information will have been passed on to PC Lever. Aside from upsetting gangsters, my disappearance has put the noses of Lever and his chums out of joint, since I rather too abruptly ceased providing them with cash and sexual favours. These bastards have come close to killing me in the past, but other than the fact that they revel in sadism there is no reason for them to do their own dirty work now. Lever is personally acquainted with Albert Redwood, the john who is sexually obsessed by me, and it is obvious that it will not take much encouragement to send this seemingly respectable businessman across the blurred line that divides delusion from murder. Likewise, the cops know that there are heavyweight gangsters out for my blood. Clearly it is no longer safe for me to stay in Cambridge Gardens, but I'm sick of running. Garrett told me to leave London but I refused. *Que sera sera*. What will be will be. I've packed more into my thirty-five years than most people manage in their three-score years and ten. I'm ready to die, and if in a few months' time I'm still alive, I will no longer need to fear anything or anyone. A life of non-stop running is not worth living. If I had a cast-iron guarantee I'd be seeing Lloyd again, then I'd have the motivation to keep moving. But seeing Lloyd is now a hope rather than a certainty, and I've had my hopes of being reunited with my son dashed so many times in the past. Right now death appears preferable to living.

I started writing this account of my life to give me something to do while I was in hiding. It is far from complete, but within the next hour I intend to mail what I've written to my sister in Falkirk. Garrett is still asleep, and if I hurry I'll catch the lunch-time post. I realise now that I began writing this because I subconsciously expected to die before the solstice. If I'm murdered then my words will become a finger pointing accusingly at my killers for the rest of eternity. Likewise, if I should die before being reunited with my son Lloyd, what I've put down is also a testimony for him, so hopefully one day he will read what I've written and know how much I loved him. As I've already said, as an account of my life these pages are far from perfect. There is nothing much here about my childhood, my trips to India or time in the States. Lloyd, Garrett and London are my only realities now. Isn't it funny that I'm from Greenock and Garrett is from Leeds, but it is London that holds us in its thrall? I can't live with London and I can't live without it. I often wonder, Lloyd, how you feel about the city in which you were born. I hope you are completely free of the overwhelming ambivalence with which I view the place.

I trust, Lloyd, I've given you a realistic account of the 60s, and I say that knowing I've not put in anything about the big events of that decade. When people speak about swinging London and what followed on from that one so often hears talk of events like *Wholly Communion* at the Albert Hall or the *14-Hour Technicolor Dream* at Alexandra Palace. If, like me, you were there at the time, these things barely registered. Indeed it was the more intimate events that I liked best; and the standout among them all must be the night I spent at the Arts Lab in 1969, when my friends Alex Trocchi, William Burroughs, Ronnie Laing, Davy Graham and Feliks Topolski all appeared on the same bill. Jamie Wadhawan included copious footage of this occasion in his documentary *Cain's Film*, and as a result it surprises me that this star-studded underground event isn't better known. There are loads of audience shots in Wadhawan's documentary, and I'm clearly visible in several of them. It was a great night, even if my friend Phil White did make a bit of a nuisance of himself because he was desperate to bed a young American girl. Wadhawan's film also features extensive footage of Trocchi's apartment, which is why I haven't described the pad in any great detail, since viewing this documentary is the best way for anyone who has never been there to discover what it is like. Moving on, the all-nighters at the UFO Club were also fun, but they pale into insignificance in comparison to Giordano and Garrett, and above all to you, Lloyd. You three are the people connected in various ways to my life in London who most matter to me, and you are of far more significance than the famous entertainers I've mentioned in these pages. The real history of the 60s has yet to be written. The faces in the crowd remain blurred, and it is only when these features are brought into focus that you can comprehend what actually happened. Anyone who thinks you can understand the history of London in the 60s by looking at the lives of Mary Quant, Twiggy, Bailey and the Shrimp, Mick Jagger, Michael Caine and Terence Stamp, is sadly deluded. These few simply rode to fame on the back of a scene that was created by thousands of anonymous hands and hearts . . . I hope we achieved something.

If I ever finish this attempt at an autobiography I think I'll call it *I Led Two Lives*. Ever since I found Guru Rampa in 1972 my existence has been Janus-faced, because I've combined spiritual striving with a previous life that I've never quite managed to escape. I'm still partially trapped in the bohemian world I first entered as a teenager; indeed my appetite for sexual and chemical excess remains as strong as ever. I'd intended to write an account of my spiritual adventures, but these seem so elusive when I'm bombed out of my box. When I do heroin I can happily stare at my shoe for hours on end, so even compiling an account of the drug haze I've been living through feels like an achievement. That said, the outward march of my life reveals little of the hidden spiritual movement that has animated the better parts of it. I'm ashamed of so many things that I've done, but it seems important to record them so that they might be put behind me. Lloyd, I'm overjoyed that I'm your mother, but giving you up has been a source of unending guilt and regret for me. The one thing I really achieved in the 60s was giving birth to you. I lost you in 1962, and by the end of that decade my life was spinning dangerously out of control. It is Guru Rampa who has been my rock throughout the 70s, my chief source of happiness and consolation. God is the First and the Last, the Alpha and Omega. He means everything to me. I feel divided, and Rampa says I am divided against myself. I am ready to die, and Rampa says that death is an illusion. I am perplexed, but Rampa will provide me with the Truth. Tomorrow I will sit down and write *The Fantastic Flight*, the chronicle of my trip with Guru Rampa in the year of our Lord nineteen-hundred and seventy-nine. Lord, teach me to be an instrument of Thy Love. Let me love only for you. Love begets love. You get what you give out. I must learn patience and perseverance. I must learn how to use the tools and remember that it's more important to know the formula than the answer. Love is beyond time and space. Love is all . . . Lloyd, if you read this after I am dead please remember that I will be in a better place than when I was still alive.

AFTERWORD BY LLOYD O'SULLIVAN: THE
SIGNIFYING JUNKIE

M y (m)other Jilly O'Sullivan died at 104 Cambridge
Gardens on 2 December 1979; she was found dead in
bed at 6 p.m. on Sunday 3 December by Marianne May –
that's officially recorded. The authorities appear to have
done very little to investigate her death, and the details they
recorded about it are remarkably scant. PC Paul Wade, the
Coroner's Officer who identified my (m)other's body and
investigated her death, appears to have gone out of his way
to find the circumstances surrounding her demise unsuspi-
cious. In his report he failed to record that Marianne May
was able to gain entry to my (m)other's ground-floor bedsit
because the street door that provided direct access to it was
open. It is perhaps superfluous to add that my (m)other
hated the cold, and she was not generally in the habit of
leaving outside doors open in December. This, and the fact
that she was found naked on her bed, certainly provide
grounds to arouse suspicions that foul play may have played
a role in her death. PC Wade spoke to only two of my
(m)other's friends in the course of his cursory investigation,

but both Marianne May and Neola Shott were aware that she had undergone a withdrawal from heroin three weeks before her death. Nonetheless, PC Wade opted instead to use my mother's fraudulent 1975 job application for the post of social worker at the Westbourne Project as conclusive proof that her use of drugs was well in the past at the time of her death.

Most cops working in west London in the late 70s would have recognised the first referee on this fraudulent document as a leading figure in the local drug subculture, and Alex Trocchi's name alone should have aroused PC Wade's suspicion about the veracity of the application. How this document came into PC Wade's hands is something about which I can only speculate, but since it was not returned to my (m)other's family it appears unlikely he found it in her flat. Indeed, while my (m)other's diary, which was with her when she died, provides evidence that her use of heroin was ongoing, most of her possessions had at the time of her death been left with family and friends. I leave readers to draw their own conclusions as to why PC Wade was sufficiently diligent to locate an obscure, fraudulent and out-of-date document to back up his contention that my (m)other was not addicted to drugs at the time of her death, while somehow overlooking more recent, accessible and compelling evidence to the contrary. One of the consequences of Wade's work was that no toxicology was performed on my (m)other's body, despite the fact that given the circumstances of her death there clearly should have been one. Had a toxicology been performed, the results would have in all probability increased the chances of there being an inquest into my (m)other's death.

Some of my (m)other's friends believe she suffered an accidental heroin overdose, whereas others including Giordano de Holstein apparently thought she'd been murdered. Unfortunately de Holstein died from cancer some years ago, so it has not been possible to quizz him about this. Neola Shott, who is mentioned in the Coroner's Report, says she was surprised by its contents, while Marianne May, who has a legal background, found it shocking. Both these women knew my (m)other through their involvement in the Church of Celestial Awakening; neither is or ever was an intravenous drug user. According to official sources, my (m)other died from natural causes, viz. bronchopneumonia. Since something will invariably be found in the lungs after death, bronchopneumonia is often given as the cause of death in instances when nothing else can be established – or where those in a position of authority prefer not to do a proper investigation for whatever reason. It is a banality to state that death is always the result of the failure of a major organ, and from a legal standpoint what should be determined by the coronary process is the chain of events leading to the fatality rather than its ultimate cause. Bronchopneumonia alone should generally only be treated as a cause of death among the elderly or the homeless. By the late 70s the authorities were perfectly well aware that in west London it was not uncommon for deaths from bronchopneumonia to be brought on by an overdose of drugs. In such cases the law requires that the circumstances be properly determined, and if there has been an overdose an inquest into the death should be set up to determine among other things whether this was accidental, suicide or the result of foul play. The autopsy performed on my (m)other's body was a standard and purely visual examination. If my (m)other had been injecting heroin into some of the less immediately accessible parts of her body, such as between her toes, the resulting scarring would have been neither seen nor noted during the course of her post-mortem examination.

The general comments at the bottom of the Coroner's Report are the most interesting part of that document, and they read as follows:

The deceased woman was separated from her husband who now lives in Hong Kong and residing at the above address alone (i.e. 104 Cambridge Gardens). There is a long history of addiction to drugs but well in the past. No recent indications of this at all. She was found dead in bed at 6 p.m. on Sunday 3.12.79 by a friend Miss Marianne May who then called the police. Miss Neola Prott is also a friend who stayed with her last week and observed that she seemed quite well although she had a bad cough . . . Enquiry re relatives still continues.

There are several errors in this. The name of my (m)other's friend who stayed with her a few days before her death was Neola Shott rather than Prott. It is probable that by 'husband' PC Wade was invoking Giordano de Holstein, who had lived in Hong Kong in the mid-70s but was based in Marseilles when my (m)other died. And again, my (m)other was living with Garrett rather than alone. Her companion was well known to local cops as a drug dealer and addict. One of my (m)other's former heroin buddies has informed me that if Garrett was present when Jilly died, it would not have been the first time he'd allowed someone he was with to suffer a fatal overdose because he considered calling an ambulance far too much trouble. Indeed, Garrett later rang Marianne May to thank her for not mentioning him to the police, although precisely why he should have done so remains a mystery. Around that time Garrett relocated to the Elephant & Castle, where he continued to retail drugs supplied to him by Alex Trocchi until the latter's death in 1984. Garrett remained active within the drug subculture until at least 1986, but I have no idea whether or not he is still alive.

Recently, there has been much media hoopla about the cursory way in which autopsies are carried out in England and Wales, and the various pressures that can lead those responsible for this work to do quick and inadequate investigations. Indeed, a failure to identify traces of drugs in dead bodies has been a specific concern with regard to this. The fact that my (m)other was a known drug addict and no toxicology was performed after her death is only one of the ways in which the work of the responsible authorities appears to be deficient. In the instance of my (m)other's death, the Coroner's Report states: 'Past drug addict but no recent indications. Found dead in bed by friend.' The most likely explanation of these errors is that the Coroner's Officer, PC Paul Wade, who performed the investigation, confused the few scraps of information he collected about my (m)other while simultaneously forgetting – deliberately or otherwise – a good many things that he knew about her. The report may well have been put together in a rush, and in many instances when a drug addict dies no one is going to question what a coroner, his deputy or his officer write about them. However, it is also possible that PC Paul Wade knew a great deal about my (m)other and did not want anyone looking too closely into her life or death. It is also worth noting that under the printed heading 'State if the case should be reported to Home Office, or other authority or person' is the following: 'Not required from this Office. H. O. Drugs notified.'

The *Middlesex Independent & West London Star* of Friday 7 December 1979 covered my (m)other's death in a single paragraph of three sentences under the heading FOUND DEAD, in which it was reported that the police said there were no suspicious circumstances. The running story in the *West London Star* through to the end of 1979 was the hunt for a schoolboy Martin Allen who'd been missing since 5 November. The lead story in the issue of the paper which carried the notice of my (m)other's death concerned a fire just off Westbourne Grove, which resulted in seven people who lived above the Rhodes Restaurant being plucked to safety from flames that engulfed the building. Other stories covered in that week's issue included a call by Labour Party councillors for the neo-Nazi organisation the League of St George to be banned from municipal buildings. Films advertised as being shown at local cinemas at the time of my (m)other's death included *Fresh, Young & Sexy*;

Prostitution Racket; *Manhattan*; *Mad Max*; *Zulu Dawn*; *Love at First Bite*; *Last Tango in Paris*; *A Wedding*; *An Unmarried Woman*; *The China Syndrome*; *The Hills Have Eyes*; *Emmanuelle & the White Slave Trade*; *Jet Sex*; *Death on The Nile*; *The Getaway*; *Way of The Dragon*; *Warriors*; *Fist of Fury* and *Death Wish*. Bruce Lee's posthumous movie *Game of Death* was at that time being advertised as opening on a double bill with the Chinese *One-Armed Swordsman* at the ABC Hammersmith two weeks after my (m)other's death, that is to say on 16 December 1979. It is probable that *Manhattan* was the last movie my (m)other saw at the cinema. This is a portrait of modern relationships set against the backdrop of New York, starring the comic actor and director Woody Allen.

After attending my (m)other's cremation in Greenock, Giordano stayed with her family for a few days. When Giordano left Scotland he took my (m)other's ashes with him and went to visit Neola Shott. After a few nights in Bath, Giordano asked Neola to hold out her hands and close her eyes. Giordano gave Neola the urn holding my (m)other's ashes and asked her what she thought he'd put in her hands. Eventually, he told Neola that he'd given her Jilly. Then they both started to laugh, because the ashes weren't Jilly; they knew she was so much more than these remains. While he was in Bath, Giordano took my (m)other's ashes to bed with him at night. After staying with Neola for a week, Giordano went to the grounds of a large house that Guru Rampa owned in Reigate and scattered my (m)other's remains there.

As for me, I realised some time ago that in order to be myself I first had to become my (m)other, and to complete this process I still need the information that will enable me to fully live out her death. Until then I will remain almost literally Alex Trocchi's illegitimate son. I first read *Young Adam* and *Cain's Book* when I was a teenager, and I may yet read them again. I know almost too well, both from first-hand experience and second-hand accounts, the world the (m)other I didn't know knew. Unknowingly I even befriended a number of her acquaintances. Baudrillard amongst others has claimed that seduction is destiny ... History repeats itself, the first time as farce, the second as tragedy. A.C.A.B. The perfection of suicide lies in ambiguity. There is no beginning, there is no end; this story goes on forever.